CANNIBALS & BLOODSUCKERS

AIRSHIP 27 PRODUCTIONS

TM

Mark Justice's The Dead Sheriff
Cannibals and Bloodsuckers © 2018 Mark Justice and Ron Fortier

Published by Airship 27 Productions
www.airship27.com
www.airship27hangar.com

Interior illustrations © 2018 Art Coooper
Cover illustration © 2018 Zachary Brunner

Editor: Ron Fortier
Associate Editor: Fred Adams Jr.
Marketing and Promotions Manager: Michael Vance
Production and design by Rob Davis

ISBN-13: 978-1-946183-52-1
ISBN-10: 1-946183-52-0

Printed in the United States of America

10 9 8 7 6 5 4 3 2 1

CANNIBALS
&
BLOODSUCKERS

BY
MARK JUSTICE
AND
RON FORTIER

CHAPTER ONE

Indian Territory, north of Texas

The Indian youth screamed when Arlo Belcher bit into his shoulder and ripped away a mouthful of flesh and muscle and blood.

"Damn it, Arlo, I ain't even got the fire built yet," his brother said.

"Cain't help it, Billy," Arlo said, around a mouthful of meat. "I was hungry and this here Injun tastes good."

"You know what you are? *Uncouth*." Billy dropped an armful of thin sticks on the pile. A whimper sounded from the Indian woman tied up on the ground. Her black hair was plastered to the side of her face with blood, a result of a blow struck moments ago by Billy with the barrel of his Colt revolver. "You shut up." He kicked the woman in the ribs, taking sweet delight in the feeling of bone and cartilage collapsing against the tip of his boot. "I don't want to be hearin' from my food until it's time to cook you."

Billy walked to the edge of the clearing for more sticks, annoyed by the wet chewing sounds coming from Arlo and his meal. *Arlo is simple so you always gotta take care of him.* That's what Mama had said time and again. So Billy dragged Arlo along with him on their grand adventure, and it was mostly a good thing. Arlo was somebody to talk to–as long as the conversation stuck to killing and stealing and cornholing. His little brother had grown into a big ol' boy, and that was a big help in their work but, damn, the kid didn't listen. "I swear to God, if you don't slow down and wait for me I'm–"

Someone yelled and slammed into Billy so hard he was thrown face-down in the dirt. Whoever hit him was on his back, spewing out thick, angry sounds that might have been words. Injun talk. Billy tried to roll over, at least until something hard connected with his skull. He didn't lose consciousness, but the world grew distant and the sounds around him seemed to come from deep in a well. That included the sound of a rifle shot. The weight of the attacker slumped against Billy's back and did not move. Billy pushed mightily with his arms, despite a sick feeling in his head and gut, and managed to roll over. The dead weight fell off of him. He blinked into the sunlight and saw Arlo standing there, the Winchester Billy had brought back from the war steady in his hands. Arlo's mouth, neck and shirt were covered in the bright blood of the Injun boy.

"Goddamn it, Arlo. Wipe your face."

•••

The Belcher boys ate good. Billy's attacker had been another Injun male, around 15 or so. He was lean and tough, but the woman and the younger boy provided enough meat to last a few days. Billy and Arlo sat against a big rock, enjoying the fullness of their bellies and watching the sun disappear behind the hills.

"You sure you're all right?" At Billy's urging–*repeated* urging–Arlo had splashed creek water on his face, which only served to smear the blood around. Now he looked like some sort of sad, crazy clown. "He hit you hard with that stick."

"I got a thick head, Arlo. That's what Mama always said." Mama said a lot of things, especially when she drank, which was most days. One of her favorite sayings was *I should've kilt you when you came outta me, you little piece of shit.* Another was *You two ain't gonna amount to nothin' but a stain in the dirt.* But of all of the things Mama said, Billy's favorite was *What are ya doin; with that knife? Get away from–Arrrrrrgh!.* That was minutes before Billy and Arlo tasted people for the first time. It was only right that they start with Mama. *Flesh of my flesh...*

Arlo licked his fingers. "Good eatin'."

"Yeah. I thought Injun would be tougher."

"But it ain't. That Injun lady was right sweet tastin'."

"Be nice to have some cornbread with her. Maybe some fried taters."

Arlo sucked on his index finger until he dislodged a tiny fleck of bloody flesh from beneath the nail. "Billy, where we goin' now?"

Billy Belcher sighed. He didn't like to plan too far ahead. After he got out of the army without being killed or captured by the Yankees, he promised himself that he would never take orders from any man again. Life was short, and Billy aimed to do what he wanted. If that meant he occasionally ate people, well, that's just the way the world worked. Everybody had his own little peccadilloes, as a fellow member of the CSA once told him. Of course, that sick freak liked to lick the feet of whores, which Billy thought made dining on human beings seem like a trip through the chuck wagon line.

Joining the army taught him about life, showed him there was a whole big world beyond the walls of that run down shack he had shared with Mama and Arlo. And that whole big world was full of death and disease and dirty, dishonest people who were lower than snakes and would kill you if you turned your back. It looked to be a brief life, so Billy aimed to do what he wanted. He would have a grand adventure, traveling across the land and write the name Belcher in blood across the plains. Out here was money to steal, good whiskey and bad women. What more did he need?

Bringing his little brother along hadn't been part of the plan; that was for sure. But Arlo tended to get in trouble when left on his own. While Billy had been shooting blue bellies, Arlo killed a sheriff and two deputies who tried to drag him out of a saloon after he'd busted the place up when a whore spurned his affections (and wouldn't give him a poke for free). Billy, fresh out of the CSA and still wearing his tattered grey uniform, arrived the morning Arlo was to be hanged. There were a few more dead deputies before the sun set that day.

After that, the Belcher brothers hit the trail together, never looking back. It turned out the two of them were virtually unstoppable. There wasn't a lawman who could get in their way, as the trail of badge-wearing, half-eaten corpses would attest.

"You ever been to Kansas, little brother?"

Arlo shook his head. "What's in Kansas?"

"Farms. Some Injuns."

"Don't sound like nothin' special."

Billy smiled. "Oh, they got some banks, too. Big uns, sittin' there full of money just waitin' for two handsome and enterprisin' young fellers to take. And you know what we'll do with all that money?"

"Whores and whiskey!" Arlo clapped his blood-stained hands together. "Whiskey and whores!" Alro laughed briefly, then grew silent.

'What's wrong with you?" Billy knew that look. Some bad idea had crawled into that large empty space between his little brother's ears and taken root. Whatever it was would worry Arlo for days and make him an annoying pest, forcing Billy to constantly try to put his mind at ease. Unless he could put a stop to it now. "Spill it, Arlo. What's got you bothered?"

Arlo shrugged and kicked the dirt. Finally, he put voice to his fear. "What if one of them masked cowboys come after us? People say they're all over the place. When we was in the New Mexico territory, I heard somebody say the Silver Paladin had been in town a couple of months before. Billy, what's a paladin?"

"A sissy boy in fancy clothes. They're all sissy boys. Ain't none of 'em can take on the Belcher brothers. Count on that." Billy glanced at Arlo to see if his words had any effect. Arlo was staring down at the ground. "What now?"

"But what about the other one? He ain't a sissy boy."

"What other one?"

"The Dead Sheriff."

The Injun meat down in Billy's belly suddenly seemed to twist into a knot. "There ain't no such thing as a Dead Sheriff. Now get some sleep."

"Okay, Billy." Arlo got the bedroll from his saddle and was soon snoring.

Billy Belcher was awake for much longer, mulling over the idea of The Dead Sheriff. The stories all said he was a murdered lawman who came back from the grave to take his revenge on the men who murdered his family. Billy knew it was horseshit. There was no such thing as magic or ghosts. If there was a Dead Sheriff–and that was an *if* as big as Texas–then it was some blowhard in a spook suit. Nobody came back from the bone orchard. Nobody.

If this Dead Sheriff ever tried to hunt down the Belcher brothers, he'd learn that anybody can be killed and eaten. Even a man pretending to be a ghost.

Billy Belcher finally sank into a light, fitful sleep, waking frequently to squint into the night, imagining he saw dark shapes dancing within the shadows.

•••

Nebraska

The Silver Paladin knew what the three coaches were as soon as he spotted them rocking and swaying over the prairie land between Omaha and Lincoln. Even worse, the kid knew.

"Lordy, is that a whorehouse? A horse-drawn whorehouse?" The boy's eyes were fairly popping from his red mask.

The Silver Paladin pulled back on the reins, halting his palomino. The kid followed suit with his own mount. The pair rode across a low ridge, a rare feature in this country. Even with the setting sun quickly dropping from the sky, they were close enough to the caravan to make out every detail on the large coaches. Each vehicle had eight wheels and was pulled by six horses. The windows framed thick, velvet curtains. Most startling were the ornate wood carvings on the sides of each coach depicting a nude woman in a lascivious pose. The carvings disgusted the Silver Paladin, while the kid's reaction was decidedly different.

"Hoo-wee! We got to check it out, Dewey!" The Silver Paladin–who had been born Dewitt Aloysius Martin in Detroit, Michigan thirty-two years earlier–felt an uncomfortable clenching in his guts, like a sick a man gets when something he wants very much is slipping away.

"Not a good idea, Bullet." He used the kid's Masked Man name to show he didn't appreciate the kid calling him Dewey. Not while the masks were on. But the kid wasn't listening. He tugged on the reigns and his Appaloosa started down the ridge. The Silver Paladin spurred his own mount after them. When he reached the boy, he grabbed the Appaloosa's bridle.

"Easy, Bullet. If those wagons are filled with whores, you have to stay away. Those women are unclean and are likely riddled with disease."

The kid jerked his reigns, pulling away from The Silver Paladin. "Stop calling me Bullet. That's a kid's name. I'm sixteen. I'm a man, and it's way past time I had my first woman. Besides, what would you know about whores, Dewey?"

The Silver Paladin turned his head as if he'd been slapped. He felt a flush spreading beneath his mask.

Bullet yanked off his mask and tossed it to the ground. The Silver Paladin couldn't look away. The mask stood out on the grassy hill like a bright splatter of blood.

"I ain't like you, Dewey," the boy said.

"What–what do you..."

"I'm goin' down there. Gonna get me my first woman. Don't try to stop me." The boy spurred his horse into a gallop.

"Bullet! Wait!"

"Don't call me that," the boy hollered back. "My name's not Bullet. It's James!"

As Bullet–James, James Bennett, orphaned five years ago in Tennessee–rode away, The Silver Paladin felt like a chunk of his own soul had been ripped from his body. How could the boy turn on him like this? They had been paired up for many a dusty mile. The Silver Paladin and Bullet were legends out here. Among all the masked men, he and Bullet got top billing. It was a good life. How could the kid throw it all away?

He couldn't. It was as simple as that. The Silver Paladin hopped off his mount to pick up Bullet's mask and quickly climbed back into the saddle. He followed his young partner down the ridge to the wagons below.

He's just feeling his oats, The Silver Paladin thought. *He'll get it out of his system and things will get back to normal.*

Young Dewitt Aloysius Martin had felt his oats, as well, though they were a distinctly different brand. Once again, the masked man's faced grew warm from the memory.

The wagons had settled into a rough circle as the sun finally set. Three men, likely the drivers, worked at lighting torches set into brackets on each of the wagons' corners.

As The Silver Paladin reached the caravan, he saw Bullet climb into one of the wagons, escorted up the steps by a curvaceous raven-haired whore. Even in the torchlight, he saw the boy's wide grin. He drew up a few yards away and dismounted. The three drivers carried fire wood to a pile near the front wagon. They did not speak and seemed to take no notice of him.

He stood there, awkwardly shifting from booted foot to booted foot, holding the reins of his palomino, Shakespeare. When one of the drivers passed close to him, The Silver Paladin said, "Nice evening, isn't it?"

The man acted as if he didn't hear the words. He walked with a lurching step, like a man strolling about in his slumber. Upon closer examination, all three men behaved in the same dream-like manner.

"They're deaf-mutes," a voice said from behind him.

The gasp that squeaked from his lips was pitched so high, he prayed no one had heard. The woman's throaty chuckle told him otherwise.

"My apologies, sir. I did not wish to startle you."

He turned to see the speaker. She was a tall woman, a bit on the thin side. Her long hair was the color of copper and she had ribbons tied throughout the tresses. In the dimness, the material looked black. Her dress was a startling shade of red; that much was clear. She appeared to be in her mid-forties, though well maintained.

"You're probably wondering about my unusual garments," he said.

"I've seen stranger," the woman said.

"I–I'm called The Silver Paladin. You may have heard of me."

"Sorry, no."

"Oh, well. You see, my partner and I–"

"The boy looking for his first taste of pussy?"

"Ah, yes." He cleared his throat. "We, that is the boy and I, are crusaders."

"For or against?"

"Excuse me?"

"I mean are you crusading for something or against something?"

"Oh, I see. I suppose we crusade for justice and against evil."

The woman smiled and extended a hand. "How very nice. I've never met a masked crusader. My name is Magdala, but my girls call me Maggie."

He took her hand and dutifully kissed the back of it. He straightened and said, "Your girls? Then you..."

"Yes. I run this establishment."

"I don't believe I have ever seen a traveling bordello."

"That's just one of the aspects in which we are unique."

The three silent drivers lit the small fire and slowly fed more wood to it. They paid no attention to The Silver Paladin or Magdala. In the distance, horses snorted and huffed.

A sound issued from the wagon, a noise that was somewhere between a moan and a scream.

"It sounds like your young friend is making a memory that will stay with him for a long time." Magdala smiled, and in the firelight her lips were the color of blood, her teeth the shade of bones bleached by the sun.

The Silver Paladin restlessly shifted from foot to foot.

"You're aren't very comfortable making small talk outside a whorehouse," Magdala said.

"Uh, not really."

"Would you care to come in?"

"No! That is, I mean, I'm perfectly fine. I can wait here until the boy... until he's finished."

"That may be a while. My girls insist on customer satisfaction."

"Be that as it may, I will wait outside."

"I see." Magdala touched the sleeve of his silk shirt. "I know men pretty well. After all, they are my business. And I feel that you don't have an interest in our services."

The Silver Paladin took a step back from the woman. "Now, hold on. I don't know what you're implying-"

"Easy, crusader. I'm not here to judge. It was just an observation. I simply wanted to offer you a drink and conversation to pass the time, since you won't be needing one of my girls."

"Oh. I appreciate that, but I'm afraid I must decline your offer. I never drink alcohol. To do my work, I must keep my body pure."

Magdala threw back her head and laughed like a cow puncher in a saloon. After catching her breath, she said, "I have not met a man like you for a very long time."

Another figure appeared at her side. It was one of the odd drivers and he carried a tin coffee pot and a china cup. He poured the coffee into the cup and held it out for The Silver Paladin.

"Surely you're not adverse to coffee on a chilly night," Magdala said.

He took the cup in both hands. "No, I suppose not." He sipped at the beverage. It was hot and delicious. When he looked up from the cup, the driver was gone. He did not know how the woman has summoned or dismissed him. Since the man was deaf, she likely used a subtle hand signal.

"Tell me, Mister Paladin, is that mask really pure silver?"

He suddenly felt ridiculous in the mask and the fancy garments, like a child caught playing dress up. He held the china cup in one hand and used the other to remove the mask. What the hell. It wasn't as if anyone in this territory would recognize Dewey Martin. "Yes, ma'am. It is pure silver. Would you like to try it on?"

He held the mask out to her, but she didn't take it. Instead, she backed away until her face was hidden in the shadows.

Embarrassed, certain he had committed some error of social graces, he apologized. "I'm so sorry. I guess...I guess my face is one that is better off covered up."

Magdala stepped forward into the light. She looked as sorry as Dewey. "No, no. It is I who should ask for your pardon. It's just that...you look like someone I once knew."

"Should I put the mask back on?"

"No, please leave it off. Let me look at you for a bit."

Dewey placed the mask on the driver's seat. Magdala smile was back and it was almost hungry. It made him uncomfortable. "So, do you think they're, ah, almost finished in there?"

She shook her head. "How old is he? Seventeen? Eighteen?"

"Sixteen."

"Then no. You know what they say about young men. They're quick on the trigger but just as fast on the reload."

He looked at the ground, the night sky, the fire. Anywhere but at her. He briefly noted that the fire was now unattended. The three drivers were no longer in sight.

"Tell me, Mister Paladin, are there many more like you?"

"There are others in this line of work," he said. "The Night Marshall. The Cyclone. The Red Ranger. Pecos Randy."

"Pecos *Randy*?"

"He was kicked in the head by a mule. More than once. Frankly, ma'am, none of these attention seeking vigilantes have the high standards of The Silver Paladin and Bullet."

"Bullet? Is that..." She nodded toward the coach.

"Well, we usually have high standards."

"Why, Mister Paladin, I feel insulted."

Dewey took off his hat. "I must apologize again. I meant no offense. You have been very polite and well-mannered." He lowered his head. "This really isn't like me. I've behaved badly."

Magdala laughed again. "Oh, not as badly as you're going to behave."

"What do you mean?"

Strong hands gripped his arms. At least two of the drivers held him tight. The china cup fell to the ground. Magdala removed his six shooters from his holsters.

The door to the coach opened and something tumbled down the steps to land with a soft thud in the dirt. The third driver appeared from behind the coach carrying a torch. He knelt by the fallen form.

"Look at it," Magdala said.

"No!" Dewey squeezed his eyes shut, afraid of what he would see. He was frightened and confused and sure his world had gone mad, suddenly aware that everything he had gained in the past few years–his confidence, skill and reputation–was nothing but a sham.

A set of strong hands turned his head toward the torch-bearing man. One of those same hands yanked back on Dewey's scalp until he opened his eyes.

Bullet lay on the ground, naked. It was a sight Dewey had often imagined. But never in his most fevered fantasies had the boy's throat been ripped away. Bullet's–Jimmy's–unseeing eyes stared up at the cold, dark sky.

"Oh, Jimmy." He couldn't stop the sobs. "Oh, no."

He knew his life was over. These people, these impossible monsters, would never let him go. He always knew he might perish following this path, yet he never envisioned an end this horrible.

And then it got worse.

The boy blinked. He sucked in a long breath, and then rolled over and pushed himself to his feet. He saw Dewey and he smiled.

For a second, a brief, deliriously happy second, Dewey thought *He's okay, he's alive.*

But when he saw the dead, empty eyes he knew the boy was not okay. Or alive.

Bullet walked to him, unsteadily at first, unsure, then with stronger steps. His young cock swung to and fro, and Dewey knew it was one of the last sights he would see on this earth. He began to pray.

Magdala heard his whispers and laughed. Bullet joined her. He stood very close to Dewey and said, "Come on, partner. Ain't this what you always wanted?"

The boy opened his mouth to display many white and very sharp teeth.

The Silver Paladin screamed for a long time.

CHAPTER TWO

FROM THE JOURNAL OF RICHARD O'MALLEY

The past six weeks seem like the dream of an opium user.

After the events in Damnation, I traveled with Sam–the young man the public knew as Cheveyo–and the unusual cargo in the back of his wagon. We headed northeast, a course of which I took little notice. The events in that hellish Texas town had been so fantastic and grueling, that I truly believe my sanity had been at risk.

Once the excitement of our adventure in that apocalyptic city left my body, I felt as weak and fearful as a small child. I had been used by forces beyond my comprehension. Even though I was not in control, I was the instrument of destruction that obliterated an entire population–men, women and children. Some were truly evil, others guilty of nothing more than living in the wrong place.

For forty nights, my sleep has been filled with visions of burning men, demonic faces and screams, and The Dead Sheriff. Unstoppable and unkillable, because he is already dead, the reanimated corpse tied securely in Sam's buckboard walks freely in my dreams, free of the reins of Sam's mystical talismans. The Dead Sheriff speaks to me in those dreams, sometimes warning me, other nights issuing a plea for salvation. In the morning I can never recall his words.

I do not know who the man was before Sam's magic resurrected him from the grave in a scheme to make money. I only know that when I left Boston to write a dime novel about the west's undead avenger, I never dreamed how bizarre the truth would actually be. I could never write the real story of The Dead Sheriff. At best, I would be labeled as a liar and a blasphemer; at worst I would be imprisoned in an asylum for the insane.

If I did write of The Dead Sheriff, it would be the story of the legend, not the truth. Of course, I could not be expected to write of the truth when I could not begin to understand it. In the first days following the events in Damnation, Sam told me of his own shock at the devastation wreaked by his magic in that doomed town. Later, I tried to engage Sam in further conversation regarding the actions that befell me and how the destruction in Damnation was even possible. His only response was a grunt. It soon became obvious that he comprehended the mystic occurrence little more than I. We seldom spoke after that.

On the other hand, he hasn't left me behind or asked me to leave. Perhaps he now considers me a useful member of his "team", or it could be that he is just as overwhelmed by what happened as I am, and one day will realize that he doesn't need a former newspaper man tagging along. If that moment occurs, I must decide either to plead my case and stay or to part company with Sam, returning to a world I understand, a world where dead men don't walk and Satanic demons don't rise from Hades to murder a town.

I am not living the life I expected.

•••

We made camp in the shadows of the mountain range the Choctaw called Ouachita, near the town of Hot Springs in Arkansas. I had been so consumed by my despair and confusion that I hadn't realized we had passed out of Texas several days before.

Sam left camp that night without explanation, as befitted our current status. I stayed behind with our meager rations, Sam's bad coffee and the contents of the wagon. The moon was bright that night and I slept fitfully. After awakening from another barely-remembered nightmare, I crawled from my cold bedroll and walked stiffly around our camp. The fire was almost out, so I placed several small tree branches on it and poked and prodded them until the flames rose warm and bright. I squatted there until the chill fled my bones, before I went to the buckboard, as though drawn by a call I did not understand.

I untied Sam's careful knots and pulled the rope away from the canvas. I yanked back the covering and let the moonlight illuminate my prize and now my bane.

The corpse was in remarkable shape, considering that it had been sliced to pieces by the Gatling guns of Reverend Ludlow Skaggs back in Damnation. Though ravaged by fire and by lead, The Dead Sheriff was whole again. Or mostly so. The effects of decomposition were still evident in the blank, sunken orbs that filled his eye sockets and the slackness of muscle and tendon that allowed his jaw to hang open. Sam had replaced the clothing that The Dead Sheriff wore before Damnation and while the undead avenger had not been active since then, the clothing was stained in places by the oily black fluid that sometimes seeped form the corpse.

Soon after the destruction of Damnation, I had awakened to see The Dead Sheriff squatting near our fire, free from the control of Sam's mystical amulet and book. The corpse stared at me as though he had the ability to observe and react. And while I stared back, transfixed, a tear rolled from one sightless eye.

Amazingly, I fell asleep then, and over time, I have become convinced that what I thought I saw was the product of the nightmare-plagued slumber of a broken man.

Please do not ask me how I could have witnessed the events of the past few months and still doubt that The Dead Sheriff could move on his own. I suppose in the midst of such madness, I needed to hold on to at least a lone strand of rationality.

I poked the dead man in the chest. The skin beneath the shirt felt as soft as a wet sponge.

"Is someone in there?" My voice sounded odd in the night: loud, coarse and with a slight edge of hysteria. "Is there a soul in this rotting shell?"

Of course, there was no response. At that moment, I felt ridiculous. Here I was, a former reporter and son of a Boston police officer, standing next to a dead man, asking him questions and expecting a response.

I started to laugh. It was an unexpected chortle, rising from my chest like something that had been trapped. Soon, I was doubled over, giggling and gasping for breath. It took a long time for my mirth to subside, and when it did, I realized that I was better. I was healing, somehow accepting the madness that had become a part of my life. For now, at least, the darkness that stained my soul had retreated.

I returned to my bedroll and fell into a deep and dreamless sleep.

•••

Sam returned with the sun. I lay there, content to watch the dawn spread across the mountains, amazed at the renewal I received from a few hours of untroubled rest. The sun was in my eyes and Sam was nearly upon me before I saw him. He tied his horse to the buckboard next to my own mount and allowed the animal to graze

The past few weeks had taken a toll on him. He was even thinner than before Damnation, though that hardly seemed possible, and the loss of weight made him appear no older than a teenager. His long black hair was untied and flowed to his shoulders. He'd told me than he was of mixed heritage, yet he appeared to be of pure Indian blood. He called no tribe his own and seemed to owe allegiance to nothing save the money he earned with The Dead Sheriff. The only other items I had learned about him were his love of whiskey, his hatred of whores and the fact that in his sleep he sometimes talked to someone named Old Luke.

He was unfriendly and uneducated, yet at the same time he had a natural intelligence and the tiniest inkling of a conscience, which surfaced in rare moments.

"You awake," he said. It was the longest sentence he had spoken in days.

"I am," I said, "and ready for whatever the day brings."

He grunted. He went to the dwindling fire to stoke enough heat to warm the coffee. With a full cup, walked to the edge of our camp and stared at the mountains. After a short time, he poured the bitter liquid upon the ground..

"We need money," he said, his back to me.

"That's three words, Sam. I bet your mouth is worn out." Any intimidation I felt months ago upon meeting the famed Cheveyo, legendary "partner" of The Dead Sheriff, had vanished even before I became a murderer of hundreds back in Texas.

He turned to favor me with a squint. I returned his gaze.

"We're getting low on provisions. Most places won't sell to Injuns, so you have to head into Hot Springs and get us stocked up."

"Okay." Apparently, Sam decided that I served a useful purpose after all. "With what money? Do you have a hidey hole near here?" During our journey I had learned that Sam had secured his earnings in several safe places around the territories. I knew he had at least three spots in Texas.

"Nope," he said. "There's a small one west of here in Injun territory and a bigger one in Kansas."

"Then why are we in Arkansas?"

"For this." He approached me with something rolled up in his hand. It was a wanted poster. He passed it over and I unfurled it. In the center was a drawing of a man with a fat face and a long mustache. He was called Duke Martin, and he was worth five hundred dollars for bank robbery and crimes against man and God.

"What does that mean?"

"He diddles children," Sam said. "And we're gonna collect the bounty on that sick asshole."

•••

I found Duke Martin in a little diner called Toledo's on the dusty central avenue of Hot Springs. I got a table nearby and used a bit of Sam's money to enjoy eggs, ham, biscuits and hot coffee. Compared to the fare of the last few weeks, it was a repast worthy of royalty.

Martin was even more corpulent in life. The flesh of his neck fell like curtains over his shirt collar. His eyes were very small and restless, like those of a cunning little animal. The ends of his mustache were stained by tobacco juice and the morning's breakfast gravy.

He sat with two other men. One of them–a thin man with a face like a rat--called Martin by the name "Harry", so at least I know part of his alias. Over the course of the meal, I heard the trio discuss the town's famed springs, supposedly the source of miraculous healing waters.

"You should try them before you leave, Harry," the other man said. He was shaped like a whiskey barrel and had small, dark eyes.

"It cleared up the ache in my shoulder after one dip, Harry," the rat-faced man added.

"Maybe I will," Martin said even as he dug at a piece of meat in his teeth with a yellowed fingernail.

"You have to try it at sunup," the first man said.

"Nothing like being in the spring when the sun rises," the second one agreed. "I think there's something about the sun that energizes the power of the water."

"In the morning, then," Martin said. He pulled a gold coin from a pocket and tossed it on the table. I understood why the two men were fawning over him.

The three of them left the restaurant. I took my time finishing my meal, paid my tab and sought out the general store. I purchased the supplies we needed. With full saddlebags, I rode back to camp.

Sam had explained that he'd carried Martin's poster for a couple of months. When we fled what remained of Damnation, he'd steered us in the direction where Duke Martin had last been spotted. Sam, being an outcast in the white man's world, used a network of similarly positioned individuals to aid him in his work. These stable boys and kitchen workers and field hands, invisibles to most, often had vital information that Sam could use. It was this network that put him on Martin's trail back before we met.

Even as I feared the events in Texas would cost me my sanity, Sam was still doing his job. He'd slipped into town the previous night and showed his poster to certain persons who were likely to trust him. Martin was quickly identified as a guest in the Wilbury, the finest hotel and gambling establishment in Hot Springs. Once Martin completed a bank job, he certainly wasn't shy about spending his ill-gotten gains. One of Sam's sources even revealed that Martin was posing as a wealthy banker from Omaha.

It was then I realized that I was acclimating to the unusual life of a bounty hunter, for now that I knew where Martin would be, I felt the thrill of the hunt and a tingle of excitement. Perhaps I would be able to hold off the black cloud of fear for another day.

I arrived at camp by midday. Sam helped me store our provisions, as I told him about my observation of Martin.

"Is it time for The Dead Sheriff to come out of retirement?" I asked.

Sam nodded.

"At the Wilbury or at the spring?"

The bed of Sam's wagon had been separated into two compartments. One held the corpse. The other was for our provisions and personal belongings. He'd allowed me a small space for my valise. Now he searched through his own things.

"Either place would work," I said. "But fewer people will be at the spring, meaning less of a chance of shooting a bystander."

Sam straightened with a bundle in his arms. It was three feet long and wrapped in a blanket. He pulled the cloth away to reveal the hidden item.

"How 'bout we try something different this time," he said.

●●●

I was in place before sunup. Steam rose from a spring large enough for three buckboards to sink within. I did not know if this was a standard size. Admittedly, this was the first hot spring I had encountered.

Shortly before the break of dawn, five figures appeared on the hillside, making their way down to the spring. I stayed back, hidden in the shadows of a distant copse of pines. When the crowd passed me, I slipped from concealment and joined the parade. I was dressed in denim pants and shirt, beneath which I wore my union suit. I expected to bathe in those. I carried a towel I had lifted from the Wilbury.

Martin and the two sycophants from Toledo's were trailed by an older couple. The man was portly with a white handlebar mustache and the woman, also advanced in age, was quite large and covered in enough fabric to wrap a circus tent,

I removed my clothes. Duke Martin had already stripped down to his skivvies and settled his flabby girth into the steaming water. The two toadies quickly followed suit. Since I wasn't wearing skivvies, I sat in the pool wearing my union suit. The woman slid into the water inch by careful inch, aided by her husband, making little gasping noises all the while, though the likelihood of water actually touching her protected corpulence was quite small. Once she was settled, her husband disrobed to reveal his own union suit and he joined her on the other side. Once Martin's pals entered the spring, everyone began to relax.

That wasn't going to last long.

Martin's rat-faced companion nudged the flabby man with an elbow. "What did I tell you, Harry? Relaxing, ain't it?"

Martin reclined against the slope of the pool with his eyes closed. His only response was a grunt.

I cleared my throat. "Harry? You're kidding me."

Martin opened one eye. His two associates both stared at me, an intruder upon their special moment with the rich man.

"You're calling yourself Harry now?"

Martin's one eye continued to examine me. "Who the fuck are you?"

The woman next to me gasped at the profanity.

"Please, Duke," I said. "There's a lady present."

Martin slowly sat up. Both of his eyes were open now.

The man who was shaped like a barrel glanced from Martin to me and back at Martin. "Harry, what's he talking about?"

Martin stood up. Water rolled down his prodigious belly and dripped back into the spring. He took a step toward me. "Yeah, what are you talking about, asshole?"

The woman made another exclamation while her husband uttered a *tsk* of disapproval.

As for me, I began to regret my participation in this affair. I cleared my throat before I spoke.

"I'm someone who can read wanted posters. And I've seen a poster that says your name is Duke Martin, and you are wanted for bank robbery."

Duke's faced grew red and I was fairly certain it wasn't due to the water temperature. The complexions of his two associates lost all color, as if Martin's rage was draining it from them.

"You fellows didn't know about 'Harry's' other life, eh? Robbing banks is pretty bad." I shook my head at the shame of it all. "Of course, robbing is one thing. It's quite another to do nasty things to children when you think no one else is watching. Right, Duke?"

The old woman fainted and slid under the water. Her husband pulled

"Yeah, what are you talking about asshole?"

her up by locking his hands beneath her ample bosom. Her head rolled loosely about her shoulders.

Duke did not respond. He stepped closer to me.

Duke's tremendous width blocked my view of his companions. I had to lean to my left in order to make eye contact with them. Rat-face's mouth hung open. Barrel Man stood as still as a statue.

"Did you boys know how big the reward is for your friend?"

Finally, Duke spoke again. "Who's gonna collect that reward, shit bag? You?

I stood up and said, "The Dead Sheriff."

I felt cold and skinny and more than a little afraid. But my words had their desired effect.

Martin whipped his thick neck around so quickly that his jowls danced a little jig.

After assuring himself that no dead vigilante loomed near, her turned his gaze back at me. His piggish eyes narrowed to slits. His mouth was touched with the hint of a cruel smile.

"I guess you and me are gonna have a little talk before your Dead Sheriff gets–"

The corners of his smile dropped and his eyebrows knitted in confusion.

Martin grunted once, then softly spoke. "Aw, hell."

A stream of blood trickled from the left side of his mouth.

He grunted more loudly, and his chest burst open.

Blood exploded from the opening, splattering me, the unconscious woman and her husband.

The hole in Martin's chest opened further and something emerged from the gory wound. It was curved metal and it was festooned with bits of dripping meat. Martin's chin fell forward. Since his eyes were closed, I suspect he never saw the sword that took his life. The big man shook. I was quite certain spring water wasn't the only thing running down his leg. The big man's body seemed to float into the cool morning air, until his feet were exposed to the rising sun. Then the sword withdrew in a flash. Martin's corpse seemed to hang in the air for a long moment, though it could not have been more than a fraction of a second, before he splashed face first into the pool. I had to step aside to avoid being struck by the body.

The splash awoke the old woman. She sputtered and coughed and tried to stand. Yet when she saw what stood where Duke Martin had been, she fainted again. Her husband did not immediately notice, transfixed as he was by the sight before him.

The Dead Sheriff was a figure from the most horrible of nightmares. His face was fixed in a grimace of angry determination; the visage of swift and brutal vengeance. In some places, the flesh upon his skull had peeled away revealing the gray and white bone beneath. His shirt and pants, now soaked and plastered to his form, were bullet-riddled and stained from the dark fluids that served as blood within his decaying body. His hair was an indeterminate color and existed in patches on the scalp, where otherwise ragged and flaking flesh held sway.

But the worst thing about the creature was the eyes. They lacked pupils, those two pale orbs. Their color was white with thin webs of yellow running through them. If you stared at them long enough, though, you grew convinced that something dark swam behind them. I believed it was a result of the dark magic that animated this undead lawman.

"Shit," Rat Face said. "Shit! Shit!" He turned to the pile of clothes on the ground beside of the pool. He rummaged through them and produced a big Colt pistol.

"Whoa!" I held up my hands. "Hold up. He doesn't want you."

Rat Face pulled the trigger. The bullet must have struck The Dead Sheriff in the lower back because it exited from his stomach and dug into the side of the spring where the old woman had been before she sank beneath the water.

Before the man could fire again, The Dead Sheriff turned and slashed with the sword. Rat Face's hand and gun splashed into the spring. A fountain of blood gushed from the stump of the man's wrist and slowly turned the spring into a lake of scarlet.

Barrel Man chose discretion. He scrambled from the pool and ran for the trees, leaving his clothes behind.

The old man was still transfixed by The Dead Sheriff. I put my arms in the water and felt around until I had a good hold on the old woman. Pulling her up strained my arms and back. It didn't seem possible but she was even heavier than she looked.

"Hey," I said to her husband. He didn't react. I took a chance and pulled one hand away from the mountain of flesh that was his spouse. I slapped the man's face. "Hey, help me before she drowns."

He shook his head and touched his cheek. Finally, he turned slowly toward me, like a man awakening from a dream.

"Get her out of the water," I said.

He stole one more glance at the corpse standing in the water and the other one floating face down before he joined me in hauling the woman to safety. When we were both on dry ground, he said, "What is that?"

"The Dead Sheriff."

His face grew ashen. "No shit?"

His wife moaned. Presumably she was awake enough to be offended once again.

"No shit," I said.

"I thought it was just a story."

"So did I. Until I met him."

I joined him in helping the woman to her feet. As he led her away, she murmured questions and I heard him trying to answer her.

Rat Face was still in the water, sobbing and cradling his bleeding wrist.

"Get your belt and tie it tightly around your lower arm," I said. "It will slow down the bleeding until you can get to a doctor."

He stared at me as though he didn't understand the words I spoke.

"Here. Let me help."

But as I stepped in his direction, he slithered out of the spring on his belly, grabbed his pile of clothes and stumbled away. I watched him run, then walk. After a hundred yards or so, he collapsed and did not move again.

I heard a splash.

The Dead Sheriff had waded to the side of the spring, where he attempted to climb out. He slipped on the wet soil and fell back in the pool. He repeated the process a few times with the same result. Finally, I took his wrist and pulled.

"Careful," a voice behind me said. "Don't yank his arm off!"

Sam had left his place of concealment in the same trees where I had waited for Duke Martin. Around his neck was the medallion that gave him control over The Dead Sheriff.

"Seriously," he said. "One time in Carson City a drunk wanted for murder tried to get hold of one of the dead guy's guns away. Instead, he ended up pulling his arm off at the shoulder. Do you know how long it took for that thing to reattach enough before I could take him out on another job?"

"What happened to the drunk guy?"

"The Dead Sheriff's got two guns," Sam said.

Except that at the moment the undead avenger's holster and guns were strung over Sam's shoulder. I carefully helped the dead man to solid ground, at one point putting an arm around his shoulders to gain better leverage. It felt like I was holding a bundle of sticks.

"Who's going to get the sheriff?"

"This town has a marshal," he said. "You get him. I'll stay here in case our friend has to perform again."

As I dressed, Sam buckled the guns on The Dead Sheriff. The corpse stood silently, as he always did. I looked for some sign of activity in those blank eyes, but saw nothing.

"At least his bath cut down on the stink," Sam said.

"Don't get any ideas."

"What does that mean?"

I laughed as I started the walk toward town. When I reached the cover of the trees, I threw up, and then sat on the ground shaking for at least ten minutes.

•••

The transaction went smoother than most. The marshal needed two days to get the reward money, which he apologized for. Like most law enforcement officials, he wasn't anxious to have something as unnatural as The Dead Sheriff staying on his town any longer than necessary.

It was late in the day when we finally got the money. Sam stored it in the wagon while I cooked dinner: chicken from one of the farmers at the edge of town, beans and biscuits from one of the local diners. Despite myself, I was becoming a passable camp cook.

As we ate, I asked Sam where we were headed next.

"Back toward Injun territory, I reckon."

Sam seemed relaxed. But there was something about the way he held himself, a certain tightness around the mouth, that spoke of worry. Perhaps he, too, was still dealing with the aftereffects of our time in Damnation

"To make a deposit in your 'bank'?"

"That's part of it," he said, holding up several wanted posters that he had poached from the marshal's office.

"Anything interesting?"

He shrugged. "A pair of brothers."

"What did they do?"

"A little thievin' and some eatin'."

"Excuse me?"

"They like to eat people."

I felt supper churning in my stomach. I coughed into my hand. "Life in your company is not especially boring."

Sam nodded. "More stories for your book. You *are* still writin' it, ain't you?"

"I am. I make extensive notes in my journal."

Honestly, I wasn't sure I even wanted to be a writer any more. My time with Sam and the incredible events I had been party to had me reconsidering the man I thought I was. If I told him I wouldn't write the book, I feared he would force me to leave. Before I came out west I had been only an observer to life. Now, finally, I felt like a participant. I was changing. And I wasn't certain I would recognize myself in a few more months, particularly if we encountered anything approaching the strangeness of what happened back in that Texas town of Damnation.

On the other hand, how many times could a man expect to experience something that unholy and other worldly?

It felt like we were going to be dealing with nothing more unusual than bandits and killers. And I would be fine with that.

CHAPTER THREE

New Orleans

The man with the long red hair, who presently called himself Mr. Labine, studied his face in the mirror. His features were angular and just a shade too rough to be considered handsome. Few lines were evident around his eyes and mouth. He'd managed to delay the effects of aging, at least so far.

I have enough dark magick for that, anyway, he thought.

Magick. Just the word caused the anger to flare. But not just anger, if he was being honest with himself. There was a touch of fear, as well. He made a sound low in his throat.

"*Quel est le problème?*"

He turned to the room's small bed.

"Nothing's wrong, my dear. I simply hate that I must leave the presence of your beauty."

The whore reclined upon the stained sheets, all of her gifts on display. Her skin was the color of coffee, tempered by cream. She still had her beauty, though he knew that would be fleeting in her profession. He couldn't remember her name. It didn't matter. Unfortunately, he wouldn't be back this way for a decade or two. By that time, she would most likely be dead thanks to disease or the violence of a customer.

Some men were addicted to whiskey, some to laudanum. He was addicted to whores. He'd had them from Europe to the States, young and old, black and white and red.

Red.

The rage rushed from the center of his chest to his head, arriving at his temples like a railroad spike driven by a steel hammer. Instantly, he desired nothing more than to strike someone, but he didn't want to ruin the whore's pretty young face. Besides, she wasn't his real target.

He ached to clasp his hands around the throat of that half-breed son of a whore from New Mexico, the one who caught him at his most vulnerable.

The boy who stole his two most powerful talismans.

He clenched his hand into fists and stared at his own reflection, willing the anger to retreat. He would store it deep inside where it would serve him well when he finally ran down his prey.

Without speaking to the whore again, Mr. Labine left the room and exited the house. The evening was cool for this time of the year, and he enjoyed his stroll east to Faubourg Marigny. The air was sweet with the scent of jasmine and honeysuckle. When he arrived at Esplanade, he found his servant standing in the shadow of a live oak behind one of the large white houses that lined the street. A section of the black iron fence had been crushed to the ground as easy as if it had been constructed of newspaper.

He could sense impatience emanating from the large figure.

"My apologies. I hope you will forgive my weakness."

The nearest gas streetlight was at least fifty feet away, yet he could see a flare of illumination from the eyes of the shadowed form.

"I know my duty," he said sharply. "I certainly hope you know yours."

A rumble issued deep within the other's chest. He imagined he could feel it through the soles of his own boots.

"I can't tell where he is now. The connection to my stolen magick has grown dim. I–"

The sensation struck Labine between the shoulder blades. From there, it spread up and down, traveling along the endings of his nerves and filling up his senses. He recognized the taste, the feel of the thing. It was his, and it was the grandest pleasure he had ever known, better than fucking.

It was his magick. The half breed was using it again. The connection was faint; only a hint of what it would be when he was near the talismans again. But for this moment, it would do.

"I feel it," he said to his companion.

There was no reaction from the dark figure.

"It's east of here. That's all I can say for now. Except...except it's on the move."

Actually, he didn't know if the half breed was moving, taking a nap or standing on his head. Fortunately, he was fairly certain his friend knew even less about the magick.

Another rumble issued from the darkness. More impatience, seasoned with hatred.

"I cannot yet determine which way it's moving. It's best to stay here for a short time, until we can be certain."

He was thinking of the lovely young mulatto whore and how she might help him pass another evening or two.

This time the rumble was louder. The large shape moved closer.

"Moloch!" Mr. Labine made his voice firm and commanding, hiding his doubts and fears. "Moloch, I say your name and in the saying bind you to this place and to my will. We will find the magick that your master gave to me and which was stolen by this cowardly youth."

He raised his hands to his chest. A wavering light–like the weak flame of a small candle–appeared between his fingertips. Within the light, a shape appeared, in shades of yellow. It was the face of a young man with long black hair. The half breed.

"This is your enemy, and the enemy of your master. Not I. This is the one we shall find. When we do, his bones will be yours to grind into powder."

The creature called Moloch stretched out an arm covered in dark fabric. Only the hand was visible, and it possessed long claws and too many fingers. The flesh was also dark, and reflected light like something wet. The hand clenched into a fist.

Moloch stepped back deeper into the shadows. Quiet. And patient. For now.

"Good," Mr. Labine said. "You and your master will both have satisfaction. This I swear. I will return when I have news."

Labine retraced his path to the French Quarter. He'd taken rooms there, within walking distance of the whorehouse. He would return for a meal and sleep. He would need his strength, both for tracking the son of a bitch who held his dear possessions, and for at least one more visit to the girl who spoke only French.

•••

Wichita, Kansas

For Claire Kingman, Wichita was the closest thing to heaven she was likely to find here on Earth.

When her husband David had proposed moving from Chicago to the untamed West, Claire had been against the idea. She pictured them living in a tent, fighting off Indian attacks and wild animals, and living like savages. But then David had introduced her to his father's friend Mr. Stevenson, who owned much land in Wichita and several businesses, including the Federated Bank of Kansas. He'd explained that Wichita was a boomtown, thanks to the cattle business and the railroad. The need for hotels, restaurants and other basic services was outstripping the available pool of workers. It was a time of tremendous opportunity; both for investors and anyone wanting to set down roots in a thriving community.

He made it sound so romantic and adventurous. And it was, at first.

Mr. Stevenson kindly gave them several acres on his ranch outside of town. His workers built the basic frame of the house and roofed it in before they arrived. David went immediately to work finishing it, while she began the job Mr. Stevenson arranged for her at the Federated Bank in Wichita.

At the end of their first week in town, she and David made love in their new home, on a blanket her mother had quilted, bathed by the light from their new fireplace. At that moment, she knew moving out West was the best thing they could have done.

As the months went on, David's duties on Mr. Stevenson's ranch grew, until he eventually had to travel in the role of cattle agent. The new home seemed far less cozy at night and the howls of shrieks off the prairie caused many sleepless nights.

At least she had her job at the bank.

It was good work and she discovered that she good at it. She had a facility for numbers. Her fellow employees and the public adored her (and after a long night cringing to the howls of coyotes, the attention she got from many of the male customers was flattering, indeed. There were benefits to being the only female employee).

Work was her escape. Until the day *they* came into the bank.

She noticed the smell before she saw them. It was a rancid odor, like spoiled meat and sweat and manure all rolled up into one tremendous stink.

She glanced up from her station behind the counter. She'd been counting out a small withdrawal for Mrs. Forrester, the wife of the Methodist preacher. Over the top one the small woman's bonnet-cloaked head, she noticed the two strangers. The one in front was slim, but the man behind him was the largest person Claire had ever seen. Both men were filthy–she was now certain they were the source of the foul odor. It wasn't the dirt of the normal workaday ranch hand, though. Their hair was plastered against the skull fine as a thick sheen of grease. Their clothes were stained with God knew what and the bigger one's face was stained with something that looked like rouge, especially his lips.

"Excuse me," the smaller one softly said. No one paid him any heed.

He pulled a Colt from his holster and shot Mrs. Forrester in the back of the head. Before Claire could understand what was happening, she was covered in warm, thick fluid. It was only later that she understood that it was the blood and the brains of the preacher's wife. Mrs. Forrester head rested on the counter in front of Claire, as though the elderly woman had chosen that moment to take a brief nap.

Her ears rang with the echo of gunfire, yet she still heard the next chilling words of the killer.

"Now that I got your attention, we aim to rob yah, then we aim to eat yah."

He casually strolled to Claire's window and shoved the corpse aside. A glistening smear of gore remained on the counter. His stench was nearly overpowering.

"And by 'eat yah'," the killer said, "I mean *eat* yah."

He grabbed her wrist, pulling her partway across the counter. She screamed in shock and surprise. The killer lowered his mouth to her forearm and bit down, tearing a chunk of her skin and muscle from her. The pain must have caused her to pass out for a second. Her vision grew gray and receded to a pinpoint of light before going completely black. The agony in her arm jolted her to consciousness almost immediately and the first thing she saw was the killer as he smiled and chewed her flesh–a piece of *her*.

He licked his blood splattered lips.

"I know, I know. I said I was going to rob yah first, but you looked so goddamned sweet I had to get me a little taste."

A man screamed somewhere in the room. It sounded like Mr. Harrison, the bank's manager, a strong and confident leader. Now he sounded like a frightened child. She imagined the other thief, the giant, was doing something horrible to him.

Claire couldn't move, couldn't tear her eyes away from the flesh-eating madman. She felt the blood running from her pounding arm. The room seemed to spin around her. And she couldn't look away from the man who was going to kill her.

Where was the town Marshall? Who was going to save them?

But she knew the answer.

No one was coming.

The man released her arm. Claire stumbled backward. Her knees buckled and she fell to the floor. She lay there, aware of the grunts and the screams and wet sounds of tearing flesh. At some point, the smaller killer came behind the counter. His boots were covered in mud and shit and bright red blood. He was gathering the cash. There was a lot of it. It was payroll day for most of the cattle companies.

"Got the cash, little brother. Finish it," the killer said.

There were gunshots. Claire's entire world now consisted of pain, of acrid smoke and the coppery scent of blood. She lacked the strength to lift her head. Her own blood pooled around her.

"We ain't got time to eat 'em all, Arlo. Pick one to take with yah," the killer, *her* killer, said.

"Okay, Billy," a deeper voice replied.

She faced the back of the counter and her work station, not really seeing anything, just waiting for the inevitable and feeling her days on Earth winding down well before she thought they would. That view was suddenly replaced by the ugly, dirty face of the killer, as he squatted next to her.

"It's a bad day, huh?"

She didn't answer.

"Gonna get worse, I'm afraid."

She thought about David and her parents back in Chicago, rebuilding after the big fire last year. She thought about the child she wished she was carrying and how unfair it was that a monster could steal away your life.

"Me and my brother are gonna take yah back to our camp and we're gonna build a fire and slow roast you over it like a hog. Then I'm gonna eat the soft and tender parts of yah. And yah got plenty of those." He brought out his gun, a long-barreled pistol. "So thank yah for the food I am about to receive."

Claire, who had been raised to be a lady, felt a stab of despair and anger deep within her heart. With her last breath, she spoke words that sounded to her ears as if they came from another person.

"Fuck you."

The world was an explosion of light and noise. And then there was darkness.

•••

One more month and then I'm done.

The thought passed through Sam's head for the hundredth time that day and it wasn't even noon.

The seat of the wagon rocked comfortably beneath him. O'Malley dozed upright next to them. The city boy was plenty rattled after that excitement in Damnation. Now he seemed to be putting it behind him.

Well, that made one of them.

That business in Texas had shaken Sam up something powerful, even more than he'd realized. After a few sleepless nights, he honestly thought he was over it.

And then the dreams started.

Sam would awake shaking, drenched in his sweat, with his mind reeling from barely-remembered images of dark, impossible shapes and inhuman screams. Yes, the dreams were bad. But not as bad as what happened next.

Sam started seeing nightmare figures when he was awake.

At first, it was a glimpse from the corner of his eye: someone in the shadows, next to a building or under a tree, someone with a silhouette that seemed...strange. Too tall or too thin. Or too many limbs. But when he turned to get a good luck at the figure, it would be gone.

The sightings increased in frequency, with the worst–and strangest– incident happening at the springs in Arkansas.

While he was hidden in the trees, preparing to guide the dead man against Duke Martin, Sam felt a crawling across the back of his neck. He turned and saw several figures standing about ten feet away.

This time, they didn't vanish.

Though they remained in sight, there was something unnatural about the group that convinced Sam they were more images from his nightmares.

Wearing dark robes, six or seven shapes watched him. He couldn't tell if they were man or woman, since they were deep within the morning shadows of the trees. The only thing he could say for sure was that they were old. He wasn't sure how he knew this. It was a certainty that sprang from his head. He thought that maybe they were judging him, gauging whether or not he was worthy.

But worthy of what?

One of the figures raised a robed arm to point at Sam, and Sam froze in place. He was sure the figure was about to speak, and he was pretty damn certain that was the last thing he ever wanted to hear.

As he stared, the silent chorus faded from sight, like fog burned away by the sun.

Sam remembered The Dead Sheriff, O'Malley and Duke Martin, and returned to his task.

He hadn't seen the robed people since. And he didn't want to see them again. He feared, though, that the choice wasn't his.

He didn't know exactly where these visions were coming from, but he knew none of it would have happened without the amulet and book he stole from the red-haired man back in that New Mexico whorehouse years earlier.

Since the resurrection of the corpse that would become The Dead Sheriff (and that was another frequent nightmare: *lightning illuminating the night of horror, the bone white hand clawing from the wet earth of the grave...*) nothing had been the same. He felt poisoned by the magic, if that was the right word for it. He was stained, maybe down to his soul, if there were such a thing.

He also wondered what happened to Old Luke.

Growing up, Sam never had friends. The closet, he supposed, was the hunch-backed piano player at the whorehouse in New Mexico territory. He was always kind to Sam, a young misfit, ignored by his mother and forced to get by on his own in a variety of brothels. Old Luke taught Sam the few lessons anyone ever shared with him, mostly about how cruel people were and how to watch out for yourself because nobody else would. Then Old Luke died and the voice of Sam's only friend was silenced.

Until the magic. Once Sam first used the amulet and the book, Old Luke spoke up inside his head, offering advice and criticism, just as he had in life. Sam believed it was simply his imagination, until Old Luke began to share facts Sam didn't know.

Old Luke guided him in the use of the magical artifacts. Sam hadn't learned much, but he would have been completely lost without the old man's help.

But after Damnation, Old Luke had not spoken to him.

When that town fell, O'Malley was in possession of the amulet and book. Sam wondered if that had something to do with the disappearance of Old Luke.

He glanced at the dozing writer.

O'Malley claimed to remember little about what happened when he was in charge of The Dead Sheriff. He said he didn't know what the creature was that pulled the town into the earth. He may have been telling the truth. Sam couldn't quite remember all of it himself. It was mostly flashes of images, indistinct and frightening, much like his nightmares.

Still, he wondered...did O'Malley now hear the voice of Old Luke?

Sam wanted to ask him. But how do you start a conversation like that? *Excuse me, but I don't hear my old dead friend in my head anymore. Has he moved to your skull?*

Sam didn't plan to bring that up anytime soon.

And he hadn't forgotten the comment by a Chinese man who worked in a little casino in a small Texas town called Drummond. That celestial told Sam that his shadow was gone and he now existed "between two worlds", whatever the hell that meant. He was pretty sure that wouldn't have happened before he stole the magical items.

And Sam's shadow was right where it was supposed to be, thank you kindly.

Still, the memory left him feeling uneasy. Just another reason to get out. If he could score a few more bounties, or one big one, Sam planned to take all of the cash and head to Mexico. He would bury the amulet and the book, find a quiet corner of the country, and spend his days drinking tequila and living a normal life. Maybe he'd even marry a Mexican woman and have a passel of fat babies. It sure beat roaming around the west with a dead guy in the back of his wagon.

It was late afternoon, and the wagon neared the invisible line that separated Arkansas from Indian Territory, when Sam saw the walking man about a hundred yards ahead. He sure had picked an odd spot for hike, this close to nowhere.

The man swayed as he took slow, measured steps. If he saw Sam's wagon he made no sign.

After a few more steps, the man collapsed to his knees.

Sam slowed the wagon as they drew close to the prone figure. He nudged O'Malley with an elbow.

"Huh?" the writer said.

"Take a look at this." He pointed to the man in the road.

O'Malley leaned his tall frame over the front of the wagon to get a better look. He straightened up with a start.

"By God," he said, "I know that man!"

•••

FROM THE JOURNAL OF RICHARD O'MALLEY

Though I had last seen the man in Boston weeks ago, Thunderstorm Parker was sprawled in the dirt in front of our wagon. The man claimed kinship with several famous gunfighters and was, at the time we spoke, an advance scout for a traveling Wild West show.

"Friend of yours?" Sam said.

"Yes. No. I mean we met once. In a way, he's the reason I'm here."

I had been at the lowest point in my life when Parker shared with me his story of witnessing The Dead Sheriff in action, which set me on the path to this place and time.

"Is he dead?" Sam asked.

"I don't know."

"If he's not, I want to kick him in the face for sending you here."

I hopped off the wagon and made my way to Parker. I rolled him onto his back. When I met him in Boston, his age had been hard to determine. That wasn't the case anymore. He appeared to be ancient, his skin lined and cracked from the sun and the wind.

I leaned close to his face to determine if he was breathing.

At that instant, Thunderstorm Parker coughed. His breath stank of old whiskey, dead animals and, perhaps, an ancient crypt. When he opened his eyes they were wide with shock.

"Are you one of them monsters?"

He was delirious. "Mr. Parker, it's me. Richard O'Malley."

Now his eyes closed to tiny slits. "Do I owe you money?"

"No, sir. We met in Boston. I bought you a few drinks."

"And I don't owe you money?"

"Not a cent."

"Then help me up, son."

I pulled the man to his feet. He dusted off his clothes and looked around.

"Who's the Injun?"

I wasn't sure how much to reveal. "That's...Sam. He's a friend of mine."

Parker and Sam stared at each other for a moment. Parker finally shrugged, and said, "Okay. Any friend of ..."

"Richard O'Malley."

"Long way from Boston, ain't yah?"

"I am. I'm writing a book."

"Uh-huh." Parker stared at the wagon. "Got anything to drink?"

"You need water. We have plenty."

I dug a canteen from the side of the wagon that didn't contain the corpse of a dead man.

Parker took a sip and made a face. "Got anything that tastes more like whiskey?"

I found a tin cup and a half empty bottle of Sam's whiskey. I poured a little into the cup and handed it to Parker. Sam glared at me, but said nothing.

Parker drained the cup and handed it back to me for a refill. He repeated the experience. When he passed the cup back to me I held up a hand.

"Before we go any further, why don't you tell us why you were walking out here so far from anything?"

"O'Mooney, would really deny a small sip to a man who has looked evil right square in the eye?"

"It's O'Malley," I said. "And what are you talking about?"

He glanced from me to Sam, his expression grave.

"I have just escaped from monsters. Vicious, blood eating monsters!"

•••

He still couldn't believe it.

The Coogan and Destry Wild West Extravaganza and Carnival had fired Thunderstorm Parker.

Bill Coogan, a fraud and thief, had the gall to accuse Parker of drinking on the job. Said job was to arrive in town a few days before the show, to fire up the locals with a few colorful stories about fancy-shooting and train robberies and Injun-fighting. Hell, the only time Coogan had fired his gun was when he accidentally shot himself in the foot trying to holster his piece.

Of course, some of that tale-spinning Parker was supposed to do happened in watering holes, and if the local rubes wanted to treat him to a drink or three, who was he to insult their courtesy?

In all honesty, Parker knew Coogan didn't do anything without the say-so of Mr. Destry. Parker had never quite figured out why Destry was a partner in the show. He dressed like a doctor or a school teacher. He never spoke and when he did look at you, it was like he was seeing a little bug. When the show would set up in a town, they said Destry was never there. He wandered the city streets as if he was looking for someone or something. A strange guy. But he seemed to have some kind of control over Coogan. Maybe he caught Ol' Bill having relations with a farm animal or something. Lord knows Parker had seen worse things in his years on Earth.

After Coogan gave him the news and twenty dollars in severance, Parker got drunk, then, fighting the worst hangover of his life, he considered his options.

Show business was a mug's game, so he was through with Wild West shows. He wasn't suited to dock work or anything else back east.

Then he remembered Slow Charlie Fordham.

He and Slow Charlie had grown up together back in Kansas. They'd worked on ranches together and had even done a little rustling, giving it up before they were ever pinched for it. Last Parker heard, Slow Charlie had his own ranch in Kingman, just north of Indian Territory.

So Thunderstorm lit out for home. He took the train to Topeka, rode a stage to Wichita then bought a horse with the last of his money and headed for Kingman.

He lingered far too long in a saloon in a little town called Harmony, relying on his story -spinning skills to talk the owner out of a lunch and a bottle. Realizing he was too inebriated to ride the rest of the way to Kingman, he decided to spend the night. That meant he lingered in the lobby of Harmony's only hotel, dozing on a comfortable sofa until the manager threw him out just after sunset, apparently not caring that Parker had been friends with Wild Bill Hickok and Kit Carson.

He stumbled out the front door of the hotel, and saw an incredible sight. Several long carriages were parked at the corner of the dirt street, near the saloon where he had earlier dined and drank. There were torches lit all around the conveyances, and slender women in fancy clothes were standing around.

Parker smelled good cigar smoke. Standing next to him with a short, broad man with a star pinned on his vest.

"What's going on there?" Parker said.

"It's a traveling whore house," the cigar-smoking fella said.

"That legal?"

"It ain't illegal," the lawman said.

"Are you a deputy?"

"I'm head constable. Also the mayor and town barber. Pake Gillum's my handle."

He didn't offer to shake.

A crowd of men had gathered near the carriages. Some of the town folks were engaged in conversation with the women. There was a lot of touching going on.

"It's a traveling whore house."

"Looks like they ain't gonna lack for customers," Parker said.

"I hope not," Gillum said. "I spoke to the head woman earlier. She's paying us a, ah, business tax based on the number of customers they get." He gestured with his cigar. "Don't be shy. Go get you a poke."

"Can't afford it."

"You don't even know how much it is."

"Don't matter," Parker said. "Still can't afford it."

Gillum eyed him for a moment. He smiled, dug a stubby finger into a vest pocket and flipped a gold coin to Parker.

"It's on me, old timer. Consider it my good deed for the year." He nodded and left the porch, sauntering down the steps and up the street, away from the rolling bordello.

Parker was in a quandary.

He was flat broke. The coin would help him out tomorrow, if he couldn't sweet talk someone into a free meal. Or he could stroll back to the saloon and get him a bottle to keep him warm tonight.

On the other hand, it had been a while since he'd lain with a woman. He didn't know her real name. Everyone at the show called her Matilda, the bearded lady sharpshooter. She wasn't a small gal. In fact, she could have made two of Parker. But she was real sweet, especially when she was drunk. Parker didn't remember much about that night, except that her beard felt funny against his cheek.

Finally, he decided to postpone his decision until after a bit of a nap. He wandered behind the hotel and found a small wooden bench someone had built next to a small creek that ran behind the buildings. If he curled up, he could just fit. He hoped that ornery hotel manager didn't check out back of his place. Maybe Parker could catch a little shut eye.

So he did, at least until the rain started.

When the first fat drops splattered down, Parker awoke and thought he could ride it out. But the heavens opened and the soft shower became a gully washer. Parker scrambled to the front of the building, trying to stay out of the mud.

The hotel manager was on his porch, looking towards the traveling whorehouse.

Parker took shelter on the front porch of the general store, two doors down. He squatted down, hoping the hotel man wouldn't spot him. The storm had driven most of the men away from the whorehouse. Or maybe the women had already serviced all of them. Only a few stragglers stood near the carriages. One of them was the lawman, Gillum. Parker figured the constable/barber was waiting for his payoff.

Tired of squatting, he sat his skinny butt down on the rough wooden planks. He was cold and wet, and that coin in his pocket was growing very warm. A bottle would be heavenly. On the other hand, so would the smooth skin of a woman, even one who was filled with the jizz of several customers. Bottle or whore? It was quite the dilemma.

Parker was suddenly struck with inspiration. It was near the end of the evening. The customers had thinned out. Maybe the whores would give him a discount. That way he might be able to afford a girl and a bottle. Invigorated by the possibilities of his brilliant plan, Parker stood and headed for the street. The rain slacked off, which was most certainly a good sign for the success for his endeavor.

He sauntered down the wooden sidewalk in the light drizzle, one hand on the coin in his pocket. He briefly considered stopping in the saloon for a shot of courage. He decided to conserve his cash until he saw how negotiations with the whores went.

As he drew closer to the carriages, he noticed three men loitering by the rear vehicle. They stood as still as statues, staring at nothing. The door to that last carriage opened. The woman who stepped out had ribbons in her hair and was dressed like she was going to some fancy theater, rather than giving blowjobs to locals. Parker decided she must be the head whore. Well, good. She'd be the one who might negotiate the price down. Hell, Parker would even take the ugliest whore for a turn. Once you'd fucked a bearded lady, your standard was pretty low.

About a hundred feet away from the rolling bordello, Parker froze, not sure of what he was seeing. Constable Gillum and the head whore were talking, when the woman leaned in. Parker guessed she was going to kiss him or give his pecker a squeeze, to maybe show him a preview of what she was offering him to make up for not having quite as much money as the lawman expected.

Instead, she bit down on Gillum's throat and shook her head to and fro like a dog with a rabbit. She jerked her head back and laughed. A fountain of crimson sprayed from Gillum's neck.

"Goddamn! You killed me! Goddam!" The constable put his hand over the wound, yet the blood continued to squirt between his fingers.

Parker must have made some sound without realizing it, for the head whore looked right at him, her mouth coated with Gillum's blood. She said something Parker couldn't hear, and the door to the next carriage opened. Two whores stepped out. The head whore pointed at Parker. The other two women smiled. They ran in his direction.

Thunderstorm Parker would never claim to be the smartest man in the world, but he had a strong sense of self-preservation. He didn't understand what just happened. Ultimately, it didn't matter. He saw the head whore kill the local law. Now she sent these other two women to kill him. His path was obvious.

He ran.

He sprinted down the middle of the street, making good time, he thought, despite his arthritic knees.

But then he heard them close behind him. Even worse was the smell. It was like a wild animal and spoiled meat. Who were these women?

That question was answered almost immediately, as three revelers stepped from the saloon between the two women and their prey.

Parker heard the laughter and raucous conversation of the trio of men turn to screams in a second. He didn't want to look and, at the same time, he couldn't help himself. He slowed to a fast walk, turning his head to see what was happening.

The three men were on the ground. One of them wasn't moving. His throat was gone. The other two struggled impotently as the two women chewed on their necks.

He didn't realize that he'd come to a complete stop until the two women—if that's what they were—finished feeding. The life blood of the three men ran down their chins and onto their clothing. They looked at each other and giggled. Parker couldn't believe his ears. They actually giggled.

Leaning forward, the two arched their backs. Parker now heard a tearing noise; like a piece of canvas would make it you tore it in your hands.

"Jesus God!" Parker took a step back as he witnessed the impossible.

Leathery wings sprouted out the backs of the women, ripping their dresses in the process.

Someone screamed. Thunderstorm Parker would not have been surprised to find that it was him. A second scream was a bit further away and he realized that other residents of Harmony had seen what had just happened. One of the winged women took to the air, the big brown wings propelling her through the night sky like she was a dark eagle. With hands that looked more like claws, she scooped up a plump woman with white hair.

As Parker looked on, unable to move, the flying creature carried the woman high above the town's biggest building (which was just three stories), chewed into her neck, then dropped the squat victim from the sky. The white-haired woman landed in the middle of the dirt street with a loud and wet explosion. The second flying whore hovered only a few feet above the head of a big rough feller who looked like a bare-knuckle fighter. He pulled a pistol from his waistband and fired at her until he was out of ammo. Parker saw the bullets tear into the neck and torso of the creature. She laughed and swooped down. Her claws gripped the large man's head and pulled him off of his feet. Parker heard the crack of his neck breaking.

There were now dozens of people in the street, men and women. Parker supposed they came from the saloon or the hotel or the one restaurant at the other end of the street. Wherever they had started the evening, all of them scattered, looking for a safe haven from the nightmare.

Back at the traveling bordello, the doors to all of the carriages opened and more women piled out, each sprouting her own wings, each taking to the air to better select their next feast.

Later, Parker would think it odd the things a man noticed at a time like that. The three unusual men at the back of the last carriage stood where they were, seemingly unaware of what was happening in the street. Also, two men exited from the first carriage, one no more than a teenager. Parker thought they were customers, but their garb was too colorful and it seemed that they both wore masks over their eyes. He didn't have any more time to wonder about it.

His original pursuers were both busy slaughtering others, but if Parker stood there like an idiot much longer, they'd take notice of him soon enough. He ran to the shadows between the hotel and the general store, looking for a dark place to hide. There was a back porch on the general store, and beneath it, what looked like a crawl space, perhaps for storage of some sort. He squeezed under the porch, using his legs to push unseen crates out of the way.

Parker was out of sight.

He sniffed the air. He hoped that those monsters did not have a sharp sense of smell, for he had shit his pants and he wasn't about to venture out to find a privy.

He lay there in the dark, listening to the screams of Harmony and the laughter of those creatures. Three times he heard the beat of those leathery wings close by. Once, he heard footsteps. A young voice said, "Ain't this great, Dewey?"

Slowly, Parker lifted his head. In the moonlight he saw the backs of the two brightly-garbed men who had been the last to exit the rolling whorehouse.

Holy Christ, he recognized them.

His teeth started chattering. He drove his chin hard against the cold earth in an effort to stop the noise. He stayed like that until the sun rose, and another hour still, until the silence meant he was safe. He carefully climbed from the crawlspace, fully expecting to see one of those winged whores waiting for him. The alley between the two buildings was empty.

He stepped very softly to the corner of the hotel. Standing there trembling, he waited ten more minutes before peering around the corner.

The traveling bordello was gone, as if it had been a dream.

Parker might have believed that, had he been drinking the previous night. It wouldn't have been the first time he'd seem inexplicable things while shit faced.

He felt confident that what he's seen in the night was exactly as he remembered it.

Because the main street of Harmony was filled with corpses. There were at least a hundred dead bodies, far more people than he'd seen in the street last night. Whatever those flying whores were, they must have dragged people from their homes back to this killing ground. He recognized the hotel manager, and the owner of the saloon, who had given Parker lunch and some booze less than a day ago. And, of course, he saw Gillum, the constable and mayor and barber of the town. At the sight of the man, Parker dug a hand into his own pocket to make sure the gold coin was still there.

Cupping his hands around his mouth, Parker shouted, "Hello? Anybody out there? I ain't no monster!" There was no answer. He repeated the call. When he again got no response, he walked to the end of the street where the body of the constable was laid out. He stepped carefully to avoid blood and other things he could not identify.

He squatted next to Gillum. Breathing through his mouth, he searched the pockets of the dead man's vest. He found ten more gold coins. Parker stood and put them into his pockets.

"Sorry, gent, but I need these more than you."

Next, he went to the saloon. He found a bottle of good whiskey and with a shaking hand, poured two shots. He wanted more, but he didn't dare risk getting drunk and still being here if those killer whores came back. With his nerves steadied a bit by the hooch, he searched through a back room until he found an empty burlap sack. He filled it with several bottles of the good stuff. He carried his treasure to the livery stable, where he saddled his horse and rode out to the south.

Slow Charlie would have to get by without Thunderstorm Parker. He wasn't having anything to do with them monster whores. He'd rather wash dishes in a restaurant in New Orleans or Philadelphia or anywhere far from where flying nightmares could kill an entire town in one night.

•••

FROM THE JOURNAL OF RICHARD O'MALLEY

"Who were they?" I asked.

"Who?" Thunderstorm Parker said.

"The two men in the masks that you saw."

I noticed that Parker's hands were trembling, whether from fear or lack of drink I could not say.

"You say we met before?"

"Yes. In Boston."

"Yeah, I recollect a saloon and a tall boy who I shared a table with. Would that be you?"

"Yes, sir. It was."

"Did I tell you about the outlaw lawmen?"

"You mean the bounty hunters who never claim the bounty?"

Sam turned to me, an eyebrow raised skeptically.

"That's right," Parker said.

"These men you saw in Harmony were, ah, outlaw lawmen."

"Used to be, anyhow. They were a fancy-dressed pair called The Silver Paladin and Bullet."

I pondered that nugget of information. "And you say there were working with these creatures?"

"They weren't workin' again 'em, that's for damn sure."

"Did they have...wings, too?"

Parker squinted at me. "Boy, you havin' fun with me?"

"No, sir. Not at all."

"Then you believe me?"

"Mr. Parker, I don't disbelieve you." That was most certainly true. In my short time in the west, I'd seen things that made me question my sanity, starting with the item covered in the back of the wagon.

"What happened to your horse?" It was the first time Parker heard Sam speak. I think the older man must have thought my traveling companion was mute. He seemed startled.

"She stepped in a gopher hole about thirty miles back. Been on foot ever since."

Sam nodded. "What about the whiskey you stole?"

"Listen, sonny, it ain't stealing if there ain't nobody to steal it from. I finished it a couple of days ago. It's awful dry out here. Speaking of whiskey..." Parker still held the tin cup.

"Where are you headed now?"

"Back east," he said. "Can I ride along with you?"

"We're not going east," Sam told him. "We have business the way you came from."

"Nope. No, sir. No way." Parker started walking away from us, heading in the direction of Arkansas. He took three steps before turning around and coming back. He waved the tin cup at me. "How about a short snort for the road?"

"You can't continue on foot," I said. Sam made a noise. I ignored it. "Ride with us until we get to the next town. You can get a horse there."

I heard Sam mutter under his breath.

"Promise me you ain't goin' to Harmony."

"I got work to do," Sam said. "Ain't got time for flying killer whores."

"What kind of work you doin', Sonny?"

Sam smiled. It wasn't a pleasant expression. "We're hunting down a pair of bank robbing brothers who like to eat people."

I heard Parker swallow. His throat made a dry clicking sound.

"But as far as I know," Sam said, "these boys don't have wings."

●●●

The Silver Paladin lay dreaming in the dirt.

His new life, the life preceded by his death, was a precious gift from his mistress. Weak Dewitt Aloysius Martin was gone, leaving only the Paladin, the best of what he could be. Never had he felt so strong, so certain. All of his doubt and his unremitting guilt had vanished with his rebirth. When he thought about the man he had been, he was amused at how fragile he was, how tormented by his conflicting desires: to please his mother and father, to give into to the passion that burned with him, to live up to the image of the man he wanted to be.

No more.

All of it drifted away like smoke on the wind.

Now there was only the Silver Paladin. Now everything was so clear.

He lived to feed. His destiny was to rule over the cattle. Magdala promised him that he would be her King, reigning over their kingdom in the west for a thousand years.

She wanted him. And he so wanted her. It was an unaccustomed feeling, yet one he eagerly embraced.

His thought flew freely as he slumbered in the dark carriage, on a bed of graveyard earth. Magdala told him it would be for a short time, just until he had adjusted to his new life.

The boy slept beside him. He'd once been very important to The Silver Paladin, perhaps the most important thing in his life.

Now he was nothing, just another foot soldier. Bullet was happy in their new life, happy to kill and feed. He had no idea of the things Magdala had promised the Paladin or the things she had done to him.

Let him hunt and feed in ignorance. Soon Magdala could put him to work with the other girls. He would be a boy whore. Bullet wouldn't mind. Not the way he was now.

But The Silver Paladin had a different path.

There were few who could stop them. In fact, it was likely that none of the masked lawmen stood a chance against Magdala's tribe. The Silver Paladin certainly hadn't, and he was the best of them.

Still, it was better safe than sorry, as Magdala said.

Soon he would be ready. He would be strong enough.

And then his hunt would begin.

•••

The Belchers rode hard and rode far, and settled in at a camp in Injun Territory. Billy cooked their dinner while Arlo buried the money. Billy preferred to handle the money himself, but he couldn't trust his little brother with the meat. Before they reached the Kansas state line, the pair chanced a stop at a watering hole, and he caught Arlo chewing off a nice chunk of the woman's ass. It made Billy so mad, that he actually pulled his gun on his brother and shot at his feet. All he did was stir up the dirt, though it was enough to make Arlo piss his pants. Good thing Billy had gotten used to the stink long ago.

Once they made camp, Billy took out his big knives from the saddle bag and carved up the bank woman, setting aside his favorite parts: the kidneys, the liver and the titties. The rest was for Arlo. He was a growing boy and he'd finish it all, including sucking the marrow from her bones.

"Leave about five hundred out, Arlo."

His brother grunted his acknowledgment. The money was going in to a hole next to the spot where Billy had buried a box full of guns and such.

Billy figured they'd lay low for a few days, then celebrate someplace in Texas, maybe. Get some good hooch and some whores. They'd need a room somewhere first, to clean up and shave. And some new clothes. That way they could have fun for a while without being recognized. Hell, if he could keep Arlo from eating anybody in whatever town they ended up in, then maybe it could be a regular rest stop for the Belcher brothers. They could do all their robbing and killing and eating somewhere else. Of course, controlling Arlo was always going to be a problem.

As he tended the fire, Billy sighed. He often imagined what life would be like if Arlo wasn't around, how much easier things would be if he parked a bullet in his brother's brain while he slept.

If he even has a brain.

On the other hand, Arlo was a big ole boy, good in a fight, and it would get mighty lonely on the road without him. Also, he knew Ma would want him to look after his older brother.

A familiar weight settled between Billy's shoulder blades. He knew he could never kill Arlo or leave him. His bother would be his responsibility until his dying day.

He sighed again, as he cut up the bank woman's heart and dropped the pieces into the frying pan.

"Don't get her too done, Billy," Arlo hollered. "You know I like my meat rare."

•••

Would this drunken cow poke ever shut up?

Since Thunderstorm Parker climbed up to sit between Sam and O'Malley, he hadn't stopped talking, filling the miles with endless stories about his friendships with famous gunfighters and the fantastic adventures they'd had. Sam hadn't heard of most of these guys and he believed almost nothing of what Parker said, particularly that ridiculous tale of flying whores. O'Malley was much more polite than Sam, and he tried to appear interested in parker's yarns, but even the writer was growing impatient. The old man was O'Malley's acquaintance, and as far as Sam was concerned that made him O'Malley's problem.

Except O'Malley was too damn nice. He wouldn't say shit even if he had a mouthful.

So it was up to Sam to get them a little peace.

"Hey, Mister Parker."

Parker was in the middle of telling O'Malley about a gold mine he discovered with Kit Carson. He gave Sam a glance that contained more than a spot of irritation at being made to interrupt his epic. "Yeah?"

"I just wanted to thank you for making this dull trip so entertaining."

Parker squinted at him, until the corners of the old coot's mouth slowly curled up.

"Why, it's my pleasure, sonny. I think a man like me, whose life has been filled with much excitement and fightin', ought to share those experiences with the young. It's kind of like goin' to school, 'cept with more killin'."

Sam forced a big smile to his face and nodded. "You are so right, sir. I bet all that experience sharing is thirsty work." O'Malley's expression was one of stunned amazement.

A light seemed to bloom in Thunderstorm Parker's red-rimmed eyes. "It shore is, sonny. Very thirsty work."

Sam tilted his head toward the wagon bed. "Back in Hot Springs. I picked up a couple of bottles. One of 'em ain't even been opened."

"Yah...yah want me to open it up?"

"Yes, sir. Consider it my way of saying thanks for the stories."

Parker turned to face Sam. His genuine smile was even bigger than Sam's fake one.

"That's mighty white of you, sonny. Mighty white."

Behind Parker, O'Malley rolled his eyes.

"Thanks," Sam said. "Help yourself."

Parker got up on his knees and pulled by the corner of the canvas sheet that covered the wagon bed. Sam heard glass and metal banging together. Part of him hated to give up the last of his whiskey to the old man, but if he drank until he passed out, the blessed silence would be worth it.

As if the contrary old windbag could read Sam's thoughts, Thunderstorm Parker screamed like he was being scalped.

•••

FROM THE JOURNAL OF RICHARD O'MALLEY

Parker threw himself against me and climbed halfway up my frame.

"It's him! It's the goddamned Dead Sheriff!"

"Yes, but he can't hurt you."

Sam pulled on the reins. The horses and wagon rolled to a gentle stop. I had to remember that in some ways, Sam was still a boy. He was enjoying Parker's discomfort.

"Calm down," I told Parker. "I can explain all of this."

"Explain how come you got a living dead man in your wagon? No thank you. This here's where I get off."

Parker was frantically attempting to untangle his limbs from mine, so he did not see Sam turn to open the small leather case he kept in the back of the wagon. I knew it contained something like a medallion and a very strange book. My skin began to crawl just thinking about it.

Sam slipped a chain around his neck. He closed his eyes, his lips moving silently. There was a slow rustling from the canvas cover behind me. Parker heard it as well.

A figure raised from the hard wooden bed. The canvas dropped away from the form, to reveal the face of The Dead Sheriff.

That battered visage had seen better days. For that matter, it had seen better years. Your attention was first drawn to those dead white eyes. Despite their blank gaze, those dead orbs were disturbing. I tried to not stare into them for too long, for if I did I began to see small dark tendrils swimming deep within them, as though I were being permitted a glimpse of a place no man should witness if he wished to remain sane. The nose was crooked and broad. It had been flattened many times, by fists and axe handles and bullets. The mouth hung only slightly open, which meant the jaw was attached for the time being. On the left side of the face, there was an opening almost three inches long, through which part of the jaw bone and the back teeth were visible. A black and brackish fluid had dried around the mouth and on the dead man's chin. I didn't know what it was other than it came from his body and seemed to take the place of blood. It poured from him anytime he was shot or stabbed. It smelled faintly of sulphur.

Sam climbed down from the wagon, walking a few steps away. Damn him for scaring the old cowboy.

An eerie voice issued from The Dead Sheriff's mouth. It was a sound that could only originate on the other side of the grave.

"Thunderstorm Parker, you are a liar and a thief. You now face my judgment."

Parker whimpered like a scared pup.

The Dead Sheriff raised an arm. A bone white finger pointed accusingly at Parker.

"Parker, prepare for the grave."

Parker screamed again, this one a high-pitched squeal of fear. He scrambled over me and fell into the dirt. He started running full out. His screaming continued as he ran.

"Parker, wait. It's okay!" He didn't hear me. I turned my attention to a grinning Sam.

"Stop it. He's an old man. His heart could give out."

"I'm just having some fun. The mouthy geezer was making me crazy."

I didn't reply. I climbed down from the wagon, giving chase to poor Parker. I half-ran in the late afternoon heat. He hadn't made it very far. He knelt down maybe a hundred feet away from the wagon, gasping for breath.

He jerked his head to see who was pursuing him. He seemed relieved to find a living man.

"It's just me," I said.

"I cain't run no more," he said between deep panting breaths. "If he's gonna kill me, I cain't stop him."

"He's not going to kill you. He doesn't do anything on his own." That wasn't entirely accurate. I had seen him show independent movement after our ordeal in Damnation. I attributed that to some sort of residual magic from those hellish events. "He's just a corpse. A big dead puppet and Sam pulls his strings."

Realization spread across Parker's face like the rising sun. "Hold on. Are you sayin' young Sam is really Cheveyo?"

In truth, it was the other way around, but I decided Sam's identity issues made for a complicated conversation. "Yes. He is."

"And you say the Injun is really in charge? I ain't ever heared of nothin' like that."

I stood there in the dust and the heat, and explained to Thunderstorm Parker the story of The Dead Sheriff. Some of it, anyway. I didn't say where Sam obtained his magic, for instance. And there were quite a few things he had never shared with me, such as the name of the dead man he used for the ruse of The Dead Sheriff.

When I finished, some of the color came back to Parker's face.

"Son of a bitch," he said. "So it's all just a money-making bidness."

"Well, we also capture some bad characters."

"What's this 'we' stuff? You got the magic, too?"

At that instant it was my own face that changed colors. I was embarrassed at how easily I included myself in the story of The Dead Sheriff. While it was true that I played a pivotal role during the events in Damnation, my role remained first and foremost that of a chronicler.

I forced a smile. "I don't have any magic. I'm just a newspaper man, I suppose."

"Okay then." Parker stood up and made a token effort to brush the dust from his clothes.

Sam had moved the wagon about a hundred yards, where a small stream ran amongst a small copse of trees. While the horses got watered, Sam filled the canteens and water skins. The Dead Sheriff was not in sight.

"That was pretty mean trick that Injun played on me."

"I'm certain he regrets it," I said.

To his credit, Sam appeared properly chagrined when we approached.

"I reckon I might've got carried away," he muttered.

"Don't worry about it," Parker said. "It ain't ever body who can say they got spooked by The Dead Sheriff and Cheveyo."

Sam wrinkled his nose. "What's that smell?"

Parker shrugged. "When I get spooked I sometimes get the backdoor trots, if you know what I mean. I better go take care of that." He headed for the creek.

"Quick! Finish getting our water," I whispered.

"You still owe me a bottle of whiskey," Parker shouted as he lowered his pants.

CHAPTER FOUR

The man who called himself Labine slept alone in his rented rooms in New Orleans, dreaming of his homeland, of the sharp mountain ranges and the chill night air.

The comforting illusion was broken by a harsh jolt that traveled the length of his body and forced him upright in the bed.

The magick. It was just used again.

Where?

Labine closed his eyes and focused on the taste of the dark force, the lingering tendril that reached out to him. It faded now, withdrawing to its origin point.

North. And west, yes?

That seemed right. The magick had not been used for a long duration, yet Labine hoped it would be enough.

He blinked his eyes and tried to focus on the world around him. It was late afternoon, judging by the light. Labine preferred to sleep through the heat of the day, better to be refreshed for evening and the height of the wicked debauchery of this most special of cities.

Moloch would have felt it. Damn it. The beast would know the magick had been used again, and despite Labine's appearance of control, Moloch ultimately answered to one more powerful than an earth-walking magician. The creature would expect an immediate departure.

Well, Labine would be ready. He and Moloch shared a master, and that master wanted the magical artifacts retrieved. Labine had a part to play in the master's plan. A large part. Along the way, he expected to have his fun, as well.

And the whore's son would no longer stand in his way.

As he dressed, he watched the sun begin to set on the city. He wanted to be out there, wading through every deviant pleasure it had to offer. But pleasure would have to wait.

Something thudded loudly against his door. The window glass rattled as though God himself had rapped upon the wood.

"One moment, you brainless monster," Labine called. "I have to find my shoes."

•••

Two days out in the middle of nowhere with his brother had made Billy Belcher feel more homicidal than usual.

Arlo didn't do anything new or unusual. He was just Arlo.

The previous night, just as Billy was drifting off to sleep with his belly full of a leftover piece of the bank woman, Arlo started his questions. He didn't do it every night, thank God, but when he did, it drove Billy crazy.

"Billy, when we die do we go to Heaven?"

"Some of us do, I reckon."

"So Ma is in Heaven?"

"I don't know. Ma was pretty damned mean. Now go to sleep."

Arlo was silent. Billy was just about asleep when his brother spoke again.

"Billy, when we eat people, do we eat their souls, too?"

Why me, he thought. "I don't know. I reckon."

"So their souls is in us?"

"For a little while."

"What do you mean?"

"Sooner or later, you shit them out, right? Then the souls float up to Heaven or fall down to Hell."

Then Arlo started whining about a belly ache. He eventually went behind a tree and shit. Even from thirty feet away, it was a revolting smell. The worst part was hearing Arlo talk during the shitting.

"Bye, Paco. Hope you go to heaven."

Billy had no idea who Paco was and he wasn't going to ask his brother. He'd had enough talk for the night.

But it was too late. When he finally slept, his dreams were troubling, full of strange images. Winged monsters. Men in robes. And people made out of shit who knelt and prayed and cried. In his dream, he knew that one of the shit men was Paco.

He awoke hours before dawn and tried, unsuccessfully to go back to sleep. Eventually, he got up and fixed a pot of coffee over a small fire. Billy was tired and cranky, apt to go off the edge for little or no reason. If ever there was a day he might shoot Arlo, this was it.

A good hour after the sun came up, Arlo finally stirred. He stood and stretched, yawned and scratched his ass. He walked a few feed from his bedroll to piss into the dirt. When he finally made his way over to Billy, he was smiling, as he usually was in the morning. It made Billy remember how things were where they were still kids, and Arlo was a regular sized feller.

"Mornin', Billy."

"Yeah."

"This the day we goin' to Texas for some whores and good drinkin'?"

Arlo wanted to say no, we should wait a couple of more days, but, in truth, he couldn't stand another day in this dusty camp with his stinking brother (not that Billy was any kind of fresh rose; it's just that nobody stunk like Arlo Belcher).

"Today's the day," Billy said. "Get you some breakfast, then we'll hit the trail."

"Whoo-hoo!" Arlo jumped up and down with his fists clenched at his side, making a noise that probably scared away every varmint for five miles.

"Calm down or we stay here another week." It was the emptiest of threats, and Arlo, even as dumb as he was, probably knew it. Yet he stopped his whooping and hopping. He chewed on a piece of meat and then started getting his belongings together.

Billy got the horses fed and watered before saddling them. He felt the tension of the last few days melt away. A good time in a city was exactly what he needed. They could blow off some steam, get their willies wet and drink a town dry. That would put them in good shape for resuming their outlaw ways. As he cinched the saddle on Arlo's big Palomino, Billy realized he was whistling. This might turn out to be a good day.

He held on to that thought right up until he heard the wagon.

It had a bad wheel and made a creaking lurch. That's what he'd heard. From their camp, the trail wound down between two small rocky hills. It would be a while before the wagon was visible.

Behind their camp was a cliff face that rose about forty feet. From a distance, the face looked sheer, but Billy had been using this spot long enough to know his way around. Decades ago some Injun had carved out narrow steps that led to the top of the rise. Billy told Arlo to keep quiet, and then he climbed the cliff face. It was slow going, but he was on top of the rocks in less than five minutes. He crouched down, shielding his eyes against the morning sun.

Goddamn if he wasn't right. It was a buckboard, pulled by two horses. The team was driven by a thin man wearing spectacles. Sitting next to him was an older gent who looked like he'd seen a lot of miles in the saddle. They might be traveling salesman, but they could just as likely be bounty hunters. The Belcher brothers were sure to be worth top dollar by now.

At the thought of how much their hides could bring him, Billy felt a tug of pride.

Not that he planned to let any bounty hunter or lawman bring him in. Maybe the pair with the wagon were just businessmen on their way to Kansas. Too bad. Their day was about to go very, very wrong.

Billy carefully made his way back down the cliff face. When he reached the bottom, he pulled Arlo close to him.

"What is it, Billy?"

"Maybe nothing. Maybe trouble. If it's nothing, we eat good tonight."

"What do you want me to do?"

"You know that crate I buried a while back next to the money?"

Arlo nodded.

"Dig it up real quick. And here's what we need..."

He finished delivering instructions to his brother. For once, Arlo didn't argue or question him.

When Billy was left alone, he slicked back his greasy hair, put on his hat and tried to look friendly. It felt strange.

"...they could just as likely be bounty hunters."

"Fuck it," he said to no one.

He stood on the middle of their camp and waited for company to arrive.

•••

After the way he treated Thunderstorm Parker, Sam found himself in a foul mood.

When did I become the kind of man I always hated?

The thought made him want to drink, but Parker was sitting right next to Sam, guzzling the last bottle of whiskey. And that made Sam feel even worse. So he concentrated on the dusty trail in front of him and drove the horses hard until sunset. They were deep into Indian Territory. He didn't know how far away his prey was. He desperately needed to get to a town, an outpost, anywhere he could mingle and ask questions and find those flesh-eating freaks, so he could collect the bounty and get one step closer to ending this crazy existence.

Parker and O'Malley chatted it up while making camp. Sam didn't join in. After they ate a jack rabbit he'd caught that morning, Sam moved his bedroll far away from the other two. All he wanted tonight was peace and quiet. After the conversation from the other two finally died down, Sam was finally able to sleep. At least for a while. When he awoke with a start, he didn't know how late it was. The night sky was salted with a million stars. Sam held his breath and listened. He was sure a sound had woken him.

There. A voice.

It was distant, and sounded like a man shouting or laughing. Maybe drunk (like Sam wished he was). He stood up and walked a few steps toward the sound, west of their camp.

O' Malley must have heard it, too, for the skinny writer called after Sam. "Where are you headed?"

"Shh." Sam held out a hand, hoping O'Malley would shut the hell up.

After creeping back to his bedroll for his gun, Sam started back toward the sound.

He guessed he'd covered three hundred yards or so when he smelled the smoke from their fire, along with something else. He couldn't be certain, but he had a pretty good guess about the source of that odor.

Sounds and smells carried far on the night air, farther even than Sam realized. When he finally reached a series of hills, he thought he'd missed his target. Then the wind shifted, and the smell was back, and he knew his destination lay beyond the nearest hill. He made no noise as he carefully climbed through the patchy grass and hard earth. When he came to the top of the rise, he flattened his body against the earth and he listened for a long time. He heard snoring from two men. Sam hoped those were the only men over the hill. He eased up and peeked over the hilltop.

The camp was down in a small bowl-like indentation, bordered in front by the hill that Sam was on and in the back by a rocky cliff. Sam saw two horses tied on the southern side of the bowl. In the center was a dying fire. On either side of the fire was a sleeping man. One was huge, the size of a small tree. The other man was smaller. In front of the fire, closest to Sam, was a pile of bones, some with the meat still on them. Human bones and human meat.

Sam had found the Belcher brothers.

He was a bit surprised that the outlaws chose the low ground for their hiding place. It seemed a nice spot for an ambush. On the other hand, he realized how well hidden the brothers were, and the surrounding high ground was narrow and rocky. There was nowhere to make camp. Anyone else but Sam would have made much more noise getting here, too.

Which meant catching these flesh eating freaks was going to be a problem. Sam lowered himself out of the line of sight. He settled against the earth, listening to the night sounds and the noises the Belchers made in their sleep. If a silent approach with the horses and the dead guy was going to be a problem, then maybe the best move was to go in the opposite direction.

Sam smiled to himself. That reward was almost in his hands. He was so close to leaving this life behind.

Carefully choosing his steps, he made his way down the hill, away from the Belcher's camp and on to his own. As he walked, Sam felt good. The night air filled his lungs and made him feel strong. He had a good plan and he knew it would work. He ran the details over a couple of more times.

Sound good to you, Old Luke?

The old man's voice was silent. *If* he had ever been there at all.

Sam shook his head. His life had too much crazy shit in it. Just another reason to move on.

The sun would soon be up. He needed coffee. And a certain dead man.

The Dead Sheriff was in the hunt once again.

•••

FROM THE JOURNAL OF RICHARD O'MALLEY

"Sheeeee-it," Thunderstorm Parker said. "I can't believe I'm on a bounty hunter." The wagon lurched and jolted along the uneven trail.

"Neither can I." My sarcasm seemed to escape Parker's notice. I felt I understood his excitement, though. The old man had been tossed aside, made to feel useless. Now he had the opportunity to redeem himself, at least in his mind. He was on his way to reasserting his manhood.

At least, *he* thought so.

"You shore you don't need me to do some of the shooting?" With his right hand, Parker mimed firing a gun.

"While I'm sure you're marksmanship is superb, The Dead Sheriff rarely misses." Actually, Parker's hands shook so much; I doubt he could shave himself without releasing a gout of arterial spray. I reminded myself to take him to a barber in the next town we visited.

Parker turned on the wagon bench to examine the bed on the wagon. The body of the dead man was covered with a canvas sheet, just awaiting Sam's magical summoning. I squinted in the morning sun, trying to spot Sam's hiding place. He'd left well before us, after explaining the plan in great detail. He seemed unusually enthusiastic about this endeavor, displaying more animation then he had in many a day.

Parker and I were meant to play the part of father and son, weary travelers on our way to meet my brother in Colorado territory, where we would join him in working a small silver mine. Truly, it was more background than we were likely to need. The most likely scenario had these cannibal men shooting on sight or ignoring us completely. Personally, I hoped for being ignored.

Despite the reception, our part of this dark play meant we needed to get close to the camp of the Belcher brothers. Once they spotted us, Parker and I would drop from our seat and take shelter behind the wagon. From his hidden vantage point, Sam would command the Dead Sheriff to rise with guns blazing. By Sam's reckoning, the Belchers would be shocked and then shot to death or they would ferociously attack and then be shot to death. Either, way, the outcome was fairly well determined in advance. The hardest part (other than trying not to get shot while cowering behind the wagon) was to haul the bodies of the cannibal brothers to the nearest law enforcement representative who was authorized to pay the bounty.

Piece of cake, as my father would say. As I thought of the man who sired me, a police official back in my native Boston, I wondered as I usually did what he would think of my life in the West. In truth, had he been here living the events of the past few weeks instead of me, I fear Father would have gone quite mad. Although he was raised in the Church and made certain that I was, as well, I never got the sense that my father was very religious. I don't think he had the imagination to conceive of forces beyond what he could witness for himself. That isn't to say he was an unintelligent man. Father was quite canny, good at his job and unafraid of violence, whether he received it or dispensed it. He was hard-nosed and pragmatic. The thought of a reanimated corpse or a creature rising from some Hell pit to swallow an entire town would not only be ridiculous to him, it would be unthinkable.

Yet here was his son, witness and participant in supernatural events and prepared to enter the fray once again.

When I made it back to Boston, I did not think I would be sharing all of my adventures with dear old Dad.

I concentrated on the task before me. The trail ahead curved around a rocky hill, the very one that Sam had scaled a short time ago, if his directions were correct.

"Get ready," I said softly. "They're around the next bend."

"Gotcha," Parker said, matching my quiet tone. He wiped the back of his hand across his mouth. "Sure would nice to have a short snort before all the excitement starts."

"Mr. Parker, as soon as we get to a town, I'll buy you a bottle."

"Much obliged."

We followed the trail around the hill, slowly rising in elevation. The path continued to curve until, at the top of the rise, it ended at a large pile of brush and tree limbs.

"It's a deadfall," Parker said. "We better turn around."

Sam hadn't mentioned this. The hills on either side of the trail were close. To get out of here, we would have to walk the horses and the wagon backwards down the path for two or three hundred yards.

"Perhaps we could move the brush and make a path," I said.

Thunderstorm Parker snorted in amusement.

There was a rustling of dry leaves and a crackling of small branches behind the deadfall. A man ducked under a limb and stepped out of the mass of brush. He was thin and of average height.

And he was filthy. I understood how life on the trail meant you had to skimp on some areas of personal hygiene, but this man went far beyond that. He wore no hat and his greasy hair was plastered to his scalp. His unkempt beard contained leaves and mud and something darker. This was the man Sam described as one of the Belcher brothers.

He wore a gun in a holster, but he didn't reach for it.

"Well, shit," he said.

"Hello, sir." I touched the brim of my hat. "My father and I are headed to Colorado. Would you mind if–"

"You two ain't got enough meat on you fer a good roast. Probably stringy, too."

"Excuse me?"

The man shook his head and turned back to the deadfall of brush.

"Sir? Could you tell us how far we are from the Kansas line?"

The man contorted his body to and fro until he was have hidden by tree limbs.

"Yah see, me and my brother were gonna eat you, but it ain't worth the trouble to clean yah."

"We ain't eatin' 'em, Billy?" The voice came from above us and to the left.

Damn. It was an ambush and we rode right into it. I heard the wet sound of flatulence. Parker had once again soiled his pants.

The one called Billy shouted from his hiding place. "They're too skinny, Arlo. Light 'em up!"

Wherever Sam was, I hoped he could see or hear us.

I shoved Parker off of the wagon.

"Sam!" I screamed.

Above me, silhouetted against the morning sun, a giant stood and threw something at us, something that sparked and sizzled.

It was dynamite. Several sticks.

I leapt from the wagon and ran down the trail. I only made it a few yards before there was a roar and a mighty hand lifted me up and threw me into the wall of rock.

•••

Sam picked a good spot. It was high on a rocky hill maybe one hundred and fifty yards from the Belchers' camp. There was enough scrub brush to hide him, if he maneuvered his body into a shape resembling a ball. Sam heard the faint creak of wagon wheels in the distance. O'Malley and Parker should reach the camp in thirty minutes. Maybe less.

A flurry of movement caught Sam's eye. It was Billy, the smaller of the two Belcher brothers. He was hauling something over the entrance to their camp. Sam caught a glimpse of wooden planks before Billy turned the mess around. Tree limbs and other brush had been attached to a wooden frame, making a natural looking fence that could be easily moved into place.

Well, hell. The Belchers were getting ready for the arrival of the wagon. Sam had misjudged them.

While Billy dragged the brush into place, movement on the hill above their camp meant the other brother was preparing an ambush.

Sam had to get away, to warn O'Malley. The reporter was bringing the dead man, sure, but both living men would be in the line of fire. Sam had to scrap the plan. If necessary he would track the Belchers until a better opportunity presented itself. These boys weren't getting away. They just bought themselves another day or two.

If Sam was careful, he could make it to the top of his hill without being spotted. Once he was down the other side, he would run as fast as he could. He had to reach the wagon before O'Malley started up the curving trail.

He started to move from his shelter when the amulet began to burn.

The medallion was one of two items Sam stole from a red-haired man in a whorehouse in New Mexico territory, not so far from where he now crouched. The other item had been a book full of strange symbols that sometimes moved on the page. That book was in the back of the wagon. The amulet was on a chain around Sam's neck. He didn't understand how it worked, yet through trial and error Sam used it to revive the corpse of the Dead Sheriff. As long as he had it he could control the movements of the corpse.

But something had changed. The medallion seared his flesh as though it had just been pulled from a fire.

Sam yanked the chain from his neck and dropped it on the rocky soil at his feet.

The skin of his hand was already blistering. He didn't want to see what damage the amulet had done to his chest.

When he lifted his eyes to see if the Belchers had noticed his frenzied movements, Sam made another unpleasant discovery.

A group of robed and hooded figures stood only a few feet away from him. Unlike their first appearance, this time Sam could see them quite clearly.

There were seven of them, wearing garments made of some rough, dark material. They were tall–taller than Sam, even taller than the largest of the cannibal brothers–but they were also delicate, a word Sam had never used in connection with a person. The seven looked as if a light wind could carry them away. While the hoods shadowed their features, he could make out thin lips, compressed into hard lines. The same expression etched on each face, as though carved there centuries ago. Even though he couldn't see the eyes, he felt them, like knives, laying him bare. Sam didn't how this could be; only that it was.

The purest fear he had ever known spread through his bones with the chill of a winter wind. He wanted to run, to get as far from these beings as possible. Yet he couldn't move. He couldn't look away.

He felt he should know them, as if they were older than anything on the world. Strangely, he wondered if he should kneel before them. Something in their bearing, their grim and solemn faces, made him think they were meant to be worshiped.

The judges (for that was how he now thought of them) stared silently at him for only another moment before, as one, turning their heads toward the enclave of the Belchers. Sam wanted to look, too, if only he could tear his gaze away from the Judges. His neck wouldn't obey.

That only changed when the figure closest to him returned its gaze to Sam. It lifted an arm and pointed in the direction of the camp. As if he had been released from a hunter's trap, he found he was free to move. The fear was thick and suffocating but it no longer froze him in place. When he turned, he uttered a small cry of anguish.

The wagon with O'Malley and Parker was at the deadfall.

How long was I motionless, staring at those tall monsters?

He wanted to shout a warning. However, the only sound he could make was no louder than a sigh.

Sam was forced to bear silent witness as the larger of the Belcher brothers tossed sticks of dynamite into the wagon.

The fury of the explosion was a fierce and awful thing to behold. Pieces of the wagon were hurled into the air. Sam could see nothing of the writer or the old cowboy, much less the corpse of the Dead Sheriff. There was plenty of fire and smoke.

Something inside of him burned. It melted the fear that made him feel beholden to those hooded Judges. They kept him from helping his friends. Sam spun around to face that shadowy group.

They were gone.

CHAPTER FIVE

L ariat Smith was different from the other masked lawmen in the west. For one thing, he didn't wear a mask. There was no way he was going to cover up a face this handsome. And the women seemed to agree. For another, he could rope like an ace. But he could also shoot the ball off a fly at a hundred yards. The rope was for show–his public expected it–the gun was for business. Lately, business had been pretty damn good.

He had a saddle bag full of bounty money from his capture of a one-handed bastard who'd had an axe blade attached to his stump. That was what his daddy would call a win by a cunt hair. But a win, it was. Moreover, it had made a great photograph by Mr. Matthew Brady himself. Smith's rope was wrapped around the man's chest, pinning his arms to his side, and Lariat held the detached axe blade over his head as he flashed a triumphant smile. Nobody smiled in photographs; Smith planned to change that. It would be only one of the changes he wanted to have on society. Smith had half a mind to have the photograph framed and hanging over his mantle. If he ever had a mantle. Or a house.

For now, he preferred life on the trail. He had a different gal in every town. Sometimes more than one. Like this dusty and dark saloon in Junction City. Every time he was in Kansas, Smith made it a point to visit Fuzzy's. He didn't know who Fuzzy was–or if he ever existed. It wasn't the cleanest place in Kansas. In fact, it smelled like stale beer, old tobacco, sweat and vomit. But the ambiance was not what drew him here. If Fuzzy had done the hiring, then Lariat Smith approved of the man's taste. Two of the cutest whores Smith had ever sampled worked here. He'd enjoyed them separately and together, and while he wasn't a religious man, sharing a bed with Myrtle and Matilda was finer than he imagined Heaven to be.

He had finished his second glass of cactus wine. The potent mix of peyote tea and tequila lit up the inside of his head like a bonfire. It put a soft glow around everything he saw and it made him ready for a double poke with his favorite gals. Right on cue, Matilda came down the stairs and leaned over the empty chair next to him, making sure those big round titties almost spilled out of her bodice.

"Myrtle's upstairs arranging for a hot bath. We thought you could watch us and then you could have us. What do you say, cowboy?"

The drink made the whore's lips give off crackling sparks, like a hundred fireflies. "I say I got a big ol' brandin' iron just looking for a couple of cute heifers."

"You got a mouth on you." She cupped her breasts. "And I know how you can use it. Give us ten minutes." She started back to the stairs, then stopped and added, "Lariat, use the back stairs, okay?"

Smith nodded. The girls didn't want the owner to catch on that they were giving it to Lariat Smith for free, a situation that just made sense to Smith. A man this good looking did not pay for pussy.

He had time for another drink, so he signaled the barkeep for a third glass of cactus wine. Smith drank it fast. The effect was almost immediate, warmth spread from his belly to his crotch. The colors in the saloon grew bright and throbbed as if in time to an unheard song. That's it, he decided. Three is just the right number of drinks. He was in as fine a mood as he could remember and he was primed for some serious fucking. Tossing a gold coin on the bar, he stood and, wobbling slightly, he made his way to the door.

The night air was a revelation. Somehow, the cactus wine filtered out the smell of piss and horseshit, and left only the clean and potent scent of blooming flowers somewhere in the distance. Lariat Smith smiled as he headed for the back of the building.

His mellow state of mind collapsed as he rounded the side of the structure. Someone was standing. Someone familiar.

"Lariat Smith," the man whispered. "It must be my lucky day."

Smith squinted, trying to force the shadows to coalesce into an image he recognized. Fancy clothes. Twin Colts. And a silver mask.

Son of a Bitch.

"I'll be goddamned. It's the Silver Pecker," Smith said. The words felt thick as they passed over his tongue.

The figure stepped close. "Aw, Lariat, your wit has all the bite of a rusty butter knife."

Smith was certain he was looking at the Silver Paladin, except something about the man seemed different. He was taller. Or maybe he just carried himself differently. There was definitely something wrong with his mouth. Smith couldn't put his finger on exactly what it was.

"I think you made a wrong turn, Dewey. All the whores at this joint are split-tails. Not your breed at all."

The Silver Paladin suddenly stood nose to nose with him. *Christ*, Smith thought. *I'm drunker than I thought. I didn't even see him move.*

"Handsome man," the man with the silver mask said, "Big hero with a big rope. Everybody likes him. The women all spread their legs for him."

"Not all of them. But your mama did."

The Silver Paladin smiled. His breath was horrible, like a mixture of every dead and rotting thing there was. And the teeth...they were long and sharp. How had that escaped Smith's notice until now?

"You sicken me, Smith. You and all the other masked lawmen who are in it for fortune and glory."

"And pussy. Don't forget that," Smith said.

"What about men like me, who do what we do because it's right? Where's my respect and my parade?"

"They don't give parades to men who diddle their boy sidekicks."

Faster than Smith could follow, the Silver Paladin grabbed the front of his shirt and lifted Smith off the ground. God, this Fancy Dan was strong. Smith felt his nice shirt begin to rip around the armpits.

"I never touched the boy!"

"My mistake, Dewey. You can set me down now. This is an expensive shirt. Surely you can appreciate that."

With no appreciable strain, the Silver Paladin slowly lowered Smith to the Earth. He let go of the shirt and tenderly smoothed out the material.

"Sorry," he said. "I guess I can be a little touchy. I think it comes from all you fellas laughing at me and making insults."

Smith raised his hands in a gesture of surrender. "I can be an asshole. But listen, the west is big. Plenty of room for everybody, that's what I say. You have a good night, my friend. I have a prior engagement."

He moved to step around the Silver Paladin, but the masked man's planted the palm of his hand in the center of Smith's chest. It felt like Smith had walked into a tree branch.

"Hell, Dewey, that smarts a bit."

"So we're friends now. That right?"

"S-sure, bud. Best friends."

The Silver Paladin shook his head. "That makes this kind of awkward, Lariat."

Smith felt a cramp in his stomach, like his bowels were about to explode. Maybe it was the drinks. Or maybe it was this strange fucking dude, who used to act like a fancy-dressed sissy boy but now was just...scary. "What... what do you mean?"

"I mean I have a new partner now. You'd like her, Lariat. She's a pretty lady. Best of all, she runs a whorehouse. See, I'm kind of like her advance agent. I check out the new towns. Make sure they're ripe for the picking. It's a good job."

Smith swallowed hard. "Does it pay good?"

The Silver Paladin smiled again; displaying those teeth that plain didn't look right in a man's mouth. They would be more at home with a mountain lion. Or a wolf. "Oh, it has its benefits. For instance, I get to rid myself of every two-bit glory hog, wearing a mask or not, whoever laughed at me."

Lariat Smith, who had faced downs dozens of bad men and killers over the past ten years, began to tremble. "N-now, Dewey, let's be reasonable. Don't do anything here that your gonna regret later." Even his voice shook, and Smith hated himself for that.

"That's the best part about my new job, Lariat. I never have regrets. Not anymore."

The Silver Paladin grabbed Smith by the shoulders. That mouth full of sharp teeth opened impossibly wide.

Smith's bowels finally let loose, along with his bladder. "Please," he whispered.

The teeth tore his throat out. At first he felt almost nothing, just a cold sting. Then the warmth flowed down his chest, a different feeling than the stuff that ran down his legs. The Silver Paladin stuck again, and the second attack was agony. Another large piece of him was torn away. Smith tried to scream but only managed a wheezing gasp.

He thought of Myrtle and Matilda in their room, waiting on him, and he knew they would soon find someone to replace him, and that realization hurt more than the tearing of the teeth.

He was on the ground. How did he get here? The night got blacker still, as the Silver Paladin bit into him again and again.

His final thought, before the darkness closed upon him for eternity, was *I'm too handsome to die like this.*

•••

Sam moved as fast as he was able, yet it seemed to take forever to cross the distance from his hiding place to the remains of the wagon.

His head felt like it was full of angry hornets, preventing clear thought. A toughness constricted his chest. Sam didn't know if what he was experiencing had something to do with the robed Judges or if this was just guilt and fear for his friends. Either way, he thought he was losing his mind.

Friends.

That was a word he never had much use for. He never had a friend, except for Old Luke, the piano player at the whorehouse. Had O'Malley managed to worm his way so far into Sam's life that it mattered what happened to the skinny writer? And what about Parker, the old drunk. He barely knew the man, for Christ's sake.

So why was Sam moving so fast?

For one thing, it's my wagon, he told himself. *And I need that book of spells.*

Sam automatically touched the amulet around his neck. He had grabbed it before he left his place of concealment. It was ordinary metal now; cool to the touch, even though his chest still burned from the heat the metal had put off earlier. He couldn't begin to understand what was happening. Those robed figures were the scariest thing he'd ever seen, and at this point he'd seen more weird shit than he cared to remember. When they appeared out of nowhere, Sam felt no more important than an ant scurrying away from a boot heel.

But it wasn't only his possessions that spurred him on, forcing him to run so fast he thought his heart might explode.

He was worried. Worried for someone else.

It was something he hadn't felt for a very long time. Not since he was a child, fearful that his mother was being harmed by the strange men who came and went into her bedroom all through the night. The noises that she made came through the thin wall and made Sam think she was being murdered, though when she finally came out of the room, she seemed happy, smiling as she whispered to the men and sometimes kissed them. If she was really in a good mood and not just acting, his mother would take Sam out for some candy or pie. If she was acting with the men, that usually meant she was headed for the bottle as soon as they left. And Sam was on his own.

When he was less than halfway to the explosion site, he heard horses riding away.

Run fast, Belchers. I'll be right behind you.

At that moment, Sam didn't know if he The Dead Sheriff was destroyed or the magic still worked. He only knew that he would track those sick white fuckers to the ends of the earth, even if he was on his own. Even if it was his final act on this world.

As he drew closer to the place where the wagon blew up, the air grew thick with the smell of gunpowder and the almost fruity odor of the dynamite. Sam's stomach lurched. If he came across the bodies of O'Malley or Parker, he wasn't sure he could keep his breakfast down.

He was more than a hundred yards from where they wagon had been and where that barricade of fake brush stood when he came across the first chunks of debris.

There were two items. The first was a ragged, blackened piece of wood from the wagon. The other was the wire spectacles that O'Malley always wore. The glass was completely gone from the left side, while the other held perhaps half of a lens. The remaining glass was a jagged shard.

Something clenched hard within Sam's chest.

He dropped the glass and stumbled as he resumed climbing the hill. The rubble from the explosion grew thick upon the path. Most of it was wood, with some metal and other things. Things that were soft and still smoking and had come from the two men or the two horses. Or both.

About halfway to the explosion site Sam almost stepped on The Dead Sheriff's hat. The crown was missing. A scrap of pale scalp hung from the wide brim. Several brown hairs dangled from the skin.

Well, that was it, then. The dead man was gone. Sure, he still had the amulet, but without the book, he didn't think he could create another one. Hell, he wasn't even sure how he did it the first time. And that was with both magical items. Now? He was a young man with a fancy necklace who had lost almost everything.

Everything, he thought, except his need for vengeance.

He crested the top of the hill. The sight was almost too much to take in. Where the wagon had sat was a black depression in the earth, ringed with pieces of wood, wheels, some metal and bloody flesh. The head of one of the horses swung from a branch is the Belchers' fake deadfall.

Sam forced his body to walk. He stood in the center of the dark ground with the thick odor of smoke and gore filling his senses.

You did this, you know. This is on you.

He swallowed hard. It was true. Everything he'd done since stealing from the red-haired magician had led to this moment of loss and despair. His desperate need to escape the shitty life he had been born into led inevitably–step by step– to the deaths of two men on this spot

"I'll get 'em," he muttered. "It won't make it right, but they won't get away."

Only the dead heard him. Only the wind responded, a low whistle in the rapidly warming morning.

Sam was utterly alone.

Until someone spoke.

"I don't mean to offend, but this plan was not your best."

Sam jumped in surprise and spun around.

Standing a few feet behind him was O'Malley, bruised and bloody and alive.

•••

FROM THE JOURNAL OF RICHARD O'MALLEY

As far as entrances went, it was far from my worst.

Sam stood as still as a statue, at least for a moment. Then he rushed forward and grabbed my shoulders. It was almost an embrace. He even smiled, for the smallest part of a second, before he caught himself. He released me and took a step back.

He opened his mouth to speak, closed it, and then he tried a second time.

"How...how did you..."

My clothes and hands were stained with dirt and black powder. My shirt suffered from dozens of small tears. I stared at my arms in fascination. Perhaps I was merely fascinated that I still had arms. Sam clenched my shoulders again and shook me quite violently.

"Hey! You okay?"

I pulled out of his grasp. "Pardon me?"

"We were talking and you fell into a trance or something."

I did feel out of sorts. I wondered if I had suffered a blow to the head.

"How did you survive the explosion?"

I had to concentrate in order to recall the details, which seemed dream-like, as substantial as gauze.

"We were talking to the filthiest man I had ever seen, when an even filthier one—and much larger, too—appeared on the hillside above. He had a lit stick of dynamite in each hand. I remember shoving Parker out of the way and...I was flying through the air." I pointed to an outcropping a rock beside of the path. "I must have been thrown behind that. It protected me from the debris. Also, I believe our hairy and unwashed friend probably tossed the dynamite too soon. Had he held onto it another second or two, then—"

I suddenly become dizzy. The light grew thin and so did the air. I felt myself tilting toward the ground. Hands–Sam's, I presumed–took hold of me and carefully sat me down. The lip of a canteen was pressed to my mouth and a sipped cool water. I swallowed, blew out my breath and opened my eyes.

"I apologize," I said. Sam grunted.

"Are you going to faint again?"

"I do not believe that the event constituted an actual faint," I said.

"Okay," Sam said. He squatted so he could look me in the eye.

"Getting blown up is not as much fun as it seems."

"Hardly seems like it could be," he said.

"Where is Thunderstorm Parker?"

Sam looked away.

"No," I said.

"I've been all over the area."

"You missed *me*," I said.

Sam shrugged. He stood up and extended his hand. I took it. He assisted me to my feet.

"You okay to stand?"

I nodded, making a mostly futile effort to brush some of the grime from my clothing.

"I have to search for him. For whatever remains," I said.

"I'll help you."

We walked in separate directions around the spot of the explosion. There was a charred circular mark on the earth, and that was our starting point. I saw no human remains, but evidence of our horses was plentiful. It saddened me. They were fine animals. We widened our hunt. I was impressed that one wagon could create such a wide field of debris.

After twenty minutes or so, I was light-headed. I asked Sam for another drink from his canteen.

He handed it to me, and said, "We should have found something."

I swallowed the water and took another greedy sip before answering. "Perhaps he was vaporized."

He glanced back at the horse head hanging from the tangle of brush. "I guess he was a pretty skinny old man."

"He was a good fellow, though. Even if he did have a tendency to defecate in his drawers."

Sam nodded solemnly. "Yeah, he was full of shit." Despite his attempt at self-control, a giggle escaped from him. Perhaps the stress and the physical toil of the explosion loosened something in my mind, but, God help me, I found his laughter contagious. Soon we both were bent nearly double with the force of our guffaws.

As it does, the humor slowly drained from the situation, leaving us breathless, and, at least in my case, feeling a bit more like myself.

Sam straightened up. He glanced around the site one time, and then he sighed. "Did Parker have any family?"

"I don't know." There was so much I did not know about the man. I believe the fact that I first made his acquaintance in Boston led me to feel a certain kinship with the man, when, in actuality, we had spent very little time together.

"Let's take one more look around," Sam said. "See if there's anything we can salvage. Then we'll get going on that walk back to camp."

He didn't mention that even when we got to camp, there would be no horses and few provisions. He also didn't mention the loss of The Dead Sheriff and the book of spells (aside: Despite all that I have been through these past few weeks, writing the words "book of spells" nearly sends my mind reeling in disbelief; I fear this life of fantastic mysteries is one with which I shall never grow comfortable). I'm certain he was inwardly grieving or, at the very least, disgusted with the loss of a tool that generated income. I am not sure how one goes about creating another animated corpse. Despite my queries, Sam had not shared that information with me.

We searched the debris one more time. I found an axe handle without the blade. Sam located a box of shells for The Dead Sheriff's guns, though how the ammunition survived the explosion defies explanation. Fifty yards from the heart of the dynamiting, I found a large section of the canvas sheet used to conceal The Dead Sheriff when he was in the back of the wagon. All four corners of it were singed.

"That's it," Sam announced.

We paused for a moment to gaze at the spectacle. Neither of us spoke. That made it easier to hear the sound.

At first I mistakenly believed it to be the buzzing of an insect. It was a low noise, slowing rising in volume. As it grew louder, Sam turned to me, in all likelihood to ask me what could be making the racket. Before either of us could speak, the sound grew to a cacophony of such intensity we were forced to slap our hands over our ears, a futile gesture, as it turned out.

The clatter seemingly grew louder with my ears covered, which lead me to an incredible thought: I was hearing the sound with my ears. It was *inside my mind.*

That chilling hypothesis was immediately followed by another disturbing realization.

I knew what the sound was.

It wasn't an insect or an army of insects. The disturbing–and deafening–noise wasn't the result of millions of beating wings. It was a chorus of voices. Voices chanting in an unknown tongue.

The voices were coarse and guttural. The strange syllables grated and tore against my mind. I did not know from which language they originated. I only knew with absolute certainty that they came from no language spoken on Earth.

When I realized my eyes were clenched shut, I forced them open to see

"That's it," Sam announced.

a reddish glow from the sky. Sam was on his knees next to me, hands over his ears, and his face contorted with pain.

The chorus grew louder, until I thought I must go mad. Then the volume lowered, as if members of the chorus were fading away one by one. Eventually, only one voice remained. It spoke in thick, coarse tones, one indecipherable word after another. The sounds were still jarring. Something about the way the notes touched each other sent shivers of revulsion through my body. Yet the noise seemed bearable now. I removed my hands from ears.

Swaying on my knees, I looked to Sam. He, too, had uncovered his ears. His head was cocked to one side, like a dog listening to a mournful howling in the distance. To my surprise, he spoke.

"Yes, I'm here. But I don't understand..."

He gasped.

"Where? I can't see you?"

The glow in the sky darkened to a deep crimson.

Suddenly, he was there. One moment there was nothing, the next the shape of a man floated above the spot where out wagon was blown up.

The light became brighter and I could see details of the floating man.

It was Thunderstorm Parker. The old cowpoke and advance man for Wild West shows was intact and motionless in the sky above us. His eyes were shut in what appeared to be peaceful repose.

Sam stood up, walking toward the eerie figure.

Parker's eyes opened. Those strange words sounded again.

Sam stopped in his tracks. His mouth hung open in surprise.

"Old Luke?" he said.

CHAPTER SIX

The coach had been, Labine reflected, a terrible idea.

Since he didn't know how long or how far they would be going, he wanted to be as comfortable as possible. It was equally as important to keep his traveling companion away from curious eyes. When people got a good look at Moloch, they tended to one of three responses: they cried, they screamed or they went mad. Earlier in the year, in a small hotel a hundred miles or so east of Damnation, Texas, one man had done all three in rapid succession. Labine decided to seek other accommodations for the evening.

Now he was stuck in this creaking, swaying cab on the hottest day of the year with a beast that smelled like the sulfurous pits of hell itself. Moloch wasn't much for conversation, either.

Labine's thoughts drifted to a fantasy of escape. How sweet it would be to once again live as his own man, spending his time and energy solely in the pursuit of pleasure.

Of course, he could slip away from Moloch. He could produce several spells of concealment or confusion, allowing him enough time to take a train or a coach, perhaps to the coast. Then he could sail to Europe, perhaps to sample the Parisian delights or the choice beauties of Saville.

It would be a lovely trip. Until his master sent Moloch to remove Labine's internal organs.

He squirmed in his seat. The contours of the wooden support had turned the base of his spine into a ball of pain. Of course, it was nothing compared to the pain he would face should be fail in his task.

Labine would forever regret making the deal with Moloch's master. Unfortunately, the magician had never been one to consider the consequences of his actions.

His companion rumbled. If that sound had come from a dog, one's instinct would be to soothe the cur. With Moloch, however, it was a simple sign of impatience.

"I've felt nothing for some time." Moloch was silent. Labine hoped the beast didn't realize that he was twisting the truth a tiny bit. Actually, he had felt something a short time ago. The sensation lacked the flavor of Labine's stolen magicks. It was something of a decidedly different nature. Older. Much stronger. It scared Labine in a way he didn't understand. Hell, he didn't want to understand it.

A force of unknown strength was out there and he and his pet monster were heading straight for it.

Labine wished for some whiskey. A drink would ease the tension that was even now traveling down the back of his neck and across his shoulders. Two drinks would halt the parade of bad thoughts that marched through his brain. And three drinks? If Labine had three snorts of fine whiskey, he wouldn't care if Moloch smelled like a dog farting out dead groundhog.

But there was no whiskey, an oversight he would correct if the coach ever came close to a town. Which did not seem likely.

For now, he was stuck in a lurching, uncomfortable box with a malodorous—

The pain hit him like a spear to the center of his face. It was more intense than anything he had ever suffered. An explosion of agony blinded Labine, even as it raced through his body, obliterating all conscious thought and memory. He was nothing but the pain. In what little remained of his power to reason, he had a dim vision of his body burning with a flame that only existed beneath his flesh. Was this Hell? Had the patience of Moloch's demonic master ended, and Labine's soul ripped been from his body to be deposited in eternal torment?

Almost as quickly as it arrived, the pain faded until only a pinpoint of agony remained in the center of his mind.

Labine blinked away tears. He was still in the coach. The light had not changed. Only seconds had passed.

He drew in a shuddering breath.

It was his magick that inflicted the agony. He recognized its flavor. Yet, his power was amplified to a degree that he had never imagined.

First, he sensed a frightening ancient force that defied description. Now his own magick was magnified to an unimaginable level. This couldn't be the doing of the whore's son.

More than ever, Labine wanted to run, to hide and live well for whatever time he had left.

But that would require an escape from his unholy watchdog.

He glanced at Moloch. The creature was fanning his hand before his grotesque face, as if to remove an odor. Perhaps the monster was finally aware of his stench.

Or perhaps not. Moloch pointed a large claw-tipped finger at Labine. The magician glanced down to discover he had soiled his trousers.

"I hate you," he muttered.

•••

Sam was confused. A moment ago there had been no sign of Thunderstorm Parker's body. Now the man was hanging in air. And he spoke with the voice of Old Luke, one of the only friends Sam ever had, and someone who had been in the grave for many years.

A part of him realized the absurdity of being shocked over the dead returning to life. It was what O'Malley called *irony*.

The floating man had said, "Listen up, boy, and listen well." It was clearly the voice of the diminutive piano player in the whorehouse where Sam had spent much of his childhood.

"Old Luke? How can that be you?"

Thunderstorm Parker titled his head to one side, like a man trying to figure out a sticky problem. His eyes were closed. "Old...Luke..."

Something was different about the voice. It seemed to come from farther away than the mouth of the man who hovered above. It had a quality that made it sound like the speaker's mouth was full of water.

"Who are you? How can you just stay in the air like that?"

Parker's head dropped until his chin touched his upper chest. The reddish glow dimmed, then brightened, over and over. Looking at it made Sam's head hurt and even thought he wanted to turn away, to cover his eyes, he couldn't look away. It wasn't the paralysis he suffered earlier when the robed judges appeared. In this case, Sam was afraid to look away. He *needed* to hear this, whether it was really Old Luke or not. For weeks, all he wanted was to leave this life of magic and horror far behind him. But when he thought O'Mallley and Parker dead, and the magic destroyed, he wanted nothing but revenge.

Maybe this is how it's supposed to go, he wondered. *Once the mystery gets a hold of you, it has you until you're dead. Maybe longer.*

Perhaps he could finally get some answers if this flying bastard would speak again.

The bastard who next spoke wasn't the one in the air.

"What did he say?" O'Malley was standing behind Sam.

"You got ears," Sam said.

"I couldn't understand. The words were...wrong."

Parker raised his head. "My words are for both of you."

O'Malley gasped. "F-father?"

Sam didn't know what he meant. The voice that issued from the floating man was Old Luke's.

"You're not Old Luke," Sam said. "Who are you?"

Thunderstorm Parker opened his eyes. The pupils rolled up, leaving only white orbs flecked with red.

"I speak for the silent men, for they have no voice."

"The silent men?" Sam thought of the hooded figures. "You mean those fellas in robes?"

"That is one aspect of the silent men. You see only a slice of existence. They see everything."

"What the hell does that mean?"

"Excuse me," O'Malley said. "Why are you speaking through our friend?"

Parker's head leaned to one side again. "Speaking to you...is difficult.

When one is dead...or close to it...a path opens."

"Parker is dead? But he's right there!" O'Malley choked on the last word.

"Why do you sound like Old Luke?" Sam said.

"My father," O'Malley said.

"We thought...a familiar voice...would make it simpler for you to understand...the power."

The voice of Old Luke had been with Sam shortly after he raised the dead man from the grave. All this time it had been the magic–the amulet and the book?

The light surrounding the floating man dimmed, and when it did the entire hilltop was shrouded in shadow. It looked like midnight instead of mid-morning. Slowly, the red glow returned, pushing the shadows away.

The man who had been Parker spoke.

"Time...grows short...my time is nearly done."

'What does that mean? O'Malley asked.

"See."

The light around the man flared to a brighter glare than before, growing in intensity until Sam and O'Malley had to shield their eyes, then cover them completely. Even through closed lids and the protection of their fingers, the light could be seen. To Sam, it felt like the Sun had fallen from the sky and now hovered right next to the floating man.

He felt a rush of heated air and a sound like the biggest dust storm he'd ever heard and the light was gone.

Lowering his hands, he opened his eyes.

The world was changed.

Where once were grassy hills, now the land was flat. Flat and black. The earth beneath Sam's feet had become some sort of stone. Every few feet a sharp protrusion rose a few inches. The now-dim sunlight was reflected in the smooth surface of the protrusions, like black glass.

And that was only the beginning. In the distance, gouts of flame erupted from the blackened surface. The closest eruption was as close as thirty feet. Multiple flaming geysers were visible for as far as Sam can see.

"O'Malley, what are those fire spouts?" Sam finished his query with a cough. The air tasted of sulfur and it burned his throat and nose.

"I don't know," the writer said. "What the hell is that?" He pointed to the sky. Sam looked upward and instantly wished he hadn't.

There was a hole in the sky, a rip in the very air above them (and the sky, Sam noticed, was no longer blue, but a sickly yellow). Something moved within that hole, something large and impossible to look at. In fact, it hurt his head to try to make sense of what he saw. Sam averted his gaze, and was left with the impression of being studied by many eyes, strange orbs with more than one pupil.

"We've got company!" O'Malley gestured toward the west. Beyond the spurts of flame came a herd of beasts, four-legged and as wide as three horses. As they rapidly drew closer, Sam saw they had only two eyes, thankfully, but beneath those eyes were a mass of tentacles, such as he had seen once in a book about sea creatures. Astride the back of each creature was a figure carrying an object that looked like a rifle, only longer and thicker.

"Shit," O'Malley said.

The figures riding the beasts may have been shaped like men, but their heads were like nothing seen on this Earth. They had the heads of bugs, large and black and covered with eyes that were even darker. Each side of the head had a hinged sort of flap with sharp edges. The flaps moved in and out. Sam couldn't help but think of a hungry animal working its jaw in anticipation of a great feast.

The lead rider pointed his rifle toward Sam and O'Malley. With a high-pitched chittering cry, he spurred his mount to a faster speed. The rest of the herd followed suit. Sam guessed there were fifty or sixty of the beasts.

"We have to run." He pulled at O'Malley's arm, but the writer didn't moved. He stared in open-mouthed astonishment at the sight of their pursuers. "Come on!"

O'Malley turned. "Where, Sam? Where can we go?"

Sam turned, as well. The land behind them was just a bleak and demolished as what lay ahead. There was no cover, no shelter. It was a dying field.

Both men resumed watching the approach of the creatures.

The lead rider pointed his rifle at Sam and O'Malley. He made that chittering shriek again and a lance of blue flame shot across the distance, slicing the air between the two men. Sam felt he intense heat on his cheek. One glance told him O'Malley felt it, too.

Despite the lack of cover, both men turned and ran. Footing was treacherous on the strange glassy ground, but they fled anyway.

It was futile move, Sam knew. But he couldn't stand and die.

More arcs of blue fire landed near them, mostly at their feet. Sam was already winded. Too many months in the wagon. He could hear O'Malley's ragged breathing just behind him.

Something grabbed Sam's feet. One instant he was upright and running and the next he was falling face down onto the slick, black earth. The rock–

or whatever it was—shattered beneath him and cut his face and hands. He rolled over and saw that O'Malley had suffered the same fate. Openings had appeared in the earth, looking like large gopher holes. But it wasn't gophers that had come out from underground. Each man was in the grasp of some vile appendage that had oozed from the openings. A tube of gray flesh, slick with an oily secretion, was wrapped around Sam's ankle and was slithering up his leg. Open sores covered the flesh and a sickly green pus ran from each lesion, mixing with the limb's greasy discharge. The tip of the appendage was blunt, with a flap of skin folded over. It looked like a wrist where the hand had been cut off.

"I can't get it off!" O'Malley kicked at the thick tube with his free foot. Sam heard a wet tearing sound. All around him more of the gopher holes opened and a greasy arm unspooled from each. They rose in the air and swayed from side to side, the flap of flesh over the ends dripped with green ichor.

The flaps peeled back. There was an eye on the end of every stalk. An eye with a black pupil. Sam bit back a scream.

The hoofbeats of their pursuers were like thunder.

"They're here," O'Malley said. He could have saved his voice.

"That's not the worst of it," Sam said.

O'Malley kicked at the flesh-stalk that wound around his thigh. "What?"

"There." Sam pointed up. Another hole had opened above them. Larger versions of the stalks descended from the sky, each one tipped with a gargantuan black eye. A screeching came from the hole in the heavens; a sound that Sam feared would shatter his mind. It was a voice. He didn't know how he could be sure of this, yet he was. It was the voice of whatever controlled the flesh-stalks. It meant to have them. It was going to pull them through that gaping maw to the bleak hell on the other side.

Sam couldn't hold back his scream any longer.

•••

The Belchers rode south, the two men they had blown up nothing but a distant memory.

All in a day's work.

"We goin' to a big city?" Arlo had talked the entire time they'd been on the trail. Every word was like a nail driven into Billy's ear.

"For the hundredth goddamned time, no," Billy said. His harsh tone made his brother shut up, but now Arlo would sulk for hours. Fine. At least there would be some quiet.

A big city had its appeal. There would sure be more opportunity for Belcher-style fun. But a lot of people meant more lawmen. And while Billy believed he and his brother were tougher than any ten badged-up bastards, he also knew that such trouble would keep them on the run for weeks. What he needed now was to blow off some steam. So a small town would have to do. Hell, if you picked the right one you could do okay. The Belchers only needed a bar and some whores. And something to eat.

Billy thought he knew just the place.

"Arlo, I ever tell you about a town in Texas called Dooley?"

Arlo didn't answer. Billy went on talking.

"It's not very big. But it has a nice hotel and a saloon with the fattest whores you ever saw."

That got his little brother's attention. "Fat? With big ol' titties?"

"Biggest you ever seen." Billy glanced over at Arlo. The big man was licking his lips. "And you know what the best thing is about Dooley?"

"What?"

"They got no peacekeepers. Just a traveling marshal who rides through every three weeks or so for a day or two."

"That's it?"

"That's it."

Arlo sat up a little straighter in his saddle. "We might be able to get into some mischief there."

"You know what, Arlo? That sounds like a fine idea. Why, I bet we could have a better time than in a big ol' crowded town."

"Yeah. Them whores have real big titties, right?"

"You bet."

Arlo chuckled.

Sure, Arlo would jabber on for the rest of the day, but Billy hated to make his kid brother sad. Mama, that evil bitch, would be proud.

Thoughts of the good times ahead should have lifted Billy's spirits. Instead. Memories of his strange dream from a few nights ago drifted into his head. Screaming was fine. As long as it was caused by Billy and Arlo, but in the dream, it seemed like the Belchers were the ones screaming. And what was that crazy shit with the flying people and the men in robes?

It was just a stupid dream. It meant nothing. But it bothered Billy all the way to the Texas border and beyond.

•••

The Silver Paladin had never felt this strong.

Flushed with the blood of Lariat Smith, he shared the dirt-filled sleeping berth of his queen. Magdala stroked him, as he recounted his conquest of the handsome bounty hunter.

Of all the others in The Silver Paladin's former field, Smith had been one of the men he hated the most. Not just for the insults and insinuations he tossed around whenever he encountered The Silver Paladin and Bullet. Smith filled him with envy; the way he moved through crowds, talking is that smooth and cocksure way with men and women alike. Everyone looked at Smith with admiration. Lariat Smith was everything Dewey Martin wasn't.

Of course, that was in the past. Now Smith was a desiccated bag of flesh.

"You did well, my prince," Magdala purred into his ear. "Doesn't it feel glorious?"

"Yes." He was sure she meant the killing of Smith. What she was doing with her hand felt pretty nice, too.

"Who is next?"

The Silver Paladin couldn't believe she was letting him make the decision. She was a goddess, and she allowed him to sit at her right side. Together they would rule the west, then the country. Who could stop them?

"There's a man," he said.

"There usually is." Everything Magdala said was tinged with laughter. In his old life, Dewey Martin would worry that he was the object of that humor. The Silver Paladin now shared Magdala's amused perspective on humanity.

"He's another fool in a mask. He calls himself Sidewinder. He wears a cape and carries a sword."

"How thrilling."

Sidewinder had been responsible for the single most humiliating moment of Dewey Martin's old life. He struck up a friendship with Dewey based on their shared line of work. He plied Dewey with drinks, opened up to him about how misunderstood he'd been. Then, when Dewey was drunk and vulnerable, Sidewinder had coerced him into an intimate encounter in the back room of a closed bar.

At least it was supposed to be closed.

When the bar owner and a couple of others walked in on them, Sidewinder accused Dewey of attacking him and called him a deviant and worse. Fortunately, Dewey hadn't been dressed as The Silver Paladin. He hadn't been dressed at all, for that matter. He fled. And the pain of that betrayal burned as hot now as it did then.

Now he could balance the books. Since Dewey Martin died, The Silver Paladin had found the strength to do so many things poor scared Dewey could never have done.

"Where is this Sidewinder?" Magdala sped up her tender ministrations.

"Mostly in Texas," The Silver Paladin said. Before he could continue, he shuddered and moaned his goddess's name.

"We shall seek him out."

The Silver Paladin smiled in the darkness. "Let's start with a little town he's fond of. It's called Dooley."

CHAPTER
SEVEN

FROM THE JOURNAL OF RICHARD O'MALLEY

I looked around. I was lying in the dust, on the charred spot where our wagon exploded. Sam was looking back at me, only a few feet away. The hole in the sky was gone, along with the horrendous tentacles and the creatures with the odd guns that fired light.

Not everything was back to normal.

The thing that had been Thunderstorm Parker still floated above us. He lifted his head from his chest, looking at Sam and I with eyes that were white orbs without pupils.

Raising to a sitting position, I tried to speak, but my throat was full of dust. I coughed and spat, and finally I said, "What did you do?"

"Showed...you..." As if he were alternating between a whisper and speaking at a normal volume, Parker's voice faded in and out.

"Why show us a nightmare?" Sam struggled to his feet. He was shaken, yet, I thought, more angry than anything.

"Not...nightmare. It is...what will come to pass...forces arrayed against you...succeed."

I stood beside Sam, uneasy on my feet. My discomfort was not caused by physical trauma. I wondered–not for the first time–how far a man's mind could be twisted before it snapped. "What we saw–the monsters, the things attacking us from the ground and the sky; that will happen?"

"If no...one...stops it."

"How?" Sam threw his hands up in frustration. "How can two men without magic, without The Dead Sheriff stop anything?"

The thing that had been Thunderstorm Parker did not answer.

"This is horseshit." Sam turned away from the floating man. I tried to take his arm. He pulled away from me. "Forget it, O'Malley. I'm tired of it all. Creatures that eat towns and this flying man and his crazy talk. I'm going to find someplace in Mexico to get drunk until the world ends."

Sam started down the hill.

Until the earth trembled.

What now, I thought. I'd read of earthquakes, though I was not aware of their likelihood in this part of the west. I backed up, determined to stay away from trees and falling rocks. Sam stood a few yards downhill.

As it turned out, it wasn't an earthquake.

Small bits of debris rose from the dirt, just a few at first, and slowly. Soon, more and more items, both large and small, floated a few feet above the ground and began to move. Other pieces from farther away flew into our sight. By now, Sam and I were huddled against the rocky hills on either side of the trail. I had nearly been decapitated by an iron brace from the back of the wagon when it soared by me inches from my neck.

What we saw was impossible. And it wasn't even the most impossible thing that day. When that particular thought blossomed into my head I had to bite off laughter, knowing that if I started, I most likely would not stop.

The wagon–blown to a thousand pieces–was reassembling in front of us. Splinters of wood became solid planks. Nails straightened and gouged into place. Shattered spokes became whole again. The activity moved so fast it became a blur.

In a short time–seconds? A minute or two?–our wagon was restored.

A looked at Sam. I'm certain my mouth fell open.

Sam didn't appear shocked. Instead, he was still angry.

"Congratulations. You can wave your hand a build a wagon. Well, everything's going to be all right now, I guess."

The floating man remained silent. The reddish light surrounding him grew blighter, losing its color in the process. Soon, it was a white glare that we could not look at.

"Here we go again," I muttered.

The world did not disappear, however, nor were we returned to that desolate land of flames and bugs the size of men.

The glare faded. I blinked.

"Son of a bitch," Sam said. He didn't sound angry anymore.

The Dead Sheriff stood next to the wagon. Not only was the corpse intact, it looked in far better shape than I had ever seen it.

The clothing, which had been riddled with holes and tears, and stained with the dark fluid inside The Dead Sheriff's body, was now intact and clean. The flap of loose skin along the undead avenger's temple had been reattached. The pale bone of the skull no longer shined through. Even the brown hair that showed beneath the brim of the hat looked fuller.

Make no mistake: I was still looking at a corpse. Yet a corpse that had been destroyed a short time ago and now stood intact and in a greatly improved condition.

Thunderstorm Parker slowly descended from his perch in the sky. His feet touched the ground between the two of us. His knees gave way and he nearly crumpled to the ground. Before that happened, he straightened. He swayed a bit as he stood staring at a space between us.

Sam shifted from foot to foot. Finally, he positioned himself in front of the man who had been Parker. It was clear that Sam was trying to hold on to his anger. Perhaps it was an anchor for him in this sea of mystery and macabre.

"Am I supposed to thank you now?" Parker did not react. Those blank eyes seemed to not see Sam or anything else. "Hooray. You brought back the dead man."

Sam grabbed the chain around his neck and yanked until the amulet came free from his shirt. "Without that book, this here's just a piece of junk. And that dead man is just another dead man. The west is full of 'em."

"The book," Parker said. Sam stopped speaking.

"The magic...cannot be destroyed." Parker's voice was fading away again. I was left with the impression that his time with us was nearly over. "The book...is gone...and its energies joined with...this one." Parker tapped his chest with the palm of one wizened hand.

Neither Sam nor I spoke. The air seemed charged, like a storm was forming. As if acknowledging his namesake, Thunderstorm Parker clasped his hands against Sam's shoulders.

Sam screamed. The air around the two of them rippled like water. I heard a sound that reminded me of frying bacon, only much louder.

Sam screamed. He fell to his knees.

I stepped toward them. The Parker-thing raised a hand to stop me.

"Tell him..it is inside him now...and look for the girl...with two faces... she...speaks... for the...silent men..." Parker collapsed in the dirt, a puppet whose string had been cut.

I rushed to him. Parker did not breathe. He showed no signs of being able to talk or walk or float into the sky. His flesh was cold.

He had been dead a long time.

I helped Sam to his feet. He stood silently for a moment, looking from the body of Parker to the standing corpse of The Dead Sheriff to the restored wagon.

He made a noise. It could have been a cough or a soft bark of laughter.

"Are you all right?"

He nodded. "The bastard couldn't have brought the damn horses back, too?"

•••

They buried Parker on the hill beside the trail. O'Malley insisted. Sam had wanted to leave immediately, but the burial seemed important to the writer.

They were both surprised to discover that the restoration of the wagon included the belongings they routinely carried, the shovel being among the contents.

O'Malley insisted on doing most of the digging. Sam was fine with that. Whatever had happened when Parker touched him left Sam feeling weak and dizzy.

When the burial was complete, O'Malley said a few words over the grave. Sam didn't pay much attention to what was said. He did add an "amen" at the end. He thought you were supposed to do that.

As they walked back to the wagon, O'Malley asked what would happen to the grave if the Belchers came back.

"They ain't coming back," Sam said.

O'Malley just stared at him. Sam had never seen the man looking so tired. He was fairly sure he looked the same way.

"We're goin' after them." Sam walked to side of the wagon where The Dead Sheriff still stood. He had not moved since his reappearance.

Sam wasn't sure how this was going to work now. Or if it even would work.

He placed his left hand over the amulet. With his right he gestured toward the standing corpse.

He felt ridiculous. He dropped his right hand.

"Get over here," he said. Sam felt an odd tingling in his head and mid-section.

The Dead Sheriff took three steps to Sam's side. He stopped.

Okay. That worked.

Sam closed his eyes. He concentrated on what he wanted the dead man to do.

Get in the wagon.

The corpse grabbed the side of the wagon and pulled himself into the bed. He sat there.

Now lie down.

The Dead Sheriff fell back into a prone position.

"Well, that's something," Sam said.

"What now?" O'Malley said.

"Now we wait."

•••

They spent just two hours hidden on the hill where Sam had watched the demolition of the wagon. It seemed like days ago. Sam found it hard to believe it had only been a few hours.

About a quarter of a mile from their position, a small pond rested in the shade of a single elm tree. When the sun was starting to set, two men on horses rode up. Sam wasn't sure what tribe they came from. Despite his appearance, he knew very little about Indian culture. That's what happened when your mother was a whore who loved the bottle more than she did her son. Sam figured the two were Apache or Caddo. He'd run into both between Kansas and Texas. The two Indians may have been father and son, a least from what he could see from his distant vantage point. Both had rifles sheathed on their saddles.

The younger man dismounted. He carried two water skins to the pond. He knelt by the water and used his hand to drink. He nodded to the older man. He filled the skins.

The Dead Sheriff left his place of concealment behind the trunk of the tree. At Sam's silent command, the dead man walked a wide path toward the two Indians, partially obscured by brush that ran along one side of the pond.

He managed to approach the older man without being seen. The mounted Indian wore a leather vest. The Dead Sheriff grabbed a handful of the material and pulled the man from his horse. The impact knocked the air from the older man. The Dead Sheriff picked the man up and tossed him into the pond, which looked to be three or four feet deep. The Indian landed face down. The younger man didn't realized what was happening until the splash of his father's landing. He leaped to his feet, looked at his father and then at the horrifying apparition that stood by their horses. He hesitated only a second. He pulled a knife from a scabbard on his belt and, with a roar, rushed toward The Dead Sheriff.

The undead avenger stood still as the young brave ran his knife into the dead man's stomach. The blade sank in to the hilt. The boy stepped back in astonishment. At Sam's mental urging, The Dead Sheriff hoisted the boy over his head, walked to the edge of the pond and hurled the boy against the trunk of the tree. The boy sank to the water. Only his face could be seen. At least he wouldn't drown. The boy's father pulled himself halfway out of the water, then collapsed face down in the mud. He may have been exhausted or unconscious. Sam couldn't tell.

The Dead Sheriff took both horses by the reins and led them away from the pond.

"It was effective," O'Malley said. "Do you think those two will be all right?"

Sam shrugged.

"At least you didn't make him use his guns. There might be a spark of mercy in you after all."

Sam shrugged again. "Didn't want to spook the horses."

Despite his comments, Sam watched the pond until the dead man returned with the horses. The older man finally revived and helped the younger one out the water. They both sat at the edge of the pond, trying to recover.

Sam and O'Malley made their way to the wagon. They hitched the horses up and Sam got The Dead Sheriff back in the wagon. They thing that had been inside Parker even restored the piece of canvas. Sam used it to cover the corpse, who still had the brave's knife stuck in his belly.

Sam climbed up beside O'Malley and took the reins.

"What a day," the writer said.

"After we get back to camp and load up, we'll see who has the worst day," Sam said. "Us or them Belchers."

•••

Labine was no longer aware of the stench in the carriage, nor did he feel the craving for drink.

Something changed.

His magic was calling to him, louder than before. In fact, the magic

The blade sank in to the hilt.

had not felt this strong even when he possessed the talismans.

Something changed.

His desires and complaints and petty thoughts were gone, all sublimated by the power that was once his. He was as an addict, craving the bottle of laudanum or the exquisite pinch of the needle.

Nothing mattered now except reaching the source of the magick.

On the periphery of his senses, Labine knew that Moloch watched him with great curiosity. This human was different, perhaps dangerous.

Inwardly, Labine smiled. He felt like a dowsing rod. He smelled the water and he would not lose the scent.

He was dangerous. Somehow, his magic was stronger. And once he reclaimed it, there would be a reckoning, first with Moloch, and then his master.

After that, the world belonged to Labine.

CHAPTER EIGHT

Dooley was a nice enough town. If your only desire in this world was to sing hymns at church or sit in the saloon and drink until you died.

Billy couldn't see much else of value here.

He'd led his brother to believe that he'd visited this humble community in the past, when he'd actually heard about it from a fellow soldier in the Second Texas Calvary, old Mervyn Tallowood. Mervyn was a pretty good guy, the sort of fellow soldier you could really count on. And Billy would have been happy to go on serving with Merv, had Billy not got a hankering for some long pork during the winter of '63, when he and Merv were on patrol alone in the Rio Grande Valley. Billy later told his captain that Mervyn had run off, said he missed his wife and their seven kids too much to stay. Merv had been from Dooley and had told Billy many stories about it, including the size of the titties on the whores. Billy never knew if the army had gone back to Dooley to look for poor old Merv (who, Billy recalled with a smile, tasted pretty damn good).

Oddly enough, years later, Billy and the Second Calvary were back in almost the same spot near Brownsville for the battle of Palmito Ranch. They called it the last battle of the War. But Billy would always remember as the day he saw good old Merv once more, standing in a field between the Yankees and Colonel Ford's troop. Merv jumped up and down and laughed and waved like a little kid. Nobody but Billy saw him. Billy assumed Merv was just a product of his sour stomach, even though he danced around that battleground until the last shot was fired.

Now that he was finally in Dooley, Billy wondered if he would receive another visit from Mervyn. The thought made him uneasy.

"Do we get to eat some people first, then find the whores?" Arlo had asked some version of this question at least twenty times.

"No, dummy. Eatin' people is the last thing we do before we vamoose. The chamber of commerce tends to frown on folks chewin' up their citizens."

"You don't have to call me dummy." Wonderful. Now the big dummy would be sulking all evening. What they needed was some hooch and a fight.

"I tell you what, Arlo. Let's find the saloon. Let's get a bottle and look for them whores."

"Okay!" His spirits lifted, Arlo practically skipped down the wooden sidewalk, making the weathered planks groan under his weight.

Dooley's downtown wasn't large. There was the livery, where the Belchers just came from sheltering their mounts, a general store, a small bank, several nice houses, a tall water tower (Billy assumed the town had burned down at least once, or someone was afraid it would), and, separated by fifty yards or so of empty ground, a bar and whorehouse. The old biddies of Dooley must want to keep their distance from the bad element in town. Billy smiled at the thought. He and Arlo might just have to pay a call on some of them biddies on their way out of Dooley.

The two brothers kicked up a cloud of dust as they crossed the open ground. As they got close to the bar, a clattering commotion headed their way. Both men stepped to the side of the dirt street to make way for a procession of fancy long coaches, the largest horse-drawn conveyances Billy had ever seen.

"Look, Billy! Ain't that the circus?" Arlo looked like a little kid, standing there pointing, with his mouth hanging open.

Billy was pretty sure it wasn't the circus. He'd worked for a circus outfit right after the war. They required much more transportation. He'd heard some of the bigger circuses even owned their own trains. No, this wasn't a circus, though he had the feeling that entertainment was involved. Each coach was carved with naked women.

The carriages slowed at the end of the street and rolled to a stop in a barren field on the other side of the whorehouse. The three drivers climbed down from their perches. It was strange. They looked like bothers or something. All tall and bald. The men stood by the doors of each coach. They didn't talk to each other, only staring straight ahead.

And folks called the Belchers odd.

Billy shrugged. He yanked on Arlo's arm to get his little brother into the saloon. He'd probably end up walking Arlo over to the coaches later to convince him that it wasn't a circus.

Inside, the saloon was dark and cool. The barkeep was lighting lanterns to hang along the walls and out on the porch. Candles were going on the tables like some kind of fancy diner. There were only a handful of people in there. Maybe it was too early for serious drinking in Dooley. Or maybe this was all that turned out. If that was the case, it would be a piss poor bar fight.

They walked up to the bar. The barkeep didn't look up from his lamp lighting. "What it be–" He glanced at them, wrinkling up his nose at the same time.

"What's wrong?" Billy said. "You cut the cheese?"

The barkeep wrinkled up his forehead like he was going get sassy, except that's when Alro leaned on the bar. The saloon man looked up and up, until his neck popped. Most of the color drained from his face.

"We wanna drink," Arlo said.

The barkeep flapped his lips soundlessly.

Billy tapped Arlo's arm. The big boy eased back a step from the bar.

"Looky," Billy said, "make it two bottles of the good stuff, and we'll set at a table way over by the wall and we probably won't even bust anybody up tonight."

The barkeep nodded real fast and found two bottles and a pair of glasses. He set them on the bar.

"Keep the glasses." Billy's two gold pieces landed with twin *plinks* on the polished bar next to the drink ware.

"I hope you meant it." The voice was smooth and low. The speaker was a few stools down, shrouded by shadows.

Billy looked around. "You talkin' to me?"

"I am." The figure stood up and walked closer. He was a little taller than Billy and a foot shorter than Arlo. Worst of all, he wore a black mask. It was shiny, like silk, and covered the top of his head down to his nose. The rest of his outfit was black, too. And the son of a bitch had a big black towel tied around his neck. Billy took note of the masked fella's gun and sword hanging from his belt.

"You goin' to some kinda party?"

"Billy, is he with the circus?" Arlo was excited. "Are yah, mister? You part of that circus?"

"I'm no circus performer. Men call me Sidewinder." He actually bowed.

"What do women call you? Needle dick?" Billy laughed at his own joke.

"Very witty," the masked dude said. "You said you didn't plan to, ah, 'bust anyone up' tonight. Please see that you don't."

Billy felt his face flush. That feeling usually led to somebody dying. "Who are you, the schoolmarm?"

The masked man stepped closer to Billy. His teeth were very white in his smile. Billy wanted to knock every one of them out. "I am someone who is very fond of this town and the drinking establishment we are in. I haven't killed anyone in a month. Don't make me break that record. I haven't gone that long in years."

Arlo grabbed a handful of the masked man's silk shirt. "Don't you know who we are?"

Sidewinder kept smiling. "In fact, I don't. I told you my name; I wish you would return the favor."

Billy looked around the dim room. There were probably a dozen people scattered around, including the bartender. All of them were watching and listening very carefully. He took Arlo's arm. "It's okay, mister. We've been on the trail for a couple of days. Got saddle sores and a throat full of dust. Maybe we're cranky. We'll talk to our bottles and keep to ourselves."

The masked man pulled his shirt out of Arlo's grasp. "See that you do."

Billy led Arlo to the table. His younger brother almost trembled with anger. "I could've crushed his face with one hand. Why'd you stop me?"

"I wanna have some fun first." Billy stared at Arlo until the bigger man sat. "Let's drink and find some whores before we gotta run."

Arlo took a long pull from the bottle. After he swallowed, twin streams of amber liquid ran from his mouth to his beard, mixing with the dirt and blood and other things there.

"Okay, Billy," he said. "But when it comes time for killin' and eatin', I got dibs on the guy with the mask."

•••

FROM THE JOURNAL OF RICHARD O'MALLEY

There was a small town with no name in unorganized Indian Territory, about fifty miles north of the Texas border. I use the term "town" rather loosely. It covered perhaps an acre, and consisted of a barn, a house that had shifted on its foundation and now tilted toward Kansas, a small number of lean-to structures and a trading post. The store was run by an old white woman named Myrna and an equally aged Cherokee man called Two Hawks. I only know his tribe because he told me, in perfect English. The woman didn't talk much, but when she spoke, the man listened intently and did exactly what she said.

They both knew Sam. Two Hawks greeted him warmly. The woman allowed one corner of her mouth to rise.

I accepted a cup of coffee from the woman while Sam haggled over the price of a few supplies and questioned the couple (for it was obvious that the man and woman were a couple, whether or not it had been consecrated by God and the law).

It turned out the Belcher brothers passed through the area earlier that very morning. They didn't stop (mostly because Two Hawks stood on the porch of the trading post with a shotgun slung over his shoulder; he'd heard of the pair and wanted nothing to do with them). The old man indicated they headed southwest.

"What's in that direction?" Sam asked.

"Nothin', 'til you hit Texas." Two Hawks spit in the direction of a tin can on the floor. He only missed it by five or six feet. The old woman's scowl grew more intense, if that were possible.

Sam paid for the few items on the counter.

"Be careful, Sam,' the old man said. "I've seen some crazy bastards in my day, but those two...I got a bad feeling offen 'em."

"I will," Sam said. Before we reached the door, the old woman intercepted Sam and hugged his neck fiercely. When she finished, she walked to a back room without speaking.

Once we were outside, I asked Sam how he knew them. His answer surprised me.

"I lived here a while after I ran away from...my old life. Worked for Myrna."

"Two Hawks wasn't here?"

"Been here as long as Myrna, but she's the boss."

"So that was before The Dead Sheriff."

He didn't reply until we were on the wagon and headed south.

"It was here that I made the amulet and the book work for the first time. Just a little. I left soon after. Found the first Dead Sheriff about twenty miles from here."

"The first?" I turn to glance at the canvas covered shape in the back of the wagon.

"The one back there is number two."

My reporter's instincts came to life. "What happened to the first one?"

Sam slowly exhaled. "Another time. After we take care of business. And I have a lot of whiskey."

I didn't press him, though I did wonder about the whiskey comment. Sam had been drinking a lot the past few weeks. But back at the trading post he hadn't even glanced at their small selection of spirits. I wondered how the experience back at the Belchers camp had changed him. After all, a magical artifact had been joined with his body, if I understood those events correctly. My experience with magic was quite limited, yet even I knew an event like that must have consequences.

I felt certain that I did not wish to know what those consequences were.

•••

The Silver Paladin grew restless waiting for the sun to set. He paced ceaselessly through the private carriage.

Magdala, whose touch had often been firm but gentle, grasped his face with a steel grip. Her long nails dug into his cheeks, drawing what little blood still coursed through his cold flesh.

"Impatience is a human trait, one you should have left behind," she said.

"I'm sorry, Goddess. You are right. But this man—"

Her nails sliced deeper. "I gave you this gift to help bury your past. Do not make me regret my generosity."

"Y-you will not," he said. She loosened her grip. Her fingers brushed along his jaw.

"Do this thing, then we will all feed. The cattle in this town will fall before sunrise." Her eyes glowed with an unholy fire.

There were times when he thought Magdala was quite mad, nothing more than a monster dressed in beautiful flesh. Perhaps she was right; his humanity was still too close. The need for revenge still burned deep within him. The hurts he suffered in life still endured. For now. After he killed Sidewinder, all would be well. The doubts would evaporate, along with the rest of his humanity, and he would sit by Magdala's side as they ruled the west together.

"Ah," Magdala said. He felt it, as well. The sun was gone. New strength flowed into his bones.

So did the hunger.

"Do you think he's here?" His voice dropped an octave. The hunger was growing within her, too.

"I hope so. Regardless, we will feed well." The Silver Paladin didn't feel as cavalier as he sounded. He not only wanted Sidewinder to be here, he needed it to happen. Killing Lariat Smith had been satisfying, of course. He represented everyone who had mocked Dewey throughout his life. But Sidewinder...that was a different story. What Sidewinder had done was betrayal of the highest order. For years, Dewey had run from it, hidden away in his mask and fancy shirts.

Things were different now. Very different.

In the gloom, he smiled.

"We will give you a short time," Magdala said. "Make good use of it. Then, we shall join you."

"It will be glorious."

"Hunt well, my prince."

He put his mask on and made certain his shirt was clean. Once satisfied, he stepped from the carriage. His senses were instantly assaulted by every sound and scent that the evening offered. This was a part of his new existence to which he had not yet grown accustomed.

He heard the slow, steady heartbeats of the drivers and the faint sweet susurration of blood pulsing through their veins. He smelled night blooming flowers and horseshit, tobacco smoke and stale beer. He heard muffled voices from the street and the saloon, where windows were open. Some of the voices laughed, others were raised in anger or frustration.

One voice was calm and soft and confident.

It was him. Sidewinder was in town, presumably at his favorite spot in his favorite saloon.

Good. Let him enjoy his beloved surroundings for the final time.

The Silver Paladin stepped onto the dry, dusty street and he felt a twinge of anxiety. It was out of place in this new life. A remnant of who he had been.

The old Dewey would have been nervous heading into a showdown in Sidewinder's home turf. But not this new man, who was more than a man. He was a prince in an army of unparalleled power. He was powerful and he demanded respect.

He drew in the scent of the small town and the smell of all of those who would die tonight, and he felt the fear blow away like smoke from a camp fire.

He laughed as he walked to the saloon.

•••

"You stay out here and I'll check out the saloon," Sam said.

They left the wagon behind the shuttered and dark livery stable, and walked the length of the town on foot. Night had fallen, and the saloon was full of light and sound.

"I should go with you," O'Malley said.

"They've seen you."

"We should have brought The Dead Sheriff."

"If I need him, I can get him here quick enough." Sam felt a confidence that was both strange and comforting at the same time. Whatever the thing-that-looked-like-Parker had done, Sam felt like he'd had a shot of miracle elixir from one of those carnival shows. If that shit really worked.

O'Malley, on the other hand, looked less than steady on his feet.

"How 'bout you? Will you be all right out here?"

They'd stopped in front of the mercantile store. O'Malley braced one hand against a banister. "I'm fine."

He sweated, despite a nice breeze. His free hand shook a little as he wiped it across his mouth.

"Looking at you, 'fine' wouldn't be the word I'd use," Sam said.

The writer surprised Sam by sitting down on the store's rickety porch. He landed like a sack of potatoes and sat there for a few seconds with his head in his hands.

"It's all a bit much, isn't it?"

Sam shrugged.

"I mean, can't we get a little time between monsters from Hell who eat a town and possessed cowpokes who float in the sky and show us a terrible future? I need time to contemplate these events."

Sam didn't say anything. He just drew in a slow breath and let it out. He tried very hard not to think about the strangeness around him. Focusing on his goal–making enough gold to leave the country–had worked for him. But lately his thoughts had strayed. He was certain the mysterious events of the past few weeks had affected him. Still, there was something else. When O'Malley and the old cowboy had been in danger, Sam felt a responsibility to them. He wasn't sure where that attitude came from. It wasn't something he'd been accustomed to. That was the problem with people and old dogs. You got attached to them.

He spat in the dirt. As soon as he collected just a few more bounties, he would hit the trail. Hell, the writer could have the Dead Sheriff for all Sam cared, though he wasn't sure how that arrangement would work, what with the magic now inside of Sam. He gritted his teeth and winced. The glow of his new power faded. Sometimes, thinking about what that Parker-thing did to him made Sam feel a little dizzy and ill at his stomach. Best to not dwell on it. Take it for what it was and move on.

"I'll go check it out. You keep an eye out for any trouble." He clapped O'Malley on the shoulder. He made his way over to the saloon, his good feeling returning with each step. It was a fine evening for bounty hunting. If he spotted either Belcher, he would get the dead man over here pronto and tear them a new asshole.

It would be fairly simple.

Sam allowed himself a smile.

He didn't see any way this could go wrong.

•••

FROM THE JOURNAL OF RICHARD O'MALLEY

I won't say that was the lowest moment of my western sojourn, especially knowing now what was still to come, yet in that instant, I saw no way forward. I valued my friendship with Sam, even as I suspected that he did not feel the same. My experiences with The Dead Sheriff changed me for the better, or so I believed. I was a stronger man than the naive, peevish reporter who left Boston.

And yet...

While I may have been stronger, I feared my strength–my mental strength–was not up to the task of continuing down this strange path of mystery. Part of me blossomed from exposure to this weird adventure, while another part seemed close to collapse.

Perhaps the time had come for me to step away. I had experienced enough fantastical occurrences for a dozen lifetimes. Did I really need to witness more?

I put that decision aside when I saw the man approach the saloon. He was dressed in expensive clothing, as far as I could tell in the dusk, and he wore a silver mask. He had be one of the vigilante bounty hunters that populated the west like beggars in Boston. But which one?

Two pistols rode low on his hips. My first thought was that he was also gunning for the Belcher brothers. If that was the case, I hoped Sam would be smart enough to stay out of the masked man's way. I was a little concerned, but not frightened.

That changed when he smiled.

The moon was nearly full and it reflected from the masked vigilante's teeth.

Teeth that were as pointed as a wolf's.

The night suddenly seemed very cold.

When a dark shadow passed across the face of the moon, I looked up.

A silhouette resembling nothing less than a winged beast glided through the sky. It was soon joined by another, and then a third.

I recalled Thunderstorm Parker's story of the town of Harmony and the monsters who attacked the residents.

And of a masked man who aided the creatures. He wore a silver mask. The Silver Paladin.

The masked man entered the bar. That's when I stood up and ran.

CHAPTER NINE

It was dark when Labine's coach rolled into the dusty little town. He was already disgusted with the place, though he had yet to exit the carriage. He knew this type of backwater place. The whiskey would be watered down and the whores would be diseased.

On the other hand, his magic was here. Of that, there could be no doubt. Being this close to his power caused a sizzling jolt from his scalp to his balls. *His power.* Well, it was. And it soon would be again, once he drained it from the Indian boy's body.

Moloch growled.

"Patience, my friend," Labine said. "It's not a large place. We'll observe for a bit and see what develops."

A low rumble echoed from his companion's chest. Moloch didn't want to wait.

Labine felt the same way, though he was more cautious. After his power was stolen from him the first time, he'd vowed to never let down his guard again, though it was a vow that was less stridently enforced when he was with one of his favorite whores. That was not going to be an issue in Dooley.

Labine climbed from the carriage and stretched his legs. It felt good to be out of that coach and to breathe air that did not smell like a demon. The driver had wandered off to find feed and water for the horses. Labine knew he would quickly return. The driver had been paid a sizable quantity of gold with a promise of more upon the return to New Orleans.

Another rumble issued from within the carriage. Labine sighed.

"Yes. He's here. Very close by. We will have him tonight."

His demon companion hissed.

"Contain yourself," Labine said. "Our search has been long and filled with unpleasant odors. This is a moment to be savored."

The wheels of the carriage creaked as the demon stepped out. Moloch ambled over to Labine's side of the vehicle.

"Some fresh air would be good for you, old fellow. In fact, a bath would be even–"

Moloch struck Labine with the speed of a viper, one purplish fist striking the magician in the forehead. Labine bounced off the carriage and fell forward on his face in the dusty street.

Moloch sniffed the night air until he found the scent he wanted. Something almost like a smile passed over his grotesque features. He disappeared in the shadows between two of the homes on the main street. In the distance, the town's drinking populace and thirsty visitors continued their evening, not suspecting the night was moments away from transforming into a nightmare.

•••

Sam walked into the saloon, expecting the smells and noise that always clung to such places. He even expected the patrons to stop what they were doing to stare at the Indian who just strolled in. What he didn't expect was the greeting he got from the bar.

"Cheveyo!" The shout came from a man in a black mask, holding up a glass.

Shit. One of *them*.

Sam glanced around. The far corners of the place were dim. The Belchers could be here and he wouldn't know it. Walking to the bar, Sam kept his eyes on the crowd. He got a few angry glances, but nothing serious, and no sign of his prey.

The masked man stood up to greet him. Dressed all in black (including a cape, Sam noted with some amusement), the man clapped Sam on the arm.

"Welcome, Cheveyo," he said. Leaning in closer, the masked man whispered, "Is The Dead Sheriff nearby?"

"Which one are you?"

The masked man straightened. "I am Sidewinder. Allow me to buy you a drink." Sidewinder wore a pistol in a black holster. A sword in a scabbard bounced against his other hip.

"I knew it was you the moment you came in," Sidewinder said. "I've followed your adventures for a while." The masked man signaled the bartender. Sam decided he would make a circuit of the bar, though he was beginning to doubt the Belchers were here. Surely there would be screaming by now or tables flying through the air.

The bartender sat a glass of whiskey in front of Sam, lingering long enough to make certain Sam saw his look of disapproval. Sam lifted the glass, drained it and slammed it down on the bar, giving the barkeep a tight smile. "Thanks," he said to Sidewinder.

"So, are you here on the trail of prey?" Sidewinder took a small sip of his whiskey.

"Maybe."

"Ah. I, too, understand discretion. Are you perhaps seeking a pair of men, one much larger than the other, both in dire need of a bath?"

"You've seen them?"

Sidewinder nodded. He used his glass to gesture in the direction of the staircase on the far side of the saloon. "Beside the stairs. Hidden in the gloom. You may recognize the silhouette of the bigger one."

Sam squinted his eyes. *Damn*. It *was* them.

He took a step away from the bar.

"Do you require any assistance?" Sidewinder had a hand on the hilt of his slender sword.

"Don't think so," Sam said. He touched the amulet through his shirt. It grew warm. Deep within him he could feel the power that had once resided in the book. He could *feel* The Dead Sheriff, slumbering in the wagon. With the slightest push, the corpse would stand and commence his short walk to the bar.

Sam was about to issue that command when the bar's front door was thrown open with such force that it struck the wall, shattering the glass in the window.

Standing in the doorway was a man wearing a silver mask.

These goddamned idiots were everywhere, Sam thought.

"Just what the evening needed," Sidewinder said with a sigh.

"Finish your drink, Sidewinder," the newcomer said in a voice that filled up the saloon. "It will be your last."

•••

FROM THE JOURNAL OF RICHARD O'MALLEY

I was nearly breathless when I reached the livery stable. Instead of resting for a moment, I began to look for something with which to use to break the lock on the stable door. I hoped to find an axe or perhaps a shovel used to muck out the stalls. Unfortunately, all useful implements were apparently safe behind the locked doors.

Left with no other options, I was prepared to stupidly attempt to kick the door down when something saved me the trouble.

I heard a loud pounding noise and the door shook.

In another second, the pounding sounded again, followed almost instantaneously by the bursting open of the stable doors. A long and pointed piece of the door whistled past my face, missing my eye by mere inches.

The Dead Sheriff strode from within the darkened stable. His clothes were clean, free from stains and bullet holes. He wore his guns and his hat. He truly had been reborn, if that was the proper terminology to use for a reanimated corpse. He marched past me.

"Sam?" I said, wondering if my friend's new power including the ability to see through the dead man's eyes.

The Dead Sheriff halted. As he turned his head toward me, I heard the tendons in his neck creak like old fiddle strings.

I looked into those blank eyes, with their pale and slightly yellowed gleam that reminded me of a hard boiled egg that had been left out in the sun. But a dark shadow seemed to float behind those featureless orbs, and I know that some intelligence was at work there. I just could not be certain it was Sam's.

The jaw of the dead man trembled, as the jaw of a living man might if he were about to speak of something painful.

The Dead Sheriff turned away from me and resumed his path to the saloon.

I followed closely behind him.

•••

When the sissy in the silver mask showed up, Arlo shoved away from the table and stood. Billy didn't say anything. He was too busy studying a situation that seemed to have gone tits up.

Now there were two of those fucking masked bounty hunters.

But that wasn't the worst part.

If Billy's instincts were correct, the masked man who tussled with Arlo earlier was standing next to that Injun that worked for The Dead Sheriff.

"What do you say now, Billy?" Arlo was breathing heavily above and behind Billy. "You still gotta have fun afore we start killin'?"

Remembering the bottle in his hand, Billy took a long swallow of whiskey and wiped the back of a hand across his mouth. All of his life he faced bad odds by going right at them. It had worked out for him so far.

"Arlo, we are gonna have fun right now," he said.

Billy stood up from the table. Everybody in the bar was staring at the newcomer in the silver mask.

Everyone expect the Injun. That one looked right at Billy and Arlo.

"Let's kill 'em all," Billy said.

•••

The Silver Paladin smiled and he didn't care if everyone saw his fangs.

Sidewinder carefully placed his glass on the bar and made his way to the doorway. Though the saloon was crowded, no one stood between the two masked men.

"Dewey," Sidewinder said.

"Don't call me that," the Silver Paladin snarled.

Sidewinder sniffed the air. "This must be the evening for the great unwashed to visit our little town. You smell like rotten meat."

The Silver Paladin growled. He could rip Sidewinder's head from his shoulders before the man in black could reach his gun. But that would end the evening far too soon. The confrontation had played out in the Silver Paladin's mind for years. Recent events only made the fantasy richer. Before his change, Dewey probably would have lost this fight. That was no longer a possibility. The only question was how long he would allow Sidewinder to live. It couldn't be too fast. The bastard had to live long enough to appreciate his defeat at the hands of someone Sidewinder considered weak. Less than a man.

The Silver Paladin smiled again.

"My, how you've changed," Sidewinder said.

"You have no idea."

"Can we do this outside? There is no need for any of those people coming to harm."

"Certainly," the Silver Paladin said. "We wouldn't want anything to happen to these fine citizens." He knew Magdala's plan for the town of Dooley. Once his business with Sidewinder was completed, Magdala's forces would feed.

After the Silver Paladin tasted first blood.

He bent in a mock bow and gestured to the open door.

"After you."

•••

The Dead Sheriff was on the way. Sam could feel it. Now he only had to stay alive until the undead avenger arrived.

The Belchers must have recognized Sam, since they were headed toward him. Or maybe they just hated Indians.

Back at the Belcher's camp, Sam had been amazed at Arlo's size. Seeing him this close only increased Sam's amazement. The man was a walking mountain. As he walked, he clenched and unclenched his fists. His eyes were tiny black holes beneath his low brow. They never glanced away from Sam.

Billy, the smaller one, pulled his gun from its holster as he walked. It was a big Colt. Sam had a Colt, too, and even though The Dead Sheriff did most of the shooting for the pair, Sam knew how to hit a target, if it came to that. Billy Belcher was maybe forty feet away. Sam didn't know how good of a shot the man was. The story was he preferred to kill with his teeth.

Sam dove over the bar. He hit the floor shoulder first just before three shots rang out. Two of them struck the long mirror behind the bar. The third hit the bartender in the center of his forehead. Blood and brains rained down on Sam. He didn't stop to examine the body. Crawling quickly, he reached the far end of the bar, drew his gun and stood up. Billy Belcher was running toward the bar, his Colt aimed for the spot where Sam had vanished. Sam aimed for Belcher's stomach and fired.

His shot struck the cannibal killer in the upper thigh of the left leg. Billy yelped and fell to the floor. The bar was filled with his agonized howl, like the baying of a wounded hound. Arlo ran to Billy's side.

"It's just my leg," Billy said through clenched teeth. "Get that fucker. Make him pay."

Arlo stood and bellowed. He rushed the bar.

Sam fired three times. He was certain he'd hit the big man, even though Arlo never slowed. Arlo reached the bar and grabbed Sam by the shirt. Sam was yanked across the bar and toward the huge man. Arlo's body odor filled Sam's senses, making his eyes water and bile rise in his throat. Arlo opened his mouth. The smell that came from there was even worse. Strings of meat dangled from between his teeth. Those teeth seemed as big as the keys on Old Luke's piano back at the whorehouse in New Mexico. Several of Arlo's teeth had broken off, leaving jagged points.

He meant to kill Sam with those teeth.

Sam raised his Colt and shot Arlo in the face. The bullet struck the big man in the jaw, causing Arlo to howl louder. He hefted Sam above his head and ran toward the front of the saloon. With a final howl, he threw Sam through the saloon's large front window.

Sam flew over the wooden sidewalk and into the street, landing with an impact that drove the air from his lungs and caused the world to fade away for a few seconds. When things swam back into focus, his head throbbed and blood ran down his face from what felt like dozens of cuts. His Colt was gone, most likely lost when he hit the glass.

Christ, did that monster really take a bullet to the face (and possibly a couple to the body) and keep fighting?

As if in response to Sam's thoughts, Arlo Belcher rushed out of the bar, roaring and knocking men aside, including the two masked bounty hunters. Torches had been lit in front of the building, and in their light, Sam saw the damage his bullet did to Arlo's face. The slug had plowed a deep furrow across the jaw, exposing bloody meat and the teeth in the back of the big man's mouth. In some way, the gaping wound reminded Sam of The Dead Sheriff on one of his bad days.

Sam spat into the dirt and saw blood in his phlegm.

Probably something busted inside, the way I feel.

Arlo spotted Sam. He smiled. Apparently, pain meant very little to the cannibal. As he lumbered toward Sam, twin streams of blood trickled from wounds in his abdomen.

At least I hit him. That would be a nice thought to carry into the afterlife, he supposed. He was pretty certain he was about to die at the hands (and teeth) of this creature. The Dead Sheriff was on his way, Sam knew, but he wouldn't get here in time.

It was funny that he got this magic stuck inside him so recently, yet it wasn't going to do one goddamned thing to stop him from being killed.

"His Colt was gone..."

All that power, and no idea how to use it.

Or maybe he *could* use it.

Forcing his way to his feet, Sam made eye contact with Arlo. He felt the power stir within him. He knew he carried something strong within him, even if he wasn't sure how to use it.

No time like the present to learn.

He extended his arms, as currents of energy seemed to swirl deep within him.

"Come on, you crazy son of a bitch," Sam said. His words were masked by Arlo's wild screams. The tips of his fingers burned. He was about to find out what this magic could do.

Then he was knocked off his feet again. He flew a good ten feet through the air, landed on his stomach with an impact so forceful that he thought he must have been hit by a train.

He shook his head and tried to focus on the thing that knocked him through the air. Unless Sam's brain had been rattled loose, he hadn't been hit by a train.

It was monster. A large, man-shaped thing with skin the color of a bruise. The odor of sulfur wafted from the demon. It was dressed in an ill-fitting suit. Its feet were bare, revealing four-toed appendages with long, black talons.

As Sam watched, the monster slapped Arlo Belcher. The big man's head rocked back. If the blow dazed the cannibal, the effect only lasted a second. Arlo, half his jaw missing, smiled and bit into the monster's neck.

If Sam survived the night, he prayed that was the last time he would hear a demon scream.

CHAPTER TEN

As he regained consciousness, Labine couldn't believe Moloch had struck him. Not that the monster was incapable of such brutality. It was the fact that they were supposedly on the same side; both serving the same unforgiving master. Climbing to his feet while slapping the dirt off his pants and coat, he was grateful the thing hadn't knocked his head clean off with his blow. Still it had been enough to make Labine hear angels singing in his head.

Then, as if to confirm his thoughts, something big and loud came out of the heavens directly above him and he felt two powerful hands grasped his shoulders; talons tearing into the material. Before he knew it, he was being whisked off his feet straight up into the night air; the sound of massive leathery wings flapping over his head.

"What the hell...?" He struggled mightily as the ground quickly diminished beneath him trying for all he was worth to see what exactly had picked him up like a stuffed rag doll. Once clear of the surrounding buildings, the stars in the velvet sky provided him with just enough illumination to see he was being hauled off by woman! A flying woman?!

And she was not at all unattractive, though why he would even consider her appearance at this point wherein his life hung literally by a thread testified to his confusion of thoughts. At which point the beautiful face looking down at him, opened her mouth to reveal sharp incisors over a blood red tongue eager to dig into his flesh.

A vampire! He was being attacked by a flying vampire woman. One very hungry for his blood unless he could do something about it.

Considering the tenuous nature of his plight, he had no time for intricate spells. His one hope of survival was to employ his dark voice.

"*Stop!*" he commanded, allowing those arcane abilities that resided within him to rise to the surface and become one powerful force that would reverberate through his vocal chords.

When the vampire's head froze from descending any further, he clung to a sliver of hope that the voice had worked. He had never used it on another creature of shadows before; only the defenseless whores he enjoyed manipulating to fulfill his twisted desires.

"*Do not let me fall!*"

The she-vampire looked at him in confusion. It was clear she had never been thwarted in such a manner, her will overridden by another. He could sense the struggle in her to break free and he had no time to waste.

"*Put me back down....slowly. I command you!*"

The vampire obeyed and turning her body began to swoop back down towards the ground.

•••

Arlo Belcher, his lower jaw ruined, felt his mouth on fire and spit out the chunk of demon flesh he'd torn from the hideous beast fighting him. Renewed anger welled up inside him as his feeble brain attempted to understand what it was he was fighting. He slammed a fist into the ugly, hideous face before him.

For his part, Moloch had never been hurt by a mere mortal and his three beady black eyes grew wide in shock as the big, powerful human hit him again. For the first time in his existence he felt pain; first from the bite that had ripped off part of his neck where it met his shoulder and now the repeated blows to the face. After the third such, Moloch shook his head, pulled the hood off his horned head and roared.

The monster's foul sulfurous breath enveloped Arlo's face and breathing it in, he began to gag trying to catch his breath. Moloch's clawed hands reached out and grabbed the dazed Arlo by the neck and crotch and with a mighty heave, picked him up off the ground. Arlo felt the world tilt around him unable to understand what was happening to him. Then Moloch raised him high over his head and with a second loud shout threw Arlo to the ground head first.

The top of Arlo's head struck hard and his neck snapped killing him instantly.

Not yet satisfied, Moloch reached down, dug his claws into Arlo's neck and with a vicious ripping tug, tore the big cannibal's neck from his lifeless body. Moloch then tossed it against the saloon wall where it was crushed and then dropped to the wooden walkway with a wet thud.

"NOOO!!!!" Billy Belcher came hobbling down the street, one hand clutching his bleeding thigh while his right held out his gun pointed at monster that had just killed his brother.

He fired off three quick shots, all of them hitting the beast squarely.

But it did not fall.

•••

Sam witnessed the end of Arlo Belcher as he stood across the street attempting to regain his equilibrium. All around him he heard people screaming and winged shapes swooped across the sky above him. He looked up dazed to see garishly painted women with leathery wings carrying off men and women who had foolishly ventured outdoors upon hearing the initial gunfire from the various participants. Now these flying things were laughing at the same time their captives were screaming at the top of their lungs.

Several of the winged devils managed to silence their prey by biting into their necks. So ferociously were their fangs wreaking destruction that blood seemed to burst out of the ruined flesh and rained from the heavens. Others, grappling with stronger male victims merely dropped them from tremendous heights and Sam watched in horror as body after body impacted with Harmony's main street. None survived the fall.

Whatever horror was overwhelming the sleepy little town of Dooley was relentless and Sam recalled Thunderstorm Parker's tale having witnessed a similar holocaust in Harmony.

Was there no way to stop any of it?

It was one thing for he and the Dead Sheriff to hunt down evildoers, the flying she demons and the monster that had destroyed Arlo Belcher weren't your typical owlhoots. Now he watched as a wounded Billy Belcher awkwardly marched to his own doom, emptying his six-shooter into the unmoving beast that towered above him. The fool was so maddened by the death of his stupid brother, he was throwing his own life away as well.

•••

Sidewinder stood with the Silver Paladin, smacking dirt off his pants as chaos blossomed all around them.

"Madre Dios," he cursed. "What in the name of the Holy Ghost is going on here?"

Dewey Morton grinned, his blanched white teeth seeming to sparkle. "Oh, it's the beginning of Armageddon, old friend." He opened his mouth wider to reveal his pointed incisors. "And you are going to be one of its first victims."

Seeing those teeth, Sidewinder took several steps back as the Silver Paladin lunged for him. But he was too slow and the undead gunslinger grabbed his shirt and drew him close. Trying desperately to push him away, Sidewinder couldn't believe how strong the man was. The Silver Paladin was known for his quick draw with a gun, not feats of inhuman strength. And yet here he was bringing his animal like fangs closer; a hideous glow in his black eyes.

There was a gunshot and half of the Silver Paladin's scalp was torn off his head.

Hurt, he released his prey and stumbled backward, hands reaching for his damaged scalp.

Both the Silver Paladin and Sidewinder turned to see the Dead Sheriff walking up to them, both hands filled with his Colt Peacemakers.

The Dead Sheriff pumped two more rounds into the Silver Paladin knocking him off his feet. He hit the dirt on his backside and screamed. Amazingly, he jumped back to his feet and in a feral like crouch faced his enemy. His fingers were extended and their nails seemed to grow into sharp, razor claws.

"Ah, the Dead Sheriff," he laughed, blood and gore sliding down the side of his face. "Now we're really going to have some fun."

In turning his attention to the undead lawman, the Silver Paladin ignored Sidewinder and that would be his last mistake in this world. As the masked vampire prepared himself to lunge at the Dead Sheriff, he heard a swooshing sound and then cold steel sliced through his neck. His decapitated head fell over and rolled a few feet before coming to a stop. Blood red eyes seemed to glare upward at the sight of the sword wielding Sidewinder, now whipping his blade about in a triumphant gesture. Meanwhile the Silver Paladin's headless body managed to take one step before toppling over.

"Adios, compadre," Sidewinder laughed before kicking the Silver Paladin's head. "Give my regards to El Diablo."

•••

Magdala stood by her gaudy wagons pacing back and forth, arms wrapped around herself trying to ward an overpowering sense of danger. But what kind of danger. Her drivers had parked the three huge carriages at the end of an alley away from the town's main boulevard to better conceal them. Thus, she was able to send out her girls without fear of any kind of immediate retaliation. By the time anyone of authority realized what was happening, most of Dooley's citizens would have been slaughtered and her vampire brood satiated once again.

Her one annoying concern was Dewitt Morton; the Silver Paladin. His obsession with personally killing all the other vigilantes in the west had become a hindrance to her well orchestrated campaigns. Before taking him on as an ally, and lover, Magdala's troop would enter a town, attack and destroy and then move on in a matter of a few short hours. But since the Silver Paladin and Bullet had joined her army of female bloodsuckers, he was forever off on his own private mission; one that always seemed to delay their operations. It wasn't that she was afraid such delays could jeopardize them; that was inconceivable. She simply preferred precision. Get in, destroy and get out.

Yet now something was bothering the Vampire Madam as she kept taking furtive glances at the street beyond the alley. She could make out fleeing townspeople and every now and then one of her wicked whores flying after them. The screams emanating from all around should have soothed her as they had done in the past. But now something was awry. Something she just couldn't quite put her finger on it. Something was not as it should be.

"Excuse me, but are you the Madam of this...aw rolling house of pleasure?"

Magdala spun around startled as a broad shouldered man in an expensive suit appeared from behind a building corner. Her men, mindless slaves she had corrupted long ago, converged on the stranger, their hands brandishing clubs and knives.

"Oh, please," the intruder indicated the thugs with a gesture of his hands. "Surely you aren't afraid of one unarmed man?"

The three deaf mutes held their position eyeing the stranger warily while awaiting further instructions from their mistress.

"Hold," Magdala conveyed with hand gestures and her men stopped their threatening approach. Now the stranger was near enough that the lanterns affixed to the roof of the tall wagon showed him to be a serious, almost handsome fellow with long, red hair. The cut of his clothing suggested the south to her. Perhaps New Orleans.

"Who are you?"

He bowed at the waist with a flourish. "My name is Labine, Madam and I believe I may be of some assistance to you."

•••

Billy Belcher realized too late he was out of bullets and the demon before showed little if any affect of those shots. The holes in his tunic oozed a greenish fluid and for the first time Billy began to understand his foe was not human. But by then they were only inches apart and Moloch was really angry with the skinny pocked-face shooter.

Sam, still across the street witnessing the encounter, fully expected to see the end of the skinny cannibal. As crazy as everything was, Sam couldn't muster an ounce of pity for Belcher. The bastard was about to get what was due him; albeit in a truly strange and bizarre fashion.

The three-eyed demon reached down and grabbed Billy's gun hand. He wrapped his huge mitt around both flesh and metal and yanked the young man off his feet. Holding him up over his own head, Moloch growled and began to squeeze. Both bones and steel crunched together and Billy Belcher's bladder let go and he screamed like a wounded alley cat. Blood squished through the demon's fist dripping down onto the dusty ground.

Suddenly there was a rumble and Sam heard horses huffing loudly. A whip cracked and he turned to see a stagecoach racing up the street. High atop the driver's box was a brown woman in buckskins spurring on the six mighty steeds with a long snaking bullwhip.

"Eyah," she cried giving the air over the horses head another loud whip crack. "Don't you nags stop now! Eyahh!"

The horses thundered past Sam and he looked up at the determined driver in bewilderment. She was turning them towards the massive demon still unaware of them. At the last possible moment, the woman dropped the bullwhip, grabbed the brake handle and at the same time pulled back on the leather reins to stop her charging team.

"WHOA!!!" she commanded, almost coming to her feet as the bridles jerked the six horses' heads and they shuddered to an earth shaking halt right next to Moloch and his bleeding victim, Billy Belcher.

Moloch snorted at the presence of the animals and turned his head to look up at the dust covered coach woman. Now she held a sawed-off double-barreled shotgun in her hands. Both barrels were pointed down at the demon like the eyes of a death itself.

"Damn, but you are one butt-ugly bastard," she proclaimed and fired both triggers. The resulting blast knocked her back on her ass, while hundreds of lead pellets obliterated Moloch's head in the blink of an eye. The headless demon collapsed with the unconscious Billy Belcher beneath it.

"Hot doggies," the woman chuckled, resting the smoking shotgun across her lap. Sam ran across the street and looked down at the unmoving demon. He shook his head. Even with dozens of past adventures with the Dead Sheriff, he'd never seen anything like this before.

"I'm guessin' you might be the one they call Cheveyo," the driver said. Sam looked up at a lean, serious face the color of deer leather centered by two piercing gray eyes. Her nose was long and thin and her lips full and pink. For the first time he saw she was wearing an old beat up Union solider's cap over coal black hair cut severely short.

"Yes...ah...I am."

"Please to meetcha," the woman nodded touching the bill of her cap. "They call me Hattie Fields."

"Hello," was all Sam could think to say.

"I don't wanna rush you or anything," Hattie Fields continued. "But I think it would be smart if you were to rustle up your friends so's we can get the hell out of here before anything else goes sour."

Friends? Of course, the Dead Sheriff and O'Malley. In all the confusion, Sam had forgotten about them. The last thing he remembered was sending the journalist to the stables to get the undead lawman.

"Right," he finally replied, holding up a finger to Hattie Fields. "Wait right there, I'll find them and be right back."

"Don't take too long, Injun," she explained as he started to dash off. "There's a lot more evil creatures flying around tonight and I can't shoot all of 'em." She reached into the leather boot under her feet and from them removed a box of shotgun shells. On the box was painted with a red cross. She tore it open and began reloading her weapon. Her six horses, uncomfortable just standing still, could sense the monsters.

"Now you boys just take it easy, you know I ain't gonna let no harm come to yah. Not while I have my trusty shotgun and these here holy bullets."

●●●

The Dead Sheriff had stopped moving, much to Richard O'Malley's satisfaction. Now he, the zombie gunfighter and the black caped Sidewinder stood around the Silver Paladin's headless corpse while the level of screams continued to rise from the nearby streets. Every now and then it was intermingled with sporadic gunfire.

"I think I owe you my life," Sidewinder gratefully acknowledged as he wiped the blood off his blade with his cape. "I think something turned my old compadre here into one of the undead."

"I never saw anything like it," O'Malley agreed. "How he took all those shots and then jumped again like they didn't bother him a lick."

"I think he was a vampire, heh, senor?"

"I suppose. You may be right."

"You did not see his teeth, my friend." The Sidewinder wiped his brow with a dry piece of his cape. "He looked like a big wolf with those fangs. And he was so damn strong."

"Well, your sword did the trick."

"Si, thanks to you and The Dead Sheriff here." At that Sidewinder tugged on his chin. "Say, why is the Sheriff with you and not my old amigo, Cheveyo?"

As if on cue, Sam appeared out of breath from running. "There you are," he gasped. "Are you all right?"

"I'm fine," O'Malley answered then nodded to Sidewinder. "The Dead

Sheriff and this gentlemen here just vanquished a vampire."

"A vampire?" Then Sam noticed the body at his feet. It was headless just like the demon he had left at the other end of the street. Damn, too many were things were losing their heads on this night of madness. He hoped he wouldn't be one of them before it was over.

"Look, O'Malley, we got to get out of here and fast."

"What about the cannibals...those Belcher boys?"

"No need to worry about them anymore."

"Huh?"

"I'll explain later. Let's just say they ran into something even more terrible then their twisted habits. But for right now, we've got to get out of here."

"Fine." Things were moving too fast for O'Malley. Maybe exiting the battle and finding someplace to regroup wasn't such a bad idea. "But what about the town?"

Sam looked around at the bodies strewn all over and then grabbed Sidewinder's arm. "Is there a sheriff in this town?"

"Yes, Manuel Savila. He's a good man."

"Find him and tell him to get all the people off the streets. To stay in their homes, with the doors and windows barricaded."

"For how long?"

It was a question Sam wasn't sure he could answer. O'Malley stepped in. "Till sunrise," he suggested. "I doubt these creatures can stand the light of day."

"Hmm, I think you are right, my friend." Sidewinder shook hands with both men and then left them to find the sheriff and carry out his mission.

Sam stepped over to the Dead Sheriff and gave him a cursory look. He appeared to be in good shape, for a dead man.

"Come," he told the Dead Sheriff and started back down the street with O'Malley walking beside him.

"Where we going? Our wagons back there on the other side of the stables."

"I know," Sam picked up his pace. "I found someone to give us a ride."

•••

"How can you help me?" Magdala asked Labine. She could sense he possessed some arcane power and she was wary of it.

"Surely you can see I am more than what I appear to be," he smiled.

She was reminded of a fox; always a trickster. Showing the world only enough to achieve its ends. But then again she was no harmless chicken either.

"Again, Mr. Labine, how can you possibly be of assistance to me?"

Labine laughed. "Please, you must realize there are forces at play here even beyond your considerable control." He pointed to the end of the alley. "You can feel it, Madam. Those things we both fear are present out there somewhere. Perhaps seeking us out at this very minute."

"That's ridiculous. I am Magdala, Daughter of Satan and Queen of the Night. I fear nothing."

"Really?" Still Labine's attitude was one of irreverence. Power or not, she would teach him to respect her.

Just then a voice called out her name.

"Magdala!" Young James Bennett came running into the alley clutching something to his chest. "We've got trouble!"

She put her hands on her hips to address him. "What kind of trouble?"

The lad opened his arms and held up the head of the Silver Paladin. "This kind."

"Who did this?" she demanded, anger rising up inside her.

"I'm not sure. He was going to kill Sidewinder in the middle of the street then The Dead Sheriff showed up out of nowhere."

"The Dead Sheriff?" Magdala was becoming more confused with each passing second. She looked from Bennett to Labine and tried to clear her thoughts. The foreboding she had felt earlier was all coming to fruition.

Nervously the boy once known as Bullet fidgeted before her still holding the head of his former partner.

With a snarl, Magdala slapped it out of his hands and it disappeared under the closet wagon. She directed her attention to her minions and with several quick hand signals set them to getting the wagons ready to roll.

"Very well," she said to Labine directly. "It seems your warning was justified. We have to leave this flea-bitten pest hole until I can understand fully who are enemies are and how to deal with them."

Labine nodded satisfied. "A wise decision, Madam. And let me repeat, I am fully at your service should you so desire."

"We'll see about that," she acquiesced. "For now, let's just go."

"What about your...er...girls?"

"I've already summoned them. They'll join us soon enough."

With that Magdala indicated the biggest wagon and Labine assisted her in climbing into it. He followed after her while James Bennett went to sit with the driver in the first wagon.

The silent driver snapped the reins and their horses started off back towards the center of Dooley.

•••

Richard O'Malley had all he could do to keep up with Sam and the Dead Sheriff. For a dead man, the Sheriff could move rather swiftly. What little light came from the retail shops had long been extinguished at the end of the day; all except the glare from the solitary saloon. Its yellow sheen spilled out on a narrow patch of the main street. There were half a dozen bodies sprawled over it, cast in its glow. Had it not been for the moon and stars, it would have been impossible to keep moving down the lane.

"There," Sam finally pointed ahead. "That stagecoach."

O'Malley looked beyond his companion and could barely see the outline of a typical Concord coach connected to six fidgety horses; all of them colored gray in the darkness.

There was a loud blast from the driver's seat and fire belched from one of shotgun barrels. He blinked, trying to clear his vision and heard an animal like yowl as a winged figure dropped to the ground next to the horses. Another flew down at the coachman only to meet the same fate as the other nightmare flier.

"Hurry," a decidedly female voice urged them on and O'Malley realized the coachman was in actuality a woman. "Get in!" she cried indicating the carriage interior.

Sam didn't have to be told twice as he reached out, grabbed the door and pulled it open. "Get in the coach," he told The Dead Sheriff who, as always obeyed immediately.

O'Malley moved forward only to hit something with his right foot and trip. On the ground, he found himself beside the body of a veritable giant....missing it's head. Around the open wound was a small pool of inky black blood and gore.

"Ahh!" he gasped, pushing himself back on his feet. "What the hell is that thing?" he asked Sam pointing down at the lifeless corpse.

"You don't want to know," Sam replied. "Come on, get in the damn coach."

O'Malley obeyed and hoisted himself into the coach dropping back quickly in the seat opposite the Dead Sheriff who simply sat upright, his lifeless eyes looking into nothing.

"GO!" Sam shouted and closed the door behind him as he jumped in and took his place next to his undead ally.

Hattie Fields cracked her whip once more and bellowed, "All right, you mule-headed critters, time to earn your oats!" The horses all neighed and bolted forward pulling the heavy wheeled Concord behind them. Soon they were racing out of Dooley and heading for the surrounding foothills.

•••

Billy Belcher groaned in pain. Pain unlike anything he had ever felt before. Not only was he shot in the thigh, but his right hand was mangled and now causing him grief. He tried to move only to discover he couldn't. Something big and heavy was atop him and at first he had no idea what it could be.

He lay in the darkness cradling his hurting right hand and tried to understand where the hell he was and what had happened to him. He began to recall the fight in the saloon, that greasy Injun shooting him and Arlo both before running outdoors.

Arlo! His beloved brother had finally met something bigger and meaner than he was. Something not of this earth for sure. Billy could see it in his mind. How it had picked up poor old Arlo and dropped him on his head. Then it had done the same to him when he tried to shoot down whatever it was. His last conscious memory was being held up in the air, the monster crushing his hand as if he were a child. Then he'd heard the sound of horses, a whip snapping…and then nothing. He'd passed out.

Now he was fully awake and trapped under something. Was it a body? It was too dark to see properly, but it stank to high heaven. Enough so Billy thought he might puke. Then he heard horses approaching and wagon wheels moving by him. They stopped and he spotted a glimmer of light around the massive torso that smothered him.

"What is that….thing?" It was a woman's voice asking the question.

"That, Madam Magdala is what remains of the demon Moloch, my, how would you say it, ah…traveling companion."

Billy tried to shove the thing off him but with one hand alone it wouldn't budge.

"Mistress, there's something under it?" This was another woman.

"Help...me," Billy croaked weakly.

Then the demon's carcass was being pulled off him and a bright light blinded him as someone stood over him with a lantern.

"What is it, Alicia?"

"It's a man, Mistress. He appears hurt and is bleeding in several places."

"Please," Billy held his good hand over his eyes to shield them from the hurting glare. "You gotta help me." He begged.

There was a moment of silence and then the lantern moved away so that he could see he was looking up at one of those long colorful wagons he and Arlo had spotted earlier. A woman, her features hidden in the darkness, sat atop the driver's box looking down at him. He wished he could see her face.

"There's not much meat on him," the woman in charge said much to Billy's surprise. "Still, with this hasty departure and all, you girls will need to feed again before the night is over."

Feed? The word shook Billy Belcher. He was all too familiar with what that actually meant.

"No," he gasped.

"Very, well, Alicia. Throw him in the back of the last wagon and be sure to share him with your sisters."

"Yes, Mistress. Of course."

Then Billy saw the woman standing over him. She had long blond hair and a ripe, full body clothed in a skimpy outfit that did little to hide her charms. As she reached down to pick him up, her tongue darted out to lick her lips and he saw her sharp edged fangs.

"Yummy," she cooed anticipating her next meal.

Billy Belcher tried to scream, but he was just too hurt and tired.

CHAPTER ELEVEN

FROM THE JOURNAL OF RICHARD O'MALLEY

I honestly don't know how long or how far we rode in Hattie Fields' stagecoach that night. Frankly, I was just happy to be out of Dooley as fast as possible. Even despite the ups and downs we endured as the coach seemed to find every dip and bump awaiting us on the road. The leather straps on which the wagon frame rested were being sorely tested. Sam for the most part simply maintained his seat next to The Dead Sheriff and remained as quiet as his charge. Me, I cursed. Often.

Here I'd thought the awful events in Damnation had been the epitome of horror only to have been proven wrong once again by what had transpired in Dooley. It seemed the West was determined to show me every sick, twisted evil the universe could conjure up and lay them all before me. The idea of returning back to staid, boring Boston was starting to have added appeal.

"Do you have any idea at all what happened back there?" I finally managed to inquire.

Sam lifted his head slightly as if my question had interrupted his silent reverie.

"The Belchers are dead," he replied softly.

"What?" At first I wasn't sure I'd heard him correctly. "How? Did you see it?"

"Yes, I did. They were both killed by a giant demon with three eyes. The thing you ran past before climbing into the coach."

Now it was my turn to look foolish. I'd just encountered a masked vampire, assisted in aiding another fellow defeat it and then seen what appeared to be flying women attacking this coach. Considering our journey thus far, I shouldn't have been one bit surprised.

"There's something else," Sam added before I could say anything else.

"What?"

"I believe that demon was here looking for me. To retrieve the amulet and the magic book."

"How can you possibly know that?"

"I stole those things from a gambler named Labine. At first I thought he'd gone back East and that was the end of it. But recently, I've begun to think that he's come back and is hunting me and The Dead Sheriff."

"That seems a bit far-fetched," I suggested. "I mean, did you actually see him back there?"

"It was hard to tell," he admitted, scratching the back of his head. "That demon monster knocked me across the street and when I started to get back on my feet I thought I saw one of those flying whores go by holding someone who looked a whole lot like him."

"But you aren't sure."

"Look, O'Malley, whatever Labine was doing with those things in the first place is something I've never thought much about until recently."

"What do you mean, Sam?"

"Well, what was he doing out here on the frontier with that amulet and book in the first place? Is he some kind of missionary preacher for the Devil or something?"

It seemed like we were going round in circles with this discussion and getting nowhere. I'd questioned Sam about the magical artifacts before and his answers had always been vague. Now that he was willing to divulge their origins, all it was doing was adding even more questions to the matter.

"Let's put that aside for later," I went on trying to keep our conversation on track. "What happened after you saw this fellow, whoever he was, get whisked off?"

"Well, I got to my feet and watched the demon tear the big Belcher apart with his bare hands. A few minutes later, the skinny one, I think his name was Billy, showed up and the demon finished him off too.

"Ain't never seen anything so savage as that thing. Them Belcher brothers never had a chance. Not that they deserved any. Seems like they both got what was coming to'em."

"Agreed. So what happened next?"

Sam pointed to the ceiling of the rolling stagecoach. "She showed up out of nowhere and just rode right up to the demon and blew its head clean off with that sawed-off shotgun of hers. Now that was something to see, O'Malley. Whoever she is, she's got more grit then most men I've met."

It was the longest conversation we had ever had up to that point and I had the feeling that Sam felt some kind of relief after having unburdened himself of all he had been keeping bottled up inside. I only hoped his sharing it with me would prove beneficial to us both. Naturally I wanted to help him and if that meant dealing with this Labine character, so be it. Though if Labine consorted with actual hell spawn demons, then we were clearly in grave danger.

The stagecoach suddenly seemed to be going downhill and then I heard splashing. I leaned my head out one of the open slots trying to glimpse ahead and saw Miss Fields was driving us through a wide creek. That the wheels weren't slowed moving through it told me it was shallow and soon we were climbing up the opposite bank and onto an open prairie.

In the sky above I could barely make out the stars hidden beneath the moving clouds. There was a distinct chill in the air that normally settles in during the long twilight hours between midnight and dawn.

"Whoa, now fellas!" Hattie Fields cried out and I felt the coach begin to slow down. Minutes later it came to a full stop. "That's it," she said amiably. "Good job. Now rest up."

With that we heard her moving around on the driver's box and then it rocked slightly from her leaping to the ground. "You gents can come on out now."

Sam wasted no time getting the door open and dropping down. I followed behind him, my back aching from the ordeal it had endured the past few hours.

Though it was still dark, by then our eyes had adjusted to the gloom and I could see we had come to rest a few yards before what appeared to be a dilapidated sod-built homestead. Next to it was an empty corral and between them and a stone well that had seen better days.

"It ain't much, but I call it home," Hattie Fields told us pointing her shotgun towards the abandoned building. "Why don't you go on in and get some rest. There's fresh kindling by the fireplace and you can get a fire going if you like."

"Thank you, Madam." I stepped past Sam and extended my hand. "I am Richard O'Malley, formerly of Boston, Massachusetts."

"Howdy do, Mr. O' Malley, like I told Cheveyo here, I'm Hattie Fields. And now if you'll excuse me, I got to see to my team." She indicated the horses, all of them breathing heavily from their long run. "They need food and water and scrubbing down."

"Perhaps, I can help," Sam volunteered.

"Why that's mighty kind of you. I can always use another hand. But what about your friend up there in the coach? Don't yah need to watch over him or something?"

Sam looked back at The Dead Sheriff and then at me. He leaned into the coach and said, "Go with O'Malley and do what he says."

At that The Dead Sheriff stiffly exited the coach and stood beside me, his grim face free of any expression. He merely awaited my command.

There were a few things I wanted to ask Hattie Fields and she seemed to read my mind. She seemed to smile. "They'll plenty of time to jabber come sunup, Mr. O'Malley. Right now I think we could all use a good night's sleep."

She then walked over to the animals and began to unhitch them from their traces, those straps by which each pulled the wagon. Sam joined her by going around the team and starting on the other side.

With nothing left to discuss, I turned to my undead companion. "Come along, my friend. Let's go see about getting a nice fire going."

"She...began to unhitch them..."

The Dead Sheriff followed me as I set about my task. The sooner it was done, the sooner I could close my eyes and get some sleep.

•••

Madam Magdala's traveling bordello caravan traveled ten miles into the hills north of Dooley and came to a stop in a heavily wooded forest. Here the Vampire Madam assembled her girls, what was left of them, to hear their reports. Three of the girls had not returned and she had to assume they had somehow been vanquished. Thus having the remaining five relate their accounts would hopefully give her some clue as to exactly what had happened to the lost ones. She was always aware that there were those who hunted her kind; some extremely skilled. She did her best to avoid them.

Thus she had her drivers build a small campfire for themselves and the one called Labine while she and the other female bloodsuckers gathered at the back of the wagons to discuss what had transpired in the little town they had just departed. Bullet joined them.

As Alicia was her senior girl, having been with her for over ten years, she let her begin first asking if she'd seen anything out of the ordinary.

"I didn't see it as much as get hit with it, Mistress," the brunette Alicia shrugged. She pointed to the small campfire in the distance. "That gent, one you let come along, has got some kind of power."

"Explain…exactly what you mean?"

"I saw him on the street and snatched him up just like I've done hundreds of others. Started getting ready to bite him when he looks up at me and tells me to put him down and I just do it. It was like his command got inside my head and I had no choice but to obey it." Alicia wrapped her arms around herself and shivered. "Ain't ever had no one do that to me before. It was like his voice was different, like it belonged to someone else."

"And you couldn't resist what it was telling you to do?" Magdala suspected what the source of Labine's magic was but she wasn't about to share that with her girls. They were spooked enough as is. In all their past attacks on settlements they had never been successfully repulsed before.

"Right!" Alicia pointed a finger at her. "That's exactly like it felt, Mistress."

"What happened after you put him down?"

"Nothing, he just walked off and after a few seconds, I got my head clear and went back to hunting. When you called us back and I saw he was riding with us, I was pretty damn surprised for sure."

Magdala tapped her booted foot on the ground nervously and nodded. She cast an eye towards the fire where Labine sat hunched near the flames drinking coffee with her three mute drivers. Somewhere high in the trees above them an owl hooted.

"All right," she finally continued. "Did anyone else see anything? Anything at all?"

"I did, Mags," the blond-haired Susie raised her hand as if she was back in school. "I saw who it was killed Jessie and Ramona. Blew them right out of the air."

"Who was it?" Magdala shouted. "Tell me what you saw?"

Enjoying being the center of attention, Susie looked at her beastly sisters and using her hands to demonstrate, mimed what she had witnessed. "This here darky came charging down the street at the other end of town on a stagecoach. She just raced right up the middle of the street holding the reins in one hand and a big ole shotgun in the d'other."

"She?" Magdala interrupted. "This darky was a woman?"

"Yes, Ma'am. Heard her yell out once or twice and you know how good we can see in the dark. She was dressed like a man, but she weren't no man. I swear to it."

An involuntary chill crawled up Magdala's spine. "Go on, what did you see?"

"Only that when she showed up, both Jessie and Romona decided to come down on her together at the same time. But before they could even get close, that damn darky whips up her shotgun and gives them both a blast up close. Shot them right out of the sky. I saw them hit the ground and knew they weren't getting up again."

Things were worse than she had originally thought. Magdala's mind was whirling with what she should do next. They were clearly in jeopardy and there was no time to waste if they were to escape who it was that was chasing them.

"All right, you girls go on back to the wagons. We're going to start traveling again at first light."

"What about the skinny dude?" Susie asked, licking her lips. "He's still moaning and a groanin'."

"Finish him…but share equally. When you've finished with him, throw him away. We don't need his carcass stinking up a wagon."

As the girls squealed with delight and started to walk away, Magdala signaled Bullet to remain. Alicia did as well.

"James, go fetch Mr. Labine for me. Then help the girls with their meal."

Young James Bennett grinned. "Yes, Ma'am."

As he walked off to get the Labine, Magdala turned her attention to Alicia who looked worried.

"It's her, isn't it? The black girl Susie saw back there."

Magdala nodded, biting her lower lip. Alicia had been with her in those early years back along the Texas panhandle. "Yes, I believe it's her."

"She won't stop, will she?"

"No, Alicia. Not until she's destroyed every last one of us."

"Then what do we do?"

"We end it…once and for all. Hattie Fields has been a thorn in my side long enough. It's time we have us an old fashion show down to see which of us wins and which of us loses. Apparently, the frontier isn't big enough after all."

Alicia agreed with her mistress but still had questions on how exactly they would achieve that particular goal. It was clear she was still anxious.

"Now don't you fret," Magdala consoled her by reaching out and caressing Alicia's cheek. "I've got a plan that will see to Miss Fields once and for all. Now go join the others. I have to talk with our guest."

Labine was approaching. Alicia took hold of Magdala's hand, gave it a gentle squeeze and then turned and walked away. Magdala wondered if she had allayed her aide's concerns. She would need Alicia's strength and savagery in the coming confrontation. Something she could always count on as long as the raven-haired vampire kept her wits about her. Still, there was no use in worrying about the future. In her hundred years of existence she'd learned it always took care of itself; one way or another.

"I don't know what other skills your teamsters may have," Labine commented as he neared her, "but making good coffee is certainly not one of them." He tipped the tin cup over and poured what remained.

"Perhaps a bit of chicory mixed in would be more to your liking," Magdala suggested whimsically.

Labine studied her expression. Even in the dark, her black eyes seemed to radiate an intense glimmer. "Yes, Madam, it certainly would. I take it you are familiar with that grand old city on the Mississippi?"

"I've enjoyed the pleasures of New Orleans many times, Mr. Labine. Enough to recognize its obvious affect on your manners and clothing."

"Very astute, Madam," he bowed at the waist. "The young man said you wished to speak with me. How may I be of assistance?"

"Assistance, yes, that is the word. Back in Dooley you said you could help me, Mr. Labine. Is that pledge still offered?"

"By all means, dear lady….as long as whatever you request does not interfere with my own mission."

"Which is what?"

"A few years ago, while on another journey through this God forsaken land, an Indian lad stole precious things from me." Labine paused. "Well, actually they belonged to my Master, and he wishes them returned."

"Is that why you, and this demon Moloch, were in Dooley?'

"Yes. You see, through my Master's considerable powers, I am able to sense the boy's presence. Wherever in this world he may be."

"Interesting. And this power led you to Dooley. He was actually back there?"

"Yes, he and his notorious puppet. Even without my Master's gift, they generally make news wherever they travel."

"Puppet?"

"The Dead Sheriff. Have you heard of him? Apparently he is a bounty hunting zombie who wears a badge."

"I have. How is he connected to this Indian you seek?"

"It is a complicated issue, Madam. Even I'm not quite sure what the connection is. Only that it has to do with the stolen items and they must be retrieved at all cost."

"I see. Very well, Labine, we may be of use to each after all. In the morning, I am going to direct my drivers to take us to a location in the hills to the north which I, and my ladies, use as our secret lair.

"As we must remain in the wagons, asleep and out of the sun, during the day, I would ask you to take charge of our little caravan. See to it that we are not stopped or hindered in our journey and if attacked along the way, use whatever powers you possess to defend us. Can you do that for me, Labine?"

"Of course." He didn't hesitate at all. "Do you feel there is any chance of such an attack occurring?"

"There is someone pursuing us," Magdala confessed. "It is vital we reach our hidden sanctuary as soon as possible. If attacked on in the open country, we would be extremely vulnerable."

"How long is this trip?"

"Three days. Barring any complications, we should reach our destination on the third night."

"All right. You can depend on me, Madam. I will guard your personage with my own life, if need be."

Madam Magdala smiled wickedly. The more she spoke with the man, the more she found herself enjoying his silly Southern Charm. "I would expect no less from a Southern gentleman, sir."

Labine realized making an ally of the vampire queen was his only option at the moment. Perhaps if he helped her with her problem, she would later return the favor. Of course it didn't hurt that she was so damn beautiful. He felt an old familiar stirring.

Magdala could see the burgeoning lust in his face. Slowly she began to unbutton her dress.

Labine's eyes widened as the sight of her alabaster white skin. Then the garment seemed to drop to the cold ground at her feet and the Vampire Queen stood naked before him.

"Do you like what you see?" she asked raising her arms to him.

Labine stepped into her embrace, lowered his head and their lips met. Fiercely they kissed and she forced his mouth open so her tongue could dart into his. He felt the sharp tip of her fangs and it only severed to fuel his passion even greater.

They fell to the hard earth as she ripped his clothes from his body. Thus began a night like none other he had ever experienced.

CHAPTER TWELVE

Manuel Savila, the sheriff of Dooley, looked at the creature in one of the two jail cells and tugged at his graying beard. It was for all intents and purposes a woman with giant, bat-like wings growing out of her back. She was lying on her side, on the hard floor, the wings wrapped around her comatose body.

She'd been breathing when they threw her in the cell. Now he wasn't so sure anymore.

"What in tarnation is thing?" he asked Sidewinder. The caped vigilante, exhausted from the long night they had struggled through, shook his head.

"Don't rightly know for sure, Manny. But that city slicker with The Dead Sheriff said they were vampires. Or least that's what the Silver Paladin had turned into before I cut off its head."

Savila looked at his friend as if he were crazy.

"Hey, don't look at me like that," Sidewinder held up his hands. "You saw what was left out there after it was all over."

"Don't remind me," Savila sighed. "We got us ten dead locals, never mind those other dead…things…and the burned remains of what looks like a three-eyed giant. Fuckin' mayor is going nuts. Gonna call a special town meeting later this morning and says I gotta explain everything.

"Like I have a fuckin' clue."

The female vampire on the floor in the jail cell began to stir. Both men reacted by taking a step back.

"She's waking up," Sidewinder stated the obvious.

"I can see that," Savila snapped. Then both were silent as the creature, still in its winged form, managed to get to its feet. She turned around holding her head where a huge gash had scarred over with dried blood."

"How the hell is it still alive, is what I want to know." The sheriff lowered his voice, not wanting to startle his dazed prisoner. "My shot took her down from a fall of over thirty feet, never mind the bullet hit her square in the …."

"AAGHHHH!!!" the vampire screamed. She stepped to the bars and took hold of them. For the first time she addressed the two men. "Let me go!"

"Sorry," Sheriff Savila tried to keep his voice steady. "But you ain't going nowheres, lady."

The vampire growled like an animal then snapped the door lock as easily as if it were made of matches when she popped it open.

Savila went for his gun; Sidewinder his sword.

The she creature opened her black leather wings wide and plowed through them knocking them both off their feet.

She pushed opened the front door and rushed out into the full daylight.

Sidewinder heard her piercing scream and scrambled to his feet. He reached the door seconds before Savila. Both stood there dumbfounded as they watched the vampire burst into flames in the middle of the street. Folks passing by froze in mid-step as the dying monster attempted to leap into the air, only to flop back on the ground and continued to be consumed by the hot flames that devoured her.

Five minutes later all that remained were smoking, black charred bones. Savila gulped. "Hot damn!"

Sidewinder turned and gave him a wry look. "No shit!"

•••

The smell of sizzling bacon woke Richard O'Malley from an uneasy dream in which he was being attacked by flying demons. He and Sam had slept on the hardwood floor of the one room cabin while Hattie Fields had bedded down in her stagecoach preferring the outdoors. She also wanted to be near her horses should any mischievous predator be on the prowl.

O'Malley had used his torn, dirty jacket as a makeshift pillow and had been asleep long before Sam and Fields were done with taking care of the team. Now he lifted his head up, sniffed and felt his stomach growl.

"Morning, Mr. O'Malley," Hattie Fields greeted as she placed an iron skillet atop a small square table in the middle of the room. Long wooden benches framed the crude table to either side. "You want some vittles?"

"Indeed, I do," O'Malley rose stiffly to his feet and raised his arms to stretch out his fine. "It does smell wonderful."

"Don't be getting your hopes up, I'm not that good a cook," she warned.

On the table beside the skillet was a hemp basket in which were a dozen small sourdough biscuits.

Fields pointed to the food. "Go on and help yourself, coffee's about done." Then she went back to the crackling blaze in the stone fireplace and wearing thick leather gloves, retrieved a black pot.

As she brought it over to the table hurriedly, O'Malley got a whiff of the strong brew.

"Ah, Miss Fields, you are most certainly an angel sent to rescue we poor mortals." In the light spilling in through the window and open door, O'Malley had his first real look at the woman who had pulled them out of the deadly battle that had raged in Dooley. He saw that despite the buckskin garb, she was really quite lovely. Her skin was a rich, warm brown, without any blemishes. Her button nose and wide mouth made her smile something truly memorable to see. It was as if Hattie Fields had no secrets and simply showed the world who she was without trepidation. He'd rarely seen such confidence in the women he knew back east.

The west, for all its hardships and loneliness, seemed to mold strong characters regardless of their gender.

"Ain't no angel, Mr. O'Malley," Fields chuckled as she brought the pot over and set it down beside the iron skillet. "But Pa always thought I had a whole lot of devil in me." Atop the fireplace were two tin cups which she grabbed and then handed one to the reporter as he was sitting down.

"Go ahead and chow down," she said as she filled both cups with the steaming hot coffee.

"Though you'll have to eat with your fingers, ain't got no fancy dishes or knives and forks."

"This is just fine, Miss Fields," O'Malley picked up a biscuit, it was still warm. "May I inquire as to the whereabouts of my companions?"

"Ifn' you mean Sam and that Dead Sheriff, they're tending to the horses. Or at least the Indian is. T'other just went along like his shadow. That thing gives me the willies."

"He does take some getting used to," O'Malley concurred after swallowing his first bite. The biscuit was tasty. Next he carefully reached for a strip of the greasy bacon. "The last few months have certainly been most memorable for me."

He heard approaching footsteps, then the door opened and Sam entered. His hands and face were wet and O'Malley rightly guessed he had washed himself at the well.

"Hmm, do I smell bacon?"

Hattie Fields pointed to the food on the table. "Sit and help yourself," she directed. "Though I've only got two of these cups. You and Mr. O'Malley gonna have to share one."

The Indian nodded and sat across from O'Malley who noticed someone was missing.

"Where's The Dead Sheriff?"

"Sitting on the end of the porch," Sam replied. "He is a good look out. I told him to come tell me if anyone rides up."

Fields sat down next to O'Malley and picked up several biscuits. "Don't he eat at all?"

"Doesn't need to," Sam bit into a strip of bacon carefully as to not burn his tongue. "Don't eat, don't drink, sleep or shit. Guess that's what being dead means to a body."

"I've heard lots of stories about him and you, Cheveyo. Are they true or just saloon bullshit passed from one drunk to another?"

Sam started to answer but O'Malley raised a hand to interrupt him. He turned to the woman and smiled. "If you don't mind, Miss Fields…"

"Call me Hattie, will yah? I ain't use to all this here manners stuff."

"Very well, Hattie. As much as you are curious about our animated dead companion, I'm much more intrigued by your own history. I mean, who are you really? What's your story?"

Hattie Fields took a bite of bacon and then looked O'Malley straight in the eye. He could see she was mulling over whether she wanted to tell that story or simply rebuff his request. After a few minutes, she drained her coffee cup and came to a decision.

"All right, if you gotta know, here it is.

"My Pa was Enos Fields. He was a slave born and raised up on a plantation in Chiksaw, Virginia. Growing up, he was taught how to blacksmith and take care of horses. Toward the end of the war, when them Rebs was on their last leg, Pa lit out of there one night and never looked back. Got no idea how old he was, slaves didn't have such records.

"After a couple years drifting west, he managed to pick up some readin' and writin' from black settlers he met on his journey. Finally he ended up in the Oklahoma badlands where he was welcomed into a tribe of Crow Indians. The chief saw that Pa had a way with horses and so for a while my daddy stayed with the red man. He always said they learned from each other.

"It was there he met my Ma, Sweet Grass. She was a medicine woman and knew more about plants and critters than you could ever find in a ton of books. After she and Pa hitched up, they traveled up to Fort Smith where Wells Fargo was setting up stagecoach stations. Pa right away got a job taking care of the station halfways between there and Yellow Springs, Nebraska. He and Ma built the station house and barn with their own two hands. By the time they was done and the coaches were running through, she was carrying me in her belly."

Fields finished her coffee and wiped her lips with the back of her gloved hand.

"Please, go on." O'Malley was upset his pencils and notebook were back in the buckboard they'd left behind in Dooley. Soon as he was able to retrieve them, he would have to jot down all she was telling them. These were the stories he had come out west to collect.

"All rightee, let me think. About the time I was six, Ma had my brother Noko. She named him after some famous war chief or some such. The station was going full guns as the coaches between the two towns were always full up. Ma would put out a spread around midday when the coach from Nebraska would roll in and feed the passengers at the same time Pa was changing the teams. Later in the afternoon she'd do it again for the wagon going east from Fort Smith. That one weren't ever full. Mostly salesmen returning east to their home offices to report their sales.

"Occasionally you'd get some widows and their young'uns going back to their families in St. Louis after losing their men folks out on the frontier. The look in their eyes was always sad, as if something inside them had broken and would never be whole again."

"White people don't belong on this land," Sam spoke up ignoring the fact that his own mother had been white. "All they do is bring trouble with them."

Fields poured herself a second cup of coffee before continuing. "I won't argue you that, though I think the land's color blind myself. It pretty much brings sorrow to all of us, white, red or black."

"Go on, Hattie. What became of your parents?" O'Malley gave Sam a disapproving glance to caution him in interrupting her again.

"Anyway, life was pretty good for us in those days. The older I got, Pa began teaching me how to take care of the horses, both alone and as wagon teams. He also taught me to hunt and shoot. By the time I was ten, I was picking off jackrabbits and rattlers every day. I pretty much kept Ma's stew pot full all the time. At night, by candle light Pa would teach me and Noko our words and numbers. Ma put no stock in book learnin'; she always said it was important to know was what the land taught you.

"When I was out hunting, or helping Pa, me and Noko would go out gathering herbs with her. She taught us both what plants were good for eating and for healing…and which would give you the runs.

"Like I says, it was good times…until the night that Madam Magdala showed up in her fancy painted wagon, she only had one back then, and just two girls. It was just after sunset when they rode up to the station. Magdala told Pa they were on their way to Fort Smith to start a whore house but had gotten lost on the road.

"Pa felt sorry for them and said they could camp out by the barn until morning. The second he came back inside the house, Ma told him she had a bad feeling, as if Magdala and her ladies were dangerous somehow. Pa just laughed it off, saying she was being silly and we should have our supper and get off to bed.

"Ma wasn't happy about it and made a point of leaving the window in the room where Noko and I slept open. As she was tucking me in, she said if anything happened during the night, I was to take Noko and go out the back and run away. I asked her what she was afraid of, but she told me to go to sleep."

Fields paused for a moment. To O'Malley she seemed lost in what was obvious a very traumatic memory. He was proven correct when she picked up her story again.

"Of course with all that, I really wasn't able to sleep at all and just lay in my bed wishing morning would come. Later, must have been shortly after the moon came out, we heard the horses in the barn make a ruckus. Through the door I could hear Pa telling Ma he was gonna go out and see what was wrong. I thought maybe a few mangy coyotes had wandered down from the hills. I got out of bed and tip-toed to the door to peek out. Pa was at the front door, a lit lantern in one hand and his long barrel shotgun in t'other. Ma, in her night dress was cautioning him to be careful. Then he was gone. She closed and barred the door behind him.

"I could still hear the horses crying. Something had really spooked them good. Then we heard the shotgun blasts…both of em. After that, I think I heard my Pa yell out. Ma rushed to our room and almost knocked me over when she pushed the door in. Seeing I was awake, she went over and shook little Noko. Once he was up, she shoved us towards the window. 'Go,' she said. 'Run and don't look back.' Just then there was a loud crash and we all knew it was the front door being busted open.

"I climbed out the window and turned to catch Noko as Ma handed him to me. There was more noise, then I saw Magdala come into the room. In the dim moonlight she was laughing and there was blood smeared all over her face and hands. She saw us at the window and jumped at Ma. Ma punched her hard in the face while yelling at me and Noko to run.

"And we did, as fast as we could. Into the bushes and the trees. Behind us we could hear more noise from the bedroom. My Ma must have fought like a mother bear against that foul bitch, but in the end there was no way she could win.

"Me, I held on to Noko's hand and pulled him along through the forest as fast as I could run. He was crying and trying to keep up, but he was to small and couldn't keep up. Somehow we let go of each other and then before I knew what was happening, one of them bloodsuckers just plucked him up into the air behind me. Poor Noko called my name once and then he was gone.

"I just kept on running. I was just so damn scared. Then all of a sudden the ground fell out from under me. I'd run right off the edge of a ravine and dropped four feet to the bottom where I smacked into a rock head first. It knocked me out."

"When I woke up the next morning, I was confused. Wondering what it was I was doing at the bottom of that gully and not in my own bed. I felt the blood on my head and then it all came back to me. What had happened and all. So I climbed out of that hole in the ground and ran home not thinking at all what I would find when I got there.

"Ma was still in the bedroom, what was left of her. I found Pa by the stables, his body all ripped up in pieces. I guess I musta went into shock 'cause all I could think of was that I was still dreaming and would wake up sooner or later. But I never did wake up.

"Two days later, several of my Ma's people showed up. I was still sitting on the ground next to my Pa. I don't recollect much after that, save they brought me back to their village and my grandmother took to healing me up. But it weren't my body that was sick, it was my head…and that took a bit longer."

Tired from her storytelling, Hattie Fields drank more of her coffee. It had gone tepid. She sighed and put the cup down.

Richard O'Malley was shaken by her tale. He looked at her with sympathy in his eyes. "And what of your brother?"

"Gone," she said matter-of-factly. "We never did find him. Those bitches just carried him off."

Footsteps sounded on the porch and everyone in the cabin turned to see it open and The Dead Sheriff standing there. He pointed out towards the road. Sam, finishing the last piece of bacon sat up straight and started to get up.

"Someone's coming."

•••

The three in the cabin rushed outside to see who it was The Dead Sheriff had sighted. Sam was relieved when he recognized his buckboard coming up the road. Driving it was a Crow brave with his painted pony tied to the back. Riding along the wagon was another Crow on a yellow Palomino. Both Indian horses were without saddles.

"Those are my Crow cousins," Hattie Fields told Sam and O'Malley as she waved to their visitors while stepping off the short porch. "They showed up last night long after you two had gone to sleep. I asked them to go back into town and fetch your wagon."

As the two braves neared, she pointed to the one driving the buckboard. "That's Wild Eagle on the wagon and the other is his older brother, Achoko. He's one ornery sonofabitch and not someone you ever want to tangle with."

Sam looked at the two men and could easily see a similarity in their sharp, rugged features. "And they are your family?"

"Yup, their Pa, Snake Who Strikes, was my Ma's brother. They took me in after my folks was killed by them blood drinkers."

The one called Wild Eagle pulled up on the reins and brought the two horses to a halt. "Hello, cousin," he greeted. "It is a fine day, is it not?"

"Yes, it is, you stealing rascal," Fields replied. Then she introduced Sam and O'Malley to her relatives. "Did you have any trouble finding the wagon?"

"No," Achoko said looking down on them from his big yellow mare. "It was where you said it would be."

"And the others? The three heavy wagons."

Achoko, dressed in leather leggings, moccasins and an old cotton shirt without buttons, slid off his horse and folded his arms over his powerful chest. "That took a little longer. Brother Moon did not help much. But we did find their trail out of the town."

Hattie Fields' face took on an anxious look. "Where they headed?"

Achoko turned his body slightly and pointed to the north. "They are going to the high country. Into the Spirit Mountains."

"Damn," she blurted out. "That bitch is going to ground."

Both Sam and O'Malley gave her a curious look and she explained her meaning. "I've suspected for a long while now that Magdala has a cave hidden away in the high country. I'm betting after that ruckus in Dooley, she's making for it right now."

"Then you're going after her?" O'Malley surmised aloud.

"You bet I am," she declared. "And would welcome anyone who wants to ride with me."

O'Malley didn't know what to say. He turned to Sam and saw his companion wasn't at all receptive to the idea.

"Hey," Wild Eagle jumped off the buckboard. "You got any coffee, cousin?"

"You bet, come on inside and let's get some," Fields suggested.

The two Crows started to follow her when Wild Eagle saw The Dead Sheriff standing on the porch motionless.

"AAH...who...is that a dead man?"

"No," Fields laughed, slapping him on the back. "That's a Dead Sheriff."

Clearly shaken by the sight of the lifeless lawman, both Indian brothers gave him a very wide berth in entering the cabin.

"This ain't none of our fight," Sam gritted his teeth. "No way am I or The Dead Sheriff gonna be a part of this hunt."

"Really?" O'Malley had not expected his friend's reaction. "And just how is this not our concern. You said yourself the fellow who stole the book and amulet was back there. You don't really think that was just a coincidence, do you?"

Sam's confusion was obvious. "No, I don't."

"He was there to find you and most likely that demon beast was with him. What if he's with this vampire queen now?"

"Exactly," Sam all but shouted. "If he is, and they are going one way, shouldn't we be going as fast as we can the other way?"

"You telling me you're afraid of him?"

"Yes, I am. Look O'Malley, I ain't got a clue what kind of magic this dude has. And I don't want to find out."

"And what, you think he's going to stop looking for you?"

"Huh?"

"If he chased you these past few years all the way to Dooley, what makes you think he's going to stop now? I'm telling you, Sam, he's not going to stop coming after you and The Dead Sheriff. Wouldn't it be smarter to turn the tables on him now. Stop running and go after him.

"Maybe get some answers while you're at it?'

Sam didn't like what O'Malley was telling him one little bit. But he realized the Boston born journalist was right. He knew in his own heart that no matter how far he went, that redheaded fellow would continue to keep coming.

Wouldn't it be better to end it all here and now?

"Look," O'Malley concluded. "Think about it, Sam. Think about it long and hard. Me, I'm going to get some more coffee and see what Hattie has got planned."

With that Richard O'Malley went back to the cabin.

Sam bit his lower lip and looked up to see The Dead Sheriff seemingly staring at him standing there, now alone.

Frustrated he pointed at The Dead Sheriff and yelled, "Just shut up!" Then he stormed off to see if all their gear was still in the bed of the buckboard.

CHAPTER THIRTEEN

The man named Labine sat with the mute driver of the second wagon in Madam Magdala's caravan. This was the wagon in which she and the boy, James Bennett, slept while Magdala's ladies were divided among the first and third wagon in the rolling troop. Labine realized the Vampire Queen had purposely placed herself in the most strategically protected wagon should they ever come under attack. Though how good her three deaf and mute servants would be in defending them against a concentrated assault was anybody's guess.

All Labine knew was the further along their journey into the hill country, the more he regretted ever having set foot beyond the Mississippi River. In the few years his gambling affairs had necessitated his visiting the wilderness west, he had come to hate the vast and open country. Where pioneers saw opportunity, Labine saw only emptiness, Indian savages and a lack of any true culture. He missed the South where he had been born and nurtured. In particular he missed New Orleans, that glorious city filled with theaters, dance halls and the exquisite French food. He also longed for the crowded saloons, gambling tables and the most beautiful women in the world.

Lost in his melancholy of hedonistic memories, he was rudely snapped back to the present by another hard bounce of the wagon wheels as they hit more deep entrenched ruts. Labine's lower back was hurting and his ass cheeks nearly numb. The padded driver's seat was nothing like the plush, comfortable coaches he was use to traveling in. And his silent companion was a lost cause from the moment they had started out. Simply staring ahead, managing the horse team with small hand tugs on the reins, the driver could have been a lifeless stature for his total lack of animation.

The man, and his two companions, didn't even acknowledge Labine's presence among them. It was as if to them, he was just another piece of the paraphernalia they were charged with taking care off for their mistress. They fulfilled that task with a minimum of effort, none of them bothering with him in the slightest. He had the thought that should he fall off the wagon at any time in their journey, the three wouldn't even stop but simply continue on without him.

Just another thing to add to his growing frustration.

His most pressing worry at the moment was the loss of the demon, Moloch. Not because he and the demon were allies. Nothing could be further from the truth. Rather Labine's Master had assigned the hell-spawn thing to accompany him on his mission to recapture the amulet and magic tome. He was too aware that conjuring demons from the netherworld wasn't a casual operation and once the Master knew Moloch was gone, Labine would feel the full brunt of the Master's wrath.

All of which came sooner than he wanted.

Along about midday, the first wagon pulled up alongside a small lake that was fed from rivers emptying out of the high mountains directly in front of them. Upon seeing this, the second driver did the same and the third followed suit. Soon all three brightly painted wagons were situated in a triangular form, with the lake twenty yards from the tip of the cone shape.

The mute trio unhitched their horse teams and led them to the water to drink. Seeing his chance to get off the rolling torture machine that was his seat, Labine carefully climbed down and walked over to a cluster of dark gray rocks near the water's edge. Here he took out a handkerchief, wet it and then mopped the road dust off his face. It felt so cool and refreshing. Then he cupped his hands and took two good swallows. Feeling much better, he backed up to the largest boulder, sat on the ground and carefully rested his back against the big rock.

He closed his eyes and sighed.

When will this nightmare ever stop?" he thought to himself. What he wasn't ready for was the response that suddenly echoed in his head.

When you achieved the task I gave you!

Labine sat up straight, his head swiveling about instinctively as if someone had come up behind him. But of course there was no one there. The three drivers were still tending to their animals and for all intents and purposes, Labine was alone.

Except in his thoughts. And that was how the Master communicated with him. He did so quite often and every time the mental touch left Labine shaken, trembling with an inner fear he could never quell. The Master could reach him anywhere, any time. That was the reality.

Sweat beaded Labine's forehead and he closed his eyes, ready for what was about to come next.

Forgive me, Master. Please. It was not my fault.

Tell me what happened to Moloch. I can no longer sense his presence. How is that possible?

The demon was destroyed, Master.

What? By who? The Indian boy you sought?

No, Master. He was shot by a negress with a shotgun blast to the head at close range.

A female colored! Open your mind to me, Labine...all of it. Let me see exactly what transpired and pray you tell me everything.

Labine took a deep breath, and clenched his hands into fists. The invasion into his mind was never a pleasant thing. It felt like a hundred needles were suddenly attaching his brain, each lancing it with excruciating pain that caused him to cry out. The needles continued jabbing into him as he relived the events of the past two days within a matter of minutes.

The Master's intrusion ended as abruptly as it had begun and Labine nearly fainted from the sudden release.

So now you travel with the vampire queen and her slaves. Why?

I was confused, Master. With Moloch gone, I feared the black woman was allied with the Indian boy and so I fled with Magdala. But I assure you, at the first chance I get, I'll leave them and return to my mission.

No.

The invasion into his mind was never a pleasant thing.

At first Labine wasn't sure he'd heard the Master's reply.

But Master, she is moving us further away from the Indian boy and the artifacts.

No, Labine. You fool, don't you see? There is a larger story unfolding here. If the Indian boy is riding with this negress and she is hunting Magdala, then the likelihood is the boy will come with her in seeking out the vampires. He will come to you. And with him he will bring the book and amulet.

Labine never argued with the Master. He'd learned the folly of doing such a long time ago. But was the Master right? Would the one calling himself Cheveyo now actually be chasing them with the black woman?

Listen carefully, Labine. The fates have decided to give you a second chance.

Yes, Master. I will not fail this time. I swear it.

Oh, you won't fail me, Labine, because I am going to provide you with another demon.

Another demon? But how Master?

You doubt me, Labine?

No, Master. But how will another such creature reach us in time before the confrontation you speak of?

Fool, I am not sending you a demon. You and this Magdala are going to create one.

Labine felt his stomach drop.

But how...Master?

You have a young male vampire traveling with you, do you not?

Yes. He traveled with some vigilante calling himself Bullet until Magdala turned him into one of her slaves.

I am aware of all that, Labine, and this boy will become my new demon. When the time comes, I will give the knowledge required to make the transformation. Is that understood?

Yes, Master. I will await your bidding.

Good. I would hate to have you fail me again, Labine.

Then there was only silence and Labine fell back against the hard rock. What was the Master going to do? At times, the gambler from New Orleans truly felt as if the whole world had gone crazy. This was very much one of those times.

•••

FROM THE JOURNAL OF RICHARD O'MALLEY

By noon I'd talked myself hoarse in convincing Sam that we should accompany Hattie Fields in her pursuit of the vampire queen she called Madam Magdala. I was fairly certain if we did indeed find them, the fellow from whom Sam had first stolen the amulet and book of spells would be with her entourage. Thus there would be a final confrontation between this man, whoever he was, and Sam. Of course I swore to Sam that I and The Dead Sheriff would be there as well to support him.

By this time in our relationship, he begrudgingly had come to know I did not make promises I could not keep. Still reluctant, he finally agreed that we would ride along with Hattie Fields.

The sun was bright in a near cloudless sky as we made ready to depart. At first Sam had wanted us to follow along in his backboard, but Miss Fields easily dissuaded him with her logic that all of us could ride in her stagecoach, with the two Indian lads, Wild Eagle and Ochoko, riding along on their mounts. She underscored her argument by going to the back of her coach and lifting the canvas top of the wagon's boot, revealed her unique arsenal stored inside it.

There were several long bows with dozens of arrows packed in leather quivers. She withdrew one of them and held it up for us to inspect. The sharp edged point glimmered in the sunlight.

"Are those tips silver?" Sam asked, his eyes widening.

"Yes," she replied. "For whatever reason, it hurts them; the bloodsuckers. Wasn't all that easy to come by, but I've managed over the years to collect enough to make these."

Sam slid the arrow back into the quiver and pointed to a bunch of long wooden stakes tied together in a large bundle. "And those?"

"A vampire will die if you drive one of those spears through its heart... then cut off its head."

"You know a great deal about combating these creatures," I added matter-of-factly to which Miss Fields simply grinned.

"If you'd been chasin' them as long as I have, Mr. O'Malley, you'd be sure to learn a thing or two yourself."

"But where exactly did you gain such lore? I'd hazard there are not too many libraries in this part of the country."

To that, Hattie Fields indicated her Indian cousins. "Their Ma is a medicine woman and lots of the things I know, she taught me. Shamans like her have been fighting evil critters like these since the Great Spirit made the mountains and plains."

It was an extremely fascinating account and once again I hoped when this particular adventure was over, I'd have time to interview her at length. If, that is, we survived.

"What's in that steel box?" Sam pointed to a rust colored box tied with thick ropes to the back of the boot.

Hattie Fields carefully unhooked the latch and lifted the cover. From it she withdrew a thin, red cylinder which I immediately recognized as a stick of dynamite.

"Whoa," Sam looked at Fields as if she were crazy. "You go riding hard and fast with a box of dynamite in the back! There's something seriously wrong with you, lady."

Hattie Fields chuckled. "Relax, Sam. Ain't nothin' gonna go boom till we shove a fuse in it and light her up. Till then, the sticks are all packed in cotton wadding in there."

"You think you'll need them?" It was my turn to ask.

"You saw that three-eyed monster back in Dooley. What do you think?"

She carefully replaced the stick of gun-powder and dropped the lid back in place securing the lock as she did so.

For the next half hour, all of us, at her instructions, loaded the stagecoach with supplies leaving one seat open. With Wild Eagle's help, Hattie hitched up her horses. Meanwhile Sam untied his own two animals from his buckboard and led them into the corral. On our way out of the valley, Ochoko would make a quick detour back to his village to make arrangements for someone to care for them while we were gone.

That settled, it was time to go.

Sam told The Dead Sheriff to get into the coach and I climbed in after him. We took our places side by side on the seat left empty. His familiar rotting stench was a palpable as ever and I did my best to keep my face turned to the small window to my left. I despised the thought that I was actually becoming accustomed to it. The space inside was fairly crowded with bags of food enough to sustain us for at least a week in the hills, if not longer.

Hattie Fields took her place atop the driver's box and Sam stepped up on the front wheel and hoisted himself up to ride shotgun.

Wild Eagle and Ochoko jumped easily on their horses and awaited us.

"Well, partners," Hattie Fields called out, grabbing her bullwhip. "Here goes nothin'!" She snapped the whip over the team's heads and spurred them to start moving. "Gittyup, you ornery four-legged bastards! Eehahh!"

The horses lifted their proud heads, snorted and charged forward. We were on our way.

In to what, only God knew.

Realizing we had a long day ahead of us, I finally dug into one of my bags and dug out my writing pad of paper and a pencil. It was time to jot down these notes in my journal. I opened the cover and began to write when the coach suddenly bounced upward and the pencil flew out of my hand.

The Dead Sheriff was shoved against me for a second, his hat titled askew. He straightened up, adjusted his Stetson and then bent over and retrieved my pencil. Without saying a word, he leaned back and handed it to me.

"Thank you," I said, looking at his lifeless, dead face. There was nothing there, and yet he'd picked up my pencil as if it was just a simple thing to do.

After a few more seconds of looking into his awkward expression, I turned back to my journal, wet the tip of the pencil on my tongue and began to write.

The Dead Sheriff remained quiet.

CHAPTER FOURTEEN

Nestled along the spine of what pioneers called the Colorado Front Range, the Spirit Mountains wove their way westward gradually climbing into the clouds to become part of the Rockies. The terrain was hard, boulder strewn with little vegetation to maintain the animals who resided within its craggy valleys and bluffs. It took Madam Magdala and her party two full days to reach them. They would reach the final destination the following day.

The sun had settled over the peaks ahead of them as the three mute drivers brought their wagons to a halt at the center of a small copse of hardy blue spruce trees. They immediately set about building a campfire as Labine looked on. He sat on a wooden crate smoking one of his last few cigars still stashed in the inner pocket of his now torn and soiled coat.

He heard rustling in the wagons and one by one the vampires stepped forth to greet the new night that draped over them like a blanket of a million shining stars. Magdala and the boy, James Bennett, who had once called himself Bullet, were the last to emerge. The lad jumped down from the wagon and turned to extend his hand to his mistress. Looking as beautiful as ever, her sharp angular features caught in the campfire's yellow glow, the Vampire Queen descended gracefully and nodded approvingly to her minions.

She spotted Labine and letting go of the boy's hand, told him to select two of the girls and set about finding them food. With their special ability to visually penetrate the darkness, all of them were adapt at night hunting. Bennett smiled and went off to comply with her wishes.

Magdala sauntered over to where Labine was waiting. Seeing her approach, he stood and bowed.

"Good evening, Madam," he graciously smiled. He clearly recalled their night of lovemaking. The Vampire Queen returned the smile. If he proved as useful to her as he had promised, she might grant him more such sexual delights.

"Good evening, Labine. I trust the journey hasn't been too severe on you?"

"Nothing a week in a New Orleans steam-bath won't cure," he blew out a puff of smoke. "Perhaps when this is all over, you'll join me there."

"An intriguing invitation, Mr. Labine." She licked her lower lip. "It well might be time I explored new places. Recruited new sisters."

"You would have no lack of such in that jewel of a city, Madam. I assure you."

"Perhaps you would also introduce to me to this all powerful Master of yours?"

Labine liked that she was direct. It was something they had in common and her suggestion opened the door for him to address the matter on his mind.

"I'm sure that can be arranged. But for now, my Master has sent me a warning that I must share with you. One of dire importance to both of us."

At that, Magdala pointed to the woods behind the wagons. "Then let us take a short walk where we can talk in private." Seeing the wisdom of her suggestion, Labine tossed his half finished cigar into the crackling flames and extended his right arm to her. Magdala took it and informed her girls she would only be gone for a few minutes. They were to aid Barrett and the others when they returned in dividing their catch.

Five minutes later the two of them were walking along a small deer path still arm in arm.

"Very well, sir, you may proceed," she said looking back at the camp now a good distance behind them. "What is this important message your Master wishes you to tell me?"

"Only that our enemies have come together to hunt us down and they are most assuredly on our tracks at the moment."

"Interesting," Magdala admitted. "I had assumed Hattie Fields, that's the black woman from Dooley, was after us. She has been a thorn in my side for several years now. And this enemy of yours, is it The Dead Sheriff and the one called they Cheveyo you mentioned earlier?"

"Yes, my Master had deduced they have joined forces to ride against us."

Magdala stopped and removed her hold on Labine. She turned to face him. "I had already surmised as much. Is that all your Master wished to tell me? If so, his information is rather irrelevant at the present moment. Wouldn't you agree?"

"It is not only this he wished to convey, Madam. You see, my Master wishes to aid you in defeating them when the time comes. To that end, he offers you assistance."

"How so? We're an awfully long ways away from New Orleans."

"The limitations of time and space do not affect the Master. You see, as his agent, I am quite capable of acting as his conduit to employ his dark arts."

"To what end, Mr. Labine? What exactly is it you can do here and now?"

"I can summon another demon, Madam. Another dark beast from the pits of hell to come forth and do our bidding."

The Vampire Queen was actually surprised. A thing that only rarely happened to her. She peered up at Labine's rugged face and knew he was totally serious about his claim.

"Really. And how would you go about doing such a....summoning?"

"I would require a sacrifice. Another soul in exchange for the demon. In all such dealings, a payment is required."

"But who? One of girls? I won't allow..."

"The boy, Madam. Bennett."

"Why him?"

"The spell requires a male sacrifice. And as the boy already possesses a dark soul, the transference can be easily achieved once he has been ritually slaughtered."

Magdala turned away from Labine and wrapped her arms around herself. She walked away from him, her head bent in thought. He wondered if she would refuse him.

"Unless," he pressed his offer, "you have some special fondness for the boy?"

Magdala spun around. "Don't be coy with me, sir. The boy means nothing to me except as another slave to do my will. He has proved useful these past few months."

"I understand. But now he can even be of much greater use to you. Don't you see, as a demon, his inhuman strength will be the very advantage we require to defeat our enemies."

Finally Magdala nodded. She moved closer to her new ally. "All right. I agree. Now tell me what it is we have to do."

•••

By the time Labine and Magdala returned to the fire, James Bennett and the two female vampires had returned from their foraging. The hunt had been good as scattered on the ground next to the blazing was a carcass of a huge buck deer and half a dozen rabbits. All of her troop, except for the three teamsters, were fidgeting, anxious to tear into the oozing life's blood of the dead forest creatures.

"An excellent bounty," Magdala approved. She turned to one of her three mute servants. Then she made several hand motions and pointed to the bodies. The little stocky man rose up from his seat on a fallen log, reached over by where the cooking utensils had been laid out and took hold of a large butcher knife. He went to kneel by the buck and carved out a fairly good chunk of meat. This he brought back to the fire and began to skin it with the assistance of his two companions.

Magdala turned to Labine. "You may join the drivers. They will cook the meat and give you a portion, while the rest us feed in our own way."

She turned to face her vampires. "Alicia, if you will, please."

The brunette vampire dropped on the buck and with her claws extended, rip off a piece and then delivered it to her mistress.

Magdala nodded and smiled. "Feed my sisters, to your heart's content." Then she bit into the raw meat to suck forth its copious amount of blood.

Labine had gone over to sit with the three silent men as the vampire pack fell on the remaining animal bodies with savage abandon like wild ravenous dogs. Each ripped and tore at the big deer and the smaller rabbits were soon nothing but tattered flesh and bones. As they drank every drop of the precious blood, they howled at the stars above, the gore dripping down their faces onto their clothing.

Labine turned his head away. Watching the driver with the knife prepare the hunk of meat for the frying pan, he was only too happy to wait until it was properly cooked.

•••

After everyone had eaten, Magdala ordered one of her girls to fly back over the route they had been traveling. She was worried that Hattie Fields and the others chasing them might be nearer than she thought. If so, it would be good to know how many were in the hunting party. Thus they could properly plan their own defenses.

The girl chosen, Lizzie, hastily morphed into her flying form and her large leather wings sprouted out from her back. She shook them to get a proper feel and then began running towards the trees. At the end of the clearing she leaped up into the air and her rapidly flapping wings catching the night breeze. Many more such beats and she was soon a tiny dot disappearing into the blackness behind them.

Watching her fly off, Magdala recalled the family she and Alicia had murdered long ago at the lonely frontier way station. The black Wells Fargo agent had been a big man and it had taken both of them to overcome him in the barn. Once wounded, his lifeblood draining from his body, Magdala had rushed to the house to feed on his wife, an Indian squaw, and her two small children. But she'd been too late and the desperate mother had managed to get them out the back window before she could break into the tiny square bedroom. In the end, Alicia had caught the boy, but the girl had fallen into a nearby river while fleeing. Magdala had assumed the little brat had drowned. It wasn't till many years later when she learned of a tough, single-minded female darky that was scouring the territories in search of her company. She quickly realized the truth of it to her own chagrin.

The woman was Hattie Fields and she hadn't drowned after all. Now she was obsessed with seeking vengeance for the deaths of her family.

Ending her reverie, Magdala went over to the campfire and standing before her three servants, she began to give them their new orders. Because she spoke softly and the flames were popping, Labine, who was wiping his greasy fingers with his only handkerchief, couldn't hear what she was telling them. Which was a puzzle in itself. He stood and walked around the fire to join her as she finished whatever it was she had told the drivers.

"How can they hear you? Aren't they all deaf?"

"Yes, but they can read lips. I have told them that once we reach the caves tomorrow, they are to obey your instructions. When you speak to them, stand directly before them so that they can see your mouth."

"And they will do whatever I tell them?"

"Yes. They would never think of disobeying my commands."

"Good, and young Bennett?"

"Don't worry about him. I will deal with him when the time comes and you will have your sacrifice."

Labine smiled knowingly. With Magdala's cooperation, all would go exactly as the Master had planned. And he would finally be back in his good graces.

Magdala extended her hand and touched Labine's face. "Come, the night is young and I am restless." Then she took his hand and led him to her wagon. The others merely watched and chuckled.

Susie and one of the other girls, Anna, fell on James Bennett and began tearing at his clothes. "Come on," Susie laughed reaching between his legs. It's time we had some fun too."

He was only too happy to oblige them.

•••

Had the young woman named Lizzie not been one of the undead, she might have been able to enjoy the wonders of flight. But she had given up her humanity long ago to become a vampire and now the pleasures of the world, even the fantastical, were beyond her reasoning. She had willingly become an animal and as such she merely repeated the same actions every day of her existence; sleep, hunt, feed, sleep. Over and over under the cover of the night, never to again experience the warmth of the sun, the smell of flowers or taste of honey.

As she glided along the wind currents, her black eyes scanning the land below, she had absolutely no sense of pleasure. She was no better than the bats her abilities mimicked. Her one thought, do Magdala's bidding and then return to their camp.

Miles disappeared beneath her, from flatlands to valleys, hills and arroyos cut deep into the soil. Within a few hours she had traversed what it had taken them an entire day to complete. All the while she remained aware of the horizon to the East, from whence that awful orb would eventually arise. Her internal clock warned her that she was nearing the extent of her range and to make it back to the others before daybreak, she would soon have to turn back.

She wondered if her mistress would be pleased that she hadn't found any signs of pursuit. Or would that anger her? It was impossible to know Magdala's mind and Lizzie never wasted any time doing so. She was a devoted vampire sister who obeyed orders and drank the blood of the living.

What else was there?

She'd made up her mind to end her search when she spotted a tiny glimmer below. It was only a few miles away, appearing to be hidden behind a wall of trees.

Was it a campfire? Was it them? The hunters?

Lizzie licked her fangs and tipping her body gracefully descended.

•••

Unaware of the danger approaching them, Richard O'Malley sat near the dying campfire lost in his thoughts. They had traveled hard all day and just before sunset chosen the base of a small hilly slope to make their camp. After getting a fire going and devouring a hastily prepared meal of beans and biscuits, all of them had retired. Each had picked out a spot around the fire and attempted to make themselves as comfortable as they could on the hard, rock strewn ground. Hattie Fields had provided both O'Malley and Sam with a thick heavy woolen blanket to ward off the night chill.

Whereas Achoko and Wild Eagle had volunteered to stand guard, each taking one half the night while the other slept. Although they believed Madam Magdala and her vampires were at least fifty to sixty miles ahead of them on the trail, there were no guarantees the wily Vampire Queen might not attempt to double back and surprise them. Better to be wary than sorry.

The Dead Sheriff, who never slept, was added insurance and Sam had ordered him to sit by the fire until morning.

Shortly after midnight, O'Malley had stirred awake, his sleep filled with nightmarish visions. Unable to go back to sleep, he had wrapped the blanket around his shoulders and gone to sit by the still smoldering logs. He chose to sit opposite The Dead Sheriff who sat unmoving like a statue and didn't react at all to his appearance but simply continued to stare into the fire with his lifeless eyes.

It was as if O'Malley was reliving that night when seated across a similar campfire, he'd witnessed The Dead Sheriff shed a tear down his pasty gray sunken cheek. He had shrugged it off then; relegating the incident to a dream. And still, after all this time, the Boston bred journalist couldn't forget the moment and that sad lonely tear. *The Dead Sheriff is just an animated corpse,* he told himself for the hundredth time. He...it.... far beyond any capability of displaying emotions of any kind.

As time went by, Wild Eagle emerged from the surrounding brush carrying one of the longbows O'Malley had seen in the coach's boot and a quiver of arrows strapped to his back. He kicked his brother to rouse him. Achoko yawned, got to his feet and Wild Eagle handed him the bow and arrows before stretching out on his own blankets.

The older Crow brave saw O'Malley by the fire and indicated the dying embers. "You might want to throw a few more twigs on the fire if you don't want it to go out," he said softly as to not wake the others.

"I will," O'Malley replied also keeping his voice low. He watched Achoko disappear into the trees and then rising stiffly, tossed off his blanket and began looking for small branches and twigs over by where Hattie Fields had tied up her horses. After ten minutes he had an arm full and quietly walked back to the campfire. Trying to minimize the noise he was making, he carefully dropped the extra fuel into the fire. Instantly the hungry flames began growing again and radiating more heat. He crouched down and opened his cold hands to its welcomed warmth.

Suddenly something big flew over him and Richard O'Malley jerked his head at the sound, wanting to see what it was. In doing so he nearly lost his balance and dropped his right hand to the ground to steady himself. As he was doing so, he looked up to see a figure land heavily atop the stagecoach.

It was a female vampire with enormous wings. They beat slowly now as she looked down about the shaken O'Malley. He was reminded of the stone gargoyles that sat atop several of the massive building in downtown Boston. Only this one moved.

"Fools!" she cried out, her voice sharp and piercing. "You are all going to die."

It was enough to rouse the others; Hattie Fields and Sam were the first out of their bedrolls followed by Wild Eagle. The only one not getting to his feet was The Dead Sheriff, who for the moment seemed content to remain seated watching the fire.

"My mistress awaits you with open arms," the creature laughed, opening up her limbs as if to offer them an embrace. "Please, don't keep her waiting."

With that, the vampire once again took to the air all the while laughing cruelly.

As she passed over them, Sam yelled at The Dead Sheriff. "Don't just sit there...shoot her!"

The Dead Sheriff jumped up and drew both his guns in one quick motion. But before he could fire one bullet, there was a distinct twanging sound followed by that of something hitting flesh.

The flying vampire cried out and plummeted to the ground only yards away from the fire. Out of the trees behind her emerged Achoko, bow in hand. The winged bloodsucker twisted on her back, clawing at the silver tipped arrow protruding from her stomach.

"Not laughing now, are you bitch!" Hattie Fields snarled as she rushed over to the fallen vampire. From behind her back she whipped out a huge Bowie knife. Seeing it, the frightened monster tried to sit up only to have Fields kick her in the chest knocking her back.

"Help me hold her down!" Fields yelled to the others.

Wild Eagle rushed over and grabbed the creature's left arm and then Sam was there holding her right. The fiendish beast struggled mightily trying to break their hold on her. Seeing her legs beating against the ground in a vain attempt to shake off her captors, Richard O'Malley fell across them with his body.

"Hurry it up, woman!" he told Hattie Fields. "Do it!"

Fields dropped to one knee, took hold of the vampire's hair with her left hand and then she swung the blade down with all her might cutting through the neck and severing monster's head clean off its body.

She stood up, looking into the reddish eyes glaring at her from hell's open gates, then went over and tossed the head into the fire.

•••

Magdala felt a sharp pain in her chest and sat up in the wagon. She gasped, pushed the naked Labine away from her and grasped her head.

Lizzie was gone. The fool had revealed herself to their enemies and paid the price for her recklessness.

"Wake up," Magdala shouted at Labine.

As the gambler rolled over, she grabbed a robe and exited out the back of the wagon. The drivers, were asleep by the fire, while her remaining sisters and James Bennett were all naked and cavorting about in hedonistic revelry. At first they didn't see her.

"All of you, cease this ridiculous behavior immediately!"

Alicia, who was entangled with the sister named Corrine, knew something was very wrong.

"What has happened?"

"Lizzie has been vanquished and the enemy is nearer than we thought. Pack your things." She turned to the three silent men, now all awake. "Hitch up the horses. We leave at once."

In the wagon, putting on his pants, Labine heard Magdala's news and for the first time detected fear in her voice. He didn't like it at all.

CHAPTER FIFTEEN

The vampire caravan reached the Spirit Mountains shortly after daybreak. Labine couldn't help but marvel at how the land simply continued to climb into the foreboding hills all around them. As the sky went from a coal black to a dull gray, massive clouds appeared directly above them mirroring the peaks they were entering. A morning breeze kicked up dirt before them and slowed their progress considerably. Each of the three drivers had to peer into the choking dust curtain while shielding their eyes with one hand.

Then, as if that curtain of grit had suddenly been pulled away, the gust of wind was gone and they were moving into a narrow ravine with sharp rock walls to either side. The wheels bumped up and down over uneven ground as the long gulch continued for several miles. Finally they rode into an open expanse through which a tiny creek ran. At the end of this was a long sandy slope at the top of which Labine sighted what appeared to be cave opening.

As the drivers halted their teams at the base of the incline, Labine corrected his initial thought. From directly below the aperture, he saw it was huge cavern; more than a mere hole in the mountain. The height of the wide upside V entrance he estimated to be at least forty feet and the width perhaps thirty.

The drivers wasted no time in alerting their passengers that they had reached their destination. Once awakened, they aided each of the vampire women in walking up the slope and into cavern. Each of the undead women wore gloves and held a shawl over their heads. Magdala was grateful for the thick cloud cover and the absence of sunlight. It was Labine who personally aided her up into the waiting gloom. She told him that had the sun been present, her drivers would have had to carefully wrap her and her company in canvas sheets kept in the wagons and then hurriedly carried them into the cavern one at a time. Any exposure to the sun's rays was both painful and ultimately lethal to any vampire.

Once inside the cavern entrance, they were enveloped by the stygian darkness within. Naturally the undead had no problem with their unique nocturnal vision but Labine worried he'd soon trip over a rock. Then there was a spark and a red-orange flame materialized atop a wooden torch being held by one of the mute servants.

Magdala approached James Bennett and held up a palm to him. "I need you to wait with the other two men by the entrance."

"Whatever you wish, Madam," he obeyed eagerly.

She turned to the fellow with the torch and mouthed the word "proceed." He led them deeper into the massive interior, his single light casting moving shadows across the stone walls all around them. Labine did his best to keep up remaining behind the others. His head kept turning back and forth as he took in the majestic passageway. Ugly fat rats and lots of spiders darted about on the floor between the boulders and crevasses while in the inky blackness high above he could hear the sound of disturbed bats.

"So what do you think of my secret sanctum?" Madam Magdala asked him when at last they came to an open space in which several beds and chairs had been arranged like some hidden military barracks. There were even several tall wooden closets overstuffed with women's clothing and small card tables on which were kerosene lanterns. The lead driver busied himself lighting two of them as the girls themselves plopped down on chairs or beds.

"Quite homey, wouldn't you say?" Magdala teased Labine.

"Rather surprising is more the word I'd have chosen. So this is your secret base?"

"Yes," she moved about the layout, her hand indicating the furniture. "If we remained out there, in the open, constantly, we'd have perished long ago."

"Really? I find that hard to believe."

"Oh, do believe it, Labine. Even with our gifts from our Dark Lord, we also have our weaknesses and they make us extremely vulnerable. Thus I reasoned if we kept our foraging trips sporadic, then we could also maintain our anonymity from those we preyed on. But that required a place where we go to retreat to; a place to disappear to every so often. That way they continue to remain blissfully ignorant of our existence."

Labine clapped his hands appreciative. "Bravo. A clever strategy indeed, Magdala. I applaud you for it. But now, we do have another matter to deal with it."

"Yes, we do." She told the girls to remain in the grotto chamber and then, with Labine and the driver, started back to the cavern's entrance.

Young James Bennett was leaning back against a slab of rock awaiting them. The other drivers had returned to the wagons and were busy unhitching the horses. On seeing Magdala approach, Bennett pushed off the boulder and stood anxiously awaiting her next command.

He was such a loyal boy.

"I have been good to you," Magdala began standing before him. "Have I not?"

"For sure, Ma'am. I ain't ever had so much fun as I done the past few months. What with them girls and all. And being able to whip anyone I choose. I like all that stuff."

Magdala smiled. "Of course you do, James. What boy wouldn't. But now you must help me in another capacity. One that will demand total obedience. Are you ready for that?"

"Oh, yes, Ma'am. Just tell me what I got to do and I'll do it."

Labine stood to Magdala's left while the driver who had carried the torch had moved around and now stood behind James Bennett.

"Then do exactly as I say, James."

"Yes, Ma'am."

"Put your hands behind your back and lift your head up." Bennett did as he was told.

"Close your eyes, my pretty boy." The boy complied and Magdala leaned down and kissed him full on the mouth.

"As she did so, she raised her right hand, and Labine watched in amazement as the nails on her first two fingers grew out a full inch. She stepped back and slashed those razor sharp tips across the boy's throat.

His eyes opened in shock. The driver grabbed his arms from behind and held them tight as blood gushed from his severed jugular. Magdala let it splash over her face. He tried to speak but his voice had been silenced. His eyes asked her why as he sank down to his knees. Then the driver released him and Jim Bennett fell over onto his face, dead once again.

Magdala wiped her blood smeared face with the palm of her hand and turned to Labine.

"There is your sacrifice. Do what you have to do and be quick about it."

She spun on her heels and walked back into the cavern. Labine looked to the silent servant and pointed to the boy's body. "Come on, you grab his shoulders and I'll take his legs."

Together they lifted the corpse and carried it outdoors.

•••

Hattie Fields' snapped her bullwhip effortlessly over her team of running horses. They were racing over the miles of flat plains that stretched out like an apron before the mountains ahead.

Wild Eagle and Achoka had started out before them so as to find the wheel tracks left by the three wagons and to scout what lay before them. Towers of ominous clouds continued to roll above the distant peaks and she could feel a storm brewing. The sky itself was a purple hue and the sun had been hidden all day. Still, despite the signs of foul weather, Fields relished the speed in which her horses carried them forward as the air rushed past them cool and brisk.

Beside her Sam clung to the padded seat stoically keeping his eyes forward.

"You ain't much for talking, are you," she stated the obvious.

Sam continued to stare at the land and for a second she wondered if he'd even heard her.

"Got nothing to say," was his response.

"Suit yourself. Just thought it might take your mind off things for a spell is all."

"You mean what's going to happen when we find them?"

"Yeah. I'm thinking it's gonna be one hell of a fight."

Again, Sam lapsed into silence as if lost in other reflections other than their present conversation. Then he sighed and said, "What's one more. Sometimes it feels that's what I've been doing my whole life. Just one fight after the other."

Fields cracked the whipped again and yelled to keep her team moving. She set the whip down and looked at Sam. He wore the expression of a sad puppy.

"Rough life, heh? Mine ain't been no picnic either."

"But at least you knew both your ma and pa, lady. Me, I was born in a whorehouse. All I know is my pa was an injun and my mother a two-bit half-breed whore. Hell, she never told me what tribe she belonged to. First part of my life was spent with her going from one town whorehouse to another. She treated me more like her personal slave than her son. I couldn't even call her Ma. I had to call her Esmeralda.

"Both white folks and injuns spit on me like I was something less than dirt. That's what my life has been all about. Until..." He looked at Fields and decided he'd already said too much.

"Until what? You got hooked up with that rotting sheriff back there?"

"Yes. Until The Dead Sheriff. And that's none of your business. All right."

"Sure, Sam. It's your life, amigo. Wasn't my idea to stir up your past like that. Just wanted you to know you ain't the only half-breed out here."

He took in her words and nodded.

Hattie Fields continued. "Lots of us black Indians on the frontier, Sam. And just like you, we have to fight to make a place for ourselves. But in the end, I think it's worth it. This here is a pretty big country and there's plenty of room for all of us.

"At least those of us that are human." Fields turned and spit away from the coach. "As for those bloodsucking critters. They all belong in Hell and that's where we're gonna send them."

Fields' declaration seemed to hang in the air between them. Then Sam picked out two riders coming their way and pointed. "Looks like them your Indian kin."

Sure enough, Achoko and Wild Eagle were riding towards them at a speedy clip and Hattie Fields tugged back on her reins at the same time pulling back on the wooden brake handle. The six powerful horses came to a gradual stop and stood motionless save for their tails twitching back and forth.

In the back, Richard O'Malley opened the door and stuck his head out. "Why we stopping?"

Sam leaned over to answer him. "Her Indian cousins are back," and pointed back over his shoulder.

Achoko reared up first with Wild Eagle coming up alongside him. He looked up at Sam and Hattie fields and grinned. "We found them."

•••

Labine watched as the two of Magdala's mute drivers dug a shallow grave half way down the rocky slope from the cavern opening. The remaining fellow had tended to the horses; unhitching them and then taking them to the creek to drink before tying them to several thorny bushes that poked through the soil at the base of the opposite cliff wall.

"We found them."

When the diggers had managed to hollow out a cavity three feet deep, Labine signaled them to stop. Then he directed them to take Bennett's body and drop it into the crude grave. This done, he again used hand gestures to have them back away from the pit. They obliged him and stood in place clutching their shovels waiting to see what would happen next.

Now it was the gambler's turn to carry out his role in the Master's grand scheme. Standing at the head of the grave, Labine lifted both his arms skyward and began to chant ancient words of power. As he did so, the clouds above seem to rumble even louder with the first sounds of thunder. Labine felt the wind stir up around him and raised his voice even louder.

Whatever the Master had planned, he could only imagine.

Over and over again he repeated the spell he'd been taught until he felt a strange warmth begin to fill his body. Sweat began beading his forehead as the internal heat rose up inside him. Then it flooded him and Labine's body jerked. His eyes rolled back into their sockets so as only the whites were visible and the voice emerging from his mouth was not his own.

Lightning crackled across the sky and the horses below jumped.

Inside the pit tiny worms began to appear, popping out of the tightly packed earth. First there were a dozen, then twice as many and then even more. They began crawling over the corpse and within minutes they had covered every inch of it, and still more continued to fill the grave.

Drops of rain began to fall.

Several hit Labine's face and suddenly, he quit chanting. His eyes returned to normal and his body temperature as well. Dizzily he shook his head to clear it. More rain fell and muddied the grave. Labine waved his hands at the two men to finish their task.

Ignoring the now heavy rains, the diggers began shoveling the excavated mound of dirt back into the hole from which it had come. Over the worms and remains of the late James Bennett they threw dirt until it was all gone from sight.

Examining the site, Labine wiped the water off his face and approved of the job. He slapped each man on the shoulder to indicate they were done and then he headed back up into the cavern.

Soon the metamorphosis would be complete and whoever it was that coming for them would have a very unpleasant surprise to greet them.

CHAPTER SIXTEEN

A s quickly as the storm had unleashed its fury on the foothills, it dissipated and a hot yellow sun broke through the clouds to shine brightly. The once wet ground sucked up the precious water it had been showered in greedily until by the time Hattie Fields and her companions reached the path into the ravine all was bone dry save for a few small brackish puddles here and there.

Pulling up on the reins, she brought the team to a stop. Wild Eagle and Achoko, who had been riding to either side turned and approached the coach. Richard O'Malley climbed out of the back and came to stand beside the left front wheel. He saw the pass ahead and commented, "Is that where we are going?"

"Yes," Hattie Fields confirmed. "Wild Eagle and Achoko followed their tracks into that ravine. I'm guessin' their hidey-hole is somewhere in them foothills. Most likely some kind of cave."

Sam shook his head. "I don't like it. Got to be lots of places them folks can set up an ambush in there."

"I agree," Fields replied. "Which is why Wild Eagle and Achoko ain't going in the front door like us." She looked down at Achoko. "What do you think, brother? Can you find another way in?'

The Crow warrior looked at the hills to either side of the ravine and then nodded. "Yes, there must be many switchbacks used by goats and big cats. Wild Eagle and I will find one."

"I thought as much. Alrigtee, you boys go on ahead. We'll give you a few minutes and then follow along."

Achoko waved his right hand towards Fields. "The Great Spirits protect us all."

"Good hunting, my brothers," she returned the salute. Then the Indians kicked their mounts and rode off to the east of the gulch and soon disappeared behind a bunch of giant boulders.

Fields looked down at O'Malley. "You know how to shoot a rifle?" she asked him.

"I can hold my own, Hattie."

"Good." She handed Sam the reins, then bent down and from the boot under their seat pulled out a Winchester carbine along with a small cardboard box. She tossed them both to O'Malley one at a time. "Here you go. Now don't be shooting until you have to. Whatever is waiting for us in those hills, I want them to show theyselves first. You understand, Mr. O'Malley?"

"Of course."

"Then get back on board and let's get on with it."

Richard O'Malley tipped his hat to her and Sam and then climbed back into the stagecoach.

Hattie Fields took the reins back. "You ready for this?"

A wry smile appeared on Sam's face. "Sure. I ain't got nothing better to do."

Fields laughed, pulled hard on the leather straps and yelled at her horses to get moving again. They began trotting for the inviting shade of the rocky passageway before them.

•••

Once inside the narrow ravine, Fields' team was forced to slow down to a cautious walk. She kept spurring them on with gentle flicks of the reins and verbal encouragement; all the while her eyes scoured the rocks above them to either side.

Sam was also scrutinizing their tight lane well aware trouble could strike at them from every bend they traversed.

They had gone only a quarter of mile when suddenly rocks began to fall around them dropping from the high ledges. Fields urged her animals forward as the missiles continued to drop closer and closer.

"Somebody's throwing those rocks!" Sam shouted, keeping an arm up over his unprotected head.

"I figured as much," Fields said, her eyes trying to find the source of the projectiles above them.

Then they heard a gunshot and then the short, squat body of a man fell out of the sky in front of them. He hit the ground hard and didn't move. Fields held up her horses.

"Who the hell was that?" Sam asked.

"I don't know, but this is as far as I want to take the coach." Fields wrapped her reins around the long wooden brake handle. "From now on I think we'd best go on foot."

She grabbed her sawed off shotgun and vaulted off the coach. Sam stepped down on the top of the front wheel and jumped down easily.

O'Malley joined them along with The Dead Sheriff under Sam's command.

"Let him go first," Sam indicated The Dead Sheriff. Fields wasn't about to argue as they still didn't know how many more bushwhackers were waiting for them. Sam ordered The Dead Sheriff to proceed and fell in behind him, then came Fields and O'Malley.

As they passed the dead man, it was obvious by the cant of his neck that it was broken.

"Who do you think he was?" O'Malley's curiosity was ever present.

"Well, them vampire ladies had to have someone drive their wagons. I'm guessin' he was one of them fellas."

"Makes sense," the writer concurred. "It also means there are probably a few more of them up ahead."

"Yep. That'd be a good bet."

They remained quiet from that point on. All of them, except The Dead Sheriff who kept gazing up the cliffs above them ready to move should another attack be launched. The sun was becoming hotter by the minute, and they were caught in its unforgiving heat.

Coming around one curvature in the ravine they spotted the three painted wagons they had been chasing.

"Hold up," Sam directed The Dead Sheriff and he obeyed instantly.

Fields and O'Malley walked up beside him just as another gunshot rang out. A bullet smacked into the ground inches in front of The Dead Sheriff's boot.

"Find cover," Sam shouted and each of them scattered to crouch behind whatever boulders they could find. The Dead Sheriff stood where he was oblivious to the threat.

"Up there!" Fields pointed and all of them looked up to see another man similarly attired as the first who had attacked them with rocks. This one had a carbine and was lining up to take another shot at them.

What the shooter didn't see was Achoko rise up behind him, knife in hand. The Crow brave gave out a blood-curdling cry but the shooter didn't react, much to all their surprises. He merely fired again, this time his bullet hitting The Dead Sheriff in the right arm. They could see the consternation in Achoko's face due to the fellow's lack of reaction to the Indian's war cry. It clearly wasn't what he'd expected. Yet having the man ignore him and still fire upon his friends was enough to raise Achoko's rage.

He jumped on the driver's back to grasp his forehead with his left hand while bringing his blade around with his right. The surprised shooter only had a second to see his doom in the glint off the knife's edge as it drove into his throat and ripped it open.

"Sunovabitch," Sam gasped watching the blood spill out of the man's throat. Then Achoko released him and he tumbled over the ledge to come crashing down right in front of the opening to what appeared to be a natural cavern.

Then Sam experienced another shock as standing just inside the cavern's entrance was Labine, the redheaded gambler from whom he had stolen the magick amulet and book of spells. He was in cahoots with the vampire bitches! O'Malley had been right all long. And now, at last, he and Labine would finally settle things once and for all.

Another shot rang out and this time the bullet seemed to come from the other side of the three wagons. It hit the rock behind which Hattie Fields was hiding and sent chips flying over her head. "Where da hell did that come from?" she cried out.

Sam saw that the three gaudy wagons were stationary. Their horses could be seen further along the tiny creek running along the base of the cliff. There was another flash of gunpowder and the Indian lad lowered his head to see a third gunman on his belly under the last wagon.

"There," he bolted out from behind his own boulder and rushed up to The Dead Sheriff. "Over there," he pointed. "Under that wagon! Get'em!"

The Dead Sheriff began marching towards the wagon. He never felt the new bullet hole in his right arm as he drew both his Colt Peacemakers from their holsters at his hips. He began shooting non-stop as he neared his target.

The last of Magdala's drivers tried to fire his rifle a second time but a slug from one of The Dead Sheriff's guns hit him in the head killing him instantly.

Then all was quiet. The Dead Sheriff looked down at his vanquished foe and slipped his pistols back in their holsters. He turned and awaited his next instructions. Cautiously Fields and O'Malley joined Sam in the open, clutching their own weapons.

They looked around and saw Achoko waving down at them. There still was no sign of Wild Eagle.

"So," O'Malley asked Hattie Fields. "What now?"

She pointed her shotgun to the slope and the cavern. "Guess we go see what's in there."

•••

Magdala came up behind Labine and startled him.

"What's going on out there?" She stayed well back inside away from the burning rays of the sun. "We heard the shots."

"All of your men are dead," he angrily reported. Magdala looked past him at the motionless body only a few yards away. She could see the gaping wound that had sliced open the man's throat. Dried blood pooled under it on the ground and the urge to taste it almost overwhelmed her.

"It's that darky, Hattie Fields, isn't it?"

"What does it matter? My demon will stop them."

"You're too sure of yourself, Labine."

"Go on back to your..ah..ladies. I'll take care of this now."

Magdala was angered by Labine's tone. She had never suffered such disrespect from any man. Still she needed Labine now. But once he had defeated her enemies, she would teach him proper manners. Without another word, she spun about and hurried back to her inner sanctuary. She refused to think about what would happen if he failed her.

Watching her go, Labine questioned whether joining forces with the Vampire Queen hadn't been a mistake on his part. But now with their mutual adversaries gathered outside, he didn't have the luxury to mull over what might have been. No. The die had been cast and it was time for his dark magick.

Rolling back the sleeves of his jacket, Labine took a few steps into the glaring sunlight and raised his hands up towards where the remains of James Bennett had been buried. Drawing upon his inner strength, he began chanting another arcane spell. At the same time he began to weave his hands about in an intricate pattern.

The words coming from his mouth were as ancient as the pyramids and the incantation they wove was soon felt.

Coming up the rise, the woman, her two male companions and The Dead Sheriff finally saw Labine and his weird arm waving.

"What in tarnation is that fella doing?" Hattie Fields uttered warily.

"It's Labine," Sam informed her. "The dude who's been after me. Sounds like he's whipping up some of his black magick."

The earth beneath their feet shook and all of them froze in their tracks. It continued to rumble beneath them as Labine's voice grew louder and his gestures more dramatic.

"I don't like this," Richard O'Malley stated what they all were thinking.

Then the ground in front of them seemed to explode upwards and from it arose a thing that could only have been conceived in a land of nightmares.

It stood well over eight feet in height; a naked monstrosity in human figure horribly twisted by demonic hands. Rather than feet, it stood upright on elongated cloven hooves. Extending from its long, sinewy arms were only four fingers; each of these ending in long, curved claws. From its head there sprouted two goat-like horns connected by a thick bony brow under which peered two fiery red eyes. But the most horrific sight was its twin rows of small, needle like teeth which filled its mouth.

Rearing its head skyward, the demon roared at the sky and then it looked upon the pathetic figures before it.

"Destroy them," Labine shouted at his creation. "Rip them to pieces."

Sam came up behind The Dead Sheriff and told him to open fire on the thing. Once more the undead lawgiver filled his cold dead hands with steel and began blasting away at the demon before him. Bullet after bullet tore into the monster's chest tearing off chunks but it merely shook them off as if annoyed more than hurt. With one long stride, it reached The Dead Sheriff and picked him up. The demon that had once been James Bennett held the zombie lawman above its head. Then it lowered its captive enough to reach up and bite off a piece of The Dead Sheriff's back before hurling him away. The Dead Sheriff flew through the air and hit the second bordello wagon hard before crashing to the ground.

The thing looked down at the others and spit out the lifeless flesh from its mouth. Again it roared.

"Get out of my way! Hattie Fields pushed past Sam and fired both barrels of the shotgun into the monster's face. It cried out in agony, as dozens of silver pellets chewed up its face. A greenish blood began to ooze from lots of wounds, but somehow, unlike Moloch, this demon managed to withstand the powerful blasts.

The new creature swiped out with its right paw, hit the brown woman and sent her sprawling onto her back. The blow left her dazed and unable to move.

Labine clapped his hands in delight. Yes, this time he would win. This time he would fulfill his mission to the Master. Victory was soon to be his.

There was a loud twanging and a long shafted arrow hit the obscene monster in the chest.

Richard O'Malley turned his head towards the direction from which the arrow had come and he saw Wild Eagle standing atop the opposite ravine wall, bow in hand and notching another arrow. He let fly and his aim was true a second time as the arrow struck the monster's throat.

It cried out in rage as the silver tip burned under its thick black hide.

O'Malley lifted up his Winchester and fired at the beast. His bullet hit it in the stomach to no affect. Then a huge rock dropped onto the monster's head and it whirled about furiously.

Sam looked up to see Achoko hefting a second big rock.

All of them were fighting for their lives but the demon still raged. O'Malley went to fire again only to have his rifle breach lock up. Sam was moving towards the unmoving Hattie Fields when the hellspawn beast turned its gaze upon him.

"Shit," he gasped and tried to dodge as the behemoth lunged at him. He almost avoided its massive hands but one latched on to his left arm. Then he was being hoisted up into the air. The monster looked up at him and wrapped its other paw about his throat and began to squeeze. As it did so, the round amulet he word about his neck flopped out of his shirt.

Labine saw the amulet and all but jumped for joy. There it was. The Master's amulet. One half of the prize the foolish half-breed had stolen from him. He felt confident once the boy was dead, he would have no problem finding the missing book of spells.

Meanwhile O'Malley, unwilling to simply watch Sam be killed, charged the demon and flipping the rifle over in his hands, swung it like a baseball bat. With all his strength, he struck the monster in the small of the back repeatedly.

Somehow he managed to bother it enough to spin around and strike at him. In the process it loosened its grip on Sam and the Indian fell to the ground coughing. At the same time the monster's blow to O'Malley dropped him like a candle pin in a bowling alley. Lying there, he saw stars swimming in his field of vision. *Never thought this is how I'd die,* he mused to himself.

Life certainly was full of surprises.

It seemed hopeless. The monster that Labine had conjured up' returned its attention to Sam. Somehow it knew he was the primary target. It bent down and reached for him.

Yet something inside Sam came alive within in his blood. It wasn't that he feared dying. That had never been an issue with the lad. No, it was knowing that his brave and noble allies would also fall beside him. Now that just wasn't fair.

"NO!!" he cried out as the brutish mitts were about to wrap around him. Then weird, unfamiliar words came flooding out of his mouth. Strange, alien words he had never even heard before and yet he was the one saying them.

Wherever they came from, they had an immediate effect on the horned demon as it found itself unable to grab Sam. A look of utter bewilderment crossed the demon's face and growling it renewed its effort to ensnare him.

Louder Sam spoke the ancient words intuitively sensing they were his salvation. He kept saying them giving his soul over to whatever force was controlling his recitation. Could this be a result of the old book having been assimilated into his very being? It had to be.

Then the monster's hands began to burn and flames appeared as if conjured up by Sam's incantation. The flames were of a bright green hue and they quickly enveloped the monster's arms and torso. Roaring out in pain, it moved away from Sam and started striking at the fire on its own arms. To no avail, the flames only grew more intense and now Sam could smell the thing's flesh beginning to burn.

Labine's mouth fell open and his eyes widen in total disbelief. No, it couldn't be happening a second time. There was no way the boy could know which spells to use. It was impossible. And yet the horned giant was now a walking torch, every inch of it engulfed in the scorching conflagration. It took several steps, lost its balance and collapsed to the earth only a few feet from the grave that had spawned it. Then, with a last feeble cry of anguish, the monster folded in on itself and was totally consumed.

With minutes all that remained of it was a charred smoking hulk.

•••

Sam got to his feet slowly. He was still shaky and never took his eyes off the blackened bones of the burnt demon. Then he saw Richard O'Malley sitting up holding his head and Sam rushed to him.

"You okay?"

"Yes, I think so," O'Malley looking over his own body. It was happily still in one piece. "What about Hattie?" They saw she was till unconscious on her back where she'd landed after having been struck.

Sam extended his hand and helped O'Malley to his feet. Then together they went over to the fallen woman. O'Malley knelt beside her and was relieved to see she was still breathing. There was an ugly purple bruise on the right side of her face where the demon had hit her. O'Malley reached down and gently shook her shoulder.

"Hattie...wake up." He shook her again and she moaned. Her eyes blinked once, twice, and then they opened wide. She looked up at O'Malley and Sam slightly confused.

"Wha…what happened?"

"You tried to dance with that monster," O'Malley reminded her. "I guess it didn't appreciate your attention and it knocked you down."

"Yep, it surely did that." She pushed up her elbows, her eyes blinking again. "Give a gal a hand up, will ya."

Both O'Malley and Sam took hold of her shoulders and pulled Hattie Fields to her feet. She thanked them and brushed dirt and mud off her trousers and shirt. Her nose wrinkled and she finally saw the demon's smoking husk.

"Damn, is that the thing?"

O'Malley nodded affirmatively.

"What happened to it?"

O'Malley slapped Sam on the arm. "Sam burned it to a crisp."

Hattie Fields cocked an eye brow and the Indian raised his palms. "Don't ask me how. I ain't rightly figured that out myself."

•••

While the three victors were conversing, neither of them had seen Labine dash back into the cavern and conceal himself in the shadows. He was confused and scared. Everything was falling apart and he knew his Master would not be forgiving. He had warned what would happen should he fail again.

Sliding his left hand over the surface of the rock behind which he was hiding, his mind frantically sought any manner of escape. He would worry about the Master later. Right now he first had to elude the Indian boy and his companions. Perhaps if he hid further back in the rocks when they came for Magdala and the others, he might be able to slip past them, steal one of the horses and get away.

It wasn't a great plan, but it was all he could think of here and now.

He heard a strange sound coming from the top of the boulder and turned his head. There was a deadly rattling noise and Labine's eyes registered the coiled diamondback just as it shot out of the blackness, its fangs carrying their message of death.

•••

Sam, O'Malley and Fields heard the man's screams and looked up to see Labine come stumbling out of the cavern holding on to his face. His wailing continued as he made his way down the incline.

"It bit me!!" he cried. Then he fell forward and rolled several feet before coming to a stop.

Sam moved close to where Labine lay on his face. With the toe of his moccasin, he pushed the body over to see the dead man's face was swollen twice its normal size and his eyes were bulging out in a grimace of pure horror. Sam recognized the two holes oozing blood.

"Snake bite," Sam told the others. "By the looks of the punctures, it was a big one."

"Well, I guess you don't have to worry about him anymore," Richard O'Malley concluded. "First the demon and now the magician. I'd say luck is on our side."

"It's not over yet," Hattie Fields reminded the reporter. She pointed to the waiting cave. "Those bloodsuckers are still in there. And that's unfinished business."

"Little sister, can you hear me?" It was Achoko's voice calling down from the high ledge above the cavern entrance.

Hattie Fields went down the slope a few yards and then turned and looked up to see her cousin waving down at her.

"Is the demon gone?" he asked, unable to get a clear view of the area directly at the base of the cliff.

"Yes," she called back. "Your rocks and Wild Eagle's arrows help us to conquer it."

"That is good."

"Now we must enter that cave to root out the blood-drinkers and we will need your help."

"Wait for us, we will join you."

"Yes, but before you do, stop at the coach and get stakes and the dynamite. Do you hear me, Achoko?"

"I hear you, little sister."

Then he was gone from sight. Fields turned around in time to see Wild Eagle on the opposite ledge holding his bow above his head and waving to her as well. He had heard her instructions and quickly disappeared behind the cliff.

At the same time this exchange was taking place, Sam and Richard O'Malley had gone to the see about The Dead Sheriff. He was seated on his butt where he had landed after having been thrown against the second bordello wagon.

"Get up," Sam ordered. The Dead Sheriff stood. "Now turn around." As the undead avenger did as he was bid, Sam move up closer to examine the injury he had suffered at the hands of the deadly monster. Actually, not at its hands, but its teeth. The Dead Sheriff's shirt had been ripped along the back and Sam peeled back a piece to examine the huge chunk missing from The Dead Sheriff. It was locked dead center of the zombie's spine, just below his protruding shoulder blades.

"Shit, that's a bad one," Sam whistled. "Probably gonna take a day or two before that heals up."

O'Malley marveled at how the Indian youth took such wounds as if they were nothing but an inconsequential scratch. "Is he okay to keep going?" he inquired, although he was fairly certain what Sam's answer would be.

"He's been shot up a whole lot worse than this, O'Malley. You should know that by now."

"Knowing it is one thing. Seeing it over and over again is another."

Sam merely shrugged. "He will do what I tell him." Then he had The Dead Sheriff turn to face them. The undead lawman still clutched both .45s in his hands. Sam told him to reload both pistols and then holster them. The Dead Sheriff complied.

•••

Ten minutes later Achoko and Wild Eagle rode up, each with his hands full. The older Crow brother held the box with the TNT, while his younger sibling a tied bundle of stakes. Handing these items down to Sam and O'Malley, they slipped off their horses and awaited Hattie Fields' marching orders.

"Sam," she began. "Are you all right with letting The Dead Sheriff lead the way once we're in there?"

"Right. He's ready to go and there ain't much harm those vampires can do to him."

"What about you?"

"I'll be right behind him. I need to just tell him what to do when the fighting starts up."

Fields shoved a long wooden stake in his hands. "All right, then hold on to this. You may need it."

"Yes, Ma'am."

The coach woman looked at her crew and was confident they would win out in the end. "So listen up, them gals are gonna be hiding down deep in that cave just waiting to pounce on us. Sam here is gonna go in first behind The Dead Sheriff. Then it's gonna be me, Achoko and Wild Eagle, with Mr. O'Malley last.

"Everyone all right with that?" No one disagreed. "Good, once we move in, keep an eye out for any kind of torch or whatever. I figure it's gonna be dark as a witch's heart in there. We need to find us some kind of light."

With that she started up the slope alongside of Sam and The Dead Sheriff. As they moved around the bodies of the gambler and the wagon driver, Sam kept his eyes glued to the ground. He reminded the others about the rattler that had killed Labine and to be very careful where they stepped.

In the natural vestibule of the cavern, Fields saw the cold torch on the ground and quickly retrieved it. From her coat pockets she withdrew a wooden match and struck it against a rock. Once lit, she used it to light the top of the torch. She could smell kerosene on it and deduced the shaft's tip had at one time been soaked in the fuel.

Holding the burning brand high over her head, she nodded at Sam to move out. He in turn told The Dead Sheriff to draw his pistols and start into the cave.

"Shoot anything that comes at yah," he commanded. The Dead Sheriff kept walking forward as if without a care in the world. In the rear, Richard O'Malley thought, *there are some things to be said about already being dead.* He still held the Winchester Fields had given him. During their wait for the Crow brothers, she had helped him clean the breach from the sand pebbles that had jammed it earlier. He felt reassured it wouldn't fail him a second time.

Deeper into the cavern they went, the flickering flames of the torch causing the shadows to dance on the rocks and walls around them.

Fields, right behind Sam, whispered to him. "Tell them were comin' for them."

Sam understood what she wanted and began to whisper, his words then came out of The Dead Sheriff's mouth.

"Prepare to pay for you sins," the eerie, cold voice declared. Its chilling words echoed throughout the various tunnels. "Justice is coming for all of you. Your days of preying on the innocent are over.

"This hole is now your final grave."

Something moved ahead of them, from one rock to another. The Dead Sheriff cocked his pistols. Loose pebbles dropped from above and then a winged vampire swooped down. The Dead Sheriff fired both guns, his bullets slamming into her torso and knocking her down before him.

"Stake her!" Fields yelled as a second female bloodsucker came at them from behind. Sam pushed past The Dead Sheriff and drove his wooden pike into the she-creatures heart before she could recover. Behind them,

O'Malley ducked as razor sharp claws missed his head by inches.

Ochoko, holding his bow and arrow at ready, followed the flying vampire and loosed his shaft. It caught her in the leg and she cried out.

The vampire Sam had staked was spitting as her clawed hands tried to pull the sharp stick out of her chest. It was futile and her head fell back dead.

"Keep going!" Hattie Fields urged. The battle had been joined and it was time to see it through to the end.

The wounded vampire managed to fly to the top of another rock and there screamed down at them. Ochoko wasted no time sending another silver-tipped arrow into her chest. She fell back out of sight.

Two down, Sam thought as their procession continued deeper into the vampires' lair. *Just how many of the damn things were there?*

"You can't hide from justice," The Dead Sheriff said, again his grave-like voice sounding all around them.

The hunters turned a corner and were suddenly facing Magdala's living area still lit by the twin lanterns. The Vampire Queen stood between her two remaining girls, boldly facing the crusaders. Unlike the other two, they were wingless, preferring to meet their enemies head on with their fangs, claws and inhuman strength.

"NO," Magdala warned, her arms out. "It is you who will die here. It is you who will be gutted and your blood that I and my sisters will drink."

Then with a flourish, she actually bowed. "So come, you pathetic fools, death awaits."

If she expected some kind of poetic response, she was disappointed. The Dead Sheriff blasted away with his guns. One bullet hit Magdala in the forehead. Her head rocked back, then she straightened up. Meanwhile Alicia and her sister vampire ran into the hunters knocking The Dead Sheriff back into Sam and they fell over in a tangle. Hattie Fields, seeing their charge, stepped back and as the nearest vampire swiped at her, she ducked and then shoved the torch into the vampire's face. It caught fire.

As for Alicia, she leaped up at Wild Eagle only to have Richard O'Malley shoot at point blank range with his rifle. The shot pushed her backward to slam against the rock wall. She fell to the ground just as Wild Eagle, recovered from the surprise of her attack, rushed over to her and slammed a wooden stake through her back into her heart. She lifted her head in pain and died.

As the burning bloodsucker ran through the cave beating at her own head, The Dead Sheriff got to his feet and as she raced past him, he struck her across the back of the head with one of his guns. She dropped to the floor before him and he emptied the pistol into her.

Within seconds, Magdala was all that was left. Standing before them, the hole in her head oozing her black blood, she opened her mouth and screeched. Maddened beyond comprehension, she attacked The Dead Sheriff and her claws raked across his face and chest. Cutting long furrows into his dead skin.

"DIE!" she cursed. "DIE!" But he merely shot her in the belly with his second gun. She staggered back a few feet.

Hattie Fields shoved past the others wielding her bowie knife in her right hand. At long last the time had come. Magdala looked up at her as the justified vigilante swung out and cut her head off. Black ichor spilled out as the Vampire Queen's head plopped to the ground, followed by her body. It twitched for a few seconds and then was still.

Hattie Fields stood over Magdala breathing heavily. She looked at the bloody knife in her hand and then simply let it go. It landed beside the vampire's head.

•••

With their enemies destroyed, the group set about ending the entire mission so that there would be no lingering evil left behind. At Hattie Fields' direction, they gathered all the vampire females and as she had done with Magdala, beheaded all of them to assure none of them would ever walk again. Then they gathered up the bodies of Labine and the three men who had been the Vampire Mistress' slaves and brought them into the secret chamber.

That done, Fields set about laying dynamite charges all around the perimeter of the cavern opening and then they all moved to take up concealment behind the bordello wagons. She took the Winchester from O'Malley, sighted along the barrel and fired. The TNT erupted violently shaking the ground throughout the ravine and then the roof of the cavern collapsed. Dust and debris were scattered outward via the concussion, lots of rock pieces striking the wagons. When the noise had died away and the dust settled, they emerged to find the entrance buried under tons of rocks. No one would ever discover what was buried inside.

The last thing they did was torch the three wagons. Nothing was to be left of Magdala's existence. Achoko and Wild Eagle rounded up the six horses and the group exited the ravine long before sunset.

Thus ended Hattie Fields' vendetta.

CHAPTER SEVENTEEN

FROM THE JOURNAL OF RICHARD O'MALLEY

The aftermath of the Spirit Mountains battle was as anticlimactic as all such endings are. The trip back to Hattie Fields' sod house was a relaxed journey for all of us. There was very little conversation as each of us seemed to want to put the entire affair as far behind us as possible.

Upon reaching her little home, Achoko and Wild Eagle bid us farewell. They had agreed, with Hattie's blessing, to take the six horses, diving them equally. That was no little matter, as ownership of three strong horses would add to their prestige back in the Crow village. Watching them riding off happily herding their new wealth on hooves, I couldn't help but think the American Indian's life was a whole lot less complicated than that of we white, so called civilized people.

As for Hattie, we spent that first night back enjoying her hospitality. Still it was obvious Sam wanted to get back on the outlaw trail as soon as possible. So at first light, we all said our good-byes to this truly one of a kind woman.

She gave Sam a long hug and then turning to me, smiled mischievously. "Would you mind a kiss from an uneducated coach driver, Mr. O'Malley?"

I was naturally taken aback by her request. "Ah, no, Hattie. Not at all."

She put her hands behind my head, pulled my head down and gave me a long, tender kiss. When she finally let me go, I realized for the first time just how beautiful her eyes were.

"Wahoo, I ain't ever kissed such a pretty man before. Thank you."

I laughed and bowed slightly. "The pleasure was sincerely all mine, Miss Fields." And with that, Sam and I climbed onto the buckboards, The Dead Sheriff already stretched in the back. As Sam had prophesied, his body was already healing itself. Make of that what you will. I wondered if I'd ever be truly able to understand any of it.

Hattie Fields waved to us as we rode away down the road. I looked back a final time and returned that wave. Would we ever see her again? Somehow I believed we would. The west has a strange way of bringing people together.

THE END

THE DEAD SHERIFF LIVES ON

The Dead Sheriff Lives On. I loved the simple irony of that title. Ron Fortier coined it in the first "Dead Sheriff and it still makes me smile. Ron, who I think of as my "Fairy Godfather" has helped me more than he'll ever know. I suppose that makes his beautiful wife Valerie, my "Fairy Godmother." I don't know what I would have done without their support, their love and kindness. Their giant shoulders and their wonderful advice.

The loss I feel, after unexpectedly losing Mark in February of 2016, seems to ebb and flow. Some days it's merely heart breaking and profoundly sad. Other days, it's excruciatingly painful and lonely. I feel him all around me, talk to him often and I don't know if I feel better or worse.

I can't walk through our house without passing book shelves. The cases are full to overflowing with stories and books written by some of the world's greatest authors. One shelf, though, is full of HIS books. The books, anthologies and magazines Mark penned and published. I can't help but look at those daily. I still see him as I did the Sunday night before he passed away. He would stroll up and down his treasured shelves, arranging rearranging, kind of like Scrooge McDuck in his vault of gold coins. If you could have only seen his face in those moments. There wasn't a room in our home that wasn't filled with books. He and I used to talk about the rooms feeling full at times with a complete fusion of the characters and places and stories, just hovering in front of those shelves. An odd sort of fusion along the lines of Philip Jose Farmer's "Riverworld." If HE could put Sam Clemens together with Sir Richard Francis Burton why was it odd to suddenly see Diana Gabaldon's Jamie Fraser hanging out with Stephen King's "Gunslinger" Roland Deschain? (Besides, it was Mark introducing me to Stephen King's "The Stand" after I graduated from college vowing to never read another book. Thank Goodness I met Mark Justice).

Mark and I had some truly fun and funny literary conversations over the years. He was often partial to westerns, though. He was weaned on them, I think. Mark, was the most intelligent, creative man, I have ever known. Other than my own father, Norman Ison. (What girl doesn't think her father Hung the Moon?) He used to say if he'd had the choice to arrange a marriage for me, he would have hunted for a Mark Justice. He just never realized there was a real man out there, like Mark. He loved to just sit and talk to Mark. They could talk for hours, and often did, especially in the summer. We'd all sit around the pool, laughing, talking. My dad often wondered if there was a single subject Mark knew nothing about. Even I was never sure of that, either. Like I said; fun, funny, wonderful conversations.

Mark left a hole in my world and crates of finished stories. Mostly completed novels or novellas. Unfinished stories in every genre imaginable. Notes. Lists. Names. Titles. There isn't a day that passes I don't wonder, what in the world he would have written next? You see, he had this method. Granted he was busy from the moment his eyes were open, till he managed to shut them at night. He had his radio show, which he loved. Radio was just one of his dream jobs. At 3, he used to carry a stick and use it as a microphone. He sometimes thought he was born too soon. He would have loved to have been at an old radio mic with Jack Benny, and a list of old actors and writers a mile long. So, he made his first dream happen. He wanted to write novels and tell stories and have people begging for more like his heroes Ray Bradbury, Harlan Ellison, Stephen King, and once again, the list would be a mile long.

Every single day, Mark needed a few minutes to himself. If it was cold outside, he'd sit in a chair with his eyes closed and before I knew it, he'd be at his computer typing away. In summer, when we grew tomatoes, he'd water them daily at the same time if possible. But not with a hose. That would be too fast. He had two favorite watering buckets, and he knew how to use them. He'd then head to the den and work on show prep for the next morning, or comedy bits, interview prep and I could always tell the difference if it were radio work or work on his own short stories, newspaper articles or even work on his latest novella or novel. If he was working on Radio, there was always a laugh or two coming from that den. Yes. He used to crack himself up. If it was storytelling, it was always quiet. Sometimes he would bring me stories he'd finished, just to see what I thought. I have to tell you, Mark could write with such intense humor, like his "Deadneck Zombies" or shockingly enough, the gore (and a little comedy) in "The Dead Sheriff." Sometimes his stories were so poignant they'd make me cry. Other times, like now with "The Dead Sheriff", it's not odd for me to say straight out loud, "Mark??? Where did you Come up with This?" However, I found myself quickly lost in that first book. I never read it. You're shocked. He showed me the box of books one day, just after they arrived. I started to read it and he grabbed it back. He said I wouldn't like it. (Laughing here) When Ron wrote to me one day and said he was almost finished with the second one and would send it, soon, I thought I better read the first one. That's when I asked him, out loud, where he got those ideas. He was wrong though. I loved the book. I couldn't put it down. Mark could sure tell a story. These days, the house is too quiet.

I mentioned earlier that Mark always seemed partial to Westerns. Books, stories, John Wayne movies, "The Magnificent Seven"—it didn't matter. (Oh, he'd have loved the remake, too with Denzel Washington.) There was always a hero and his horse.

Mark loved horror, too. I wasn't surprised at all when he started writing "The Dead Sheriff." (It sure wasn't a John Wayne, title, was it?) He really didn't have a title. Just an idea. As a short working title, he just called it "The Dead Sheriff." I think he started out intending for it to be a graphic novel or maybe a comic book series. I can most definitely tell you how the title stuck, though. He was working one afternoon. I went shopping for groceries before making dinner. While walking into the store, our Greenup County Sheriff at the time, Keith Cooper, was on his way out of the store. We stopped to talk a few minutes and he asked what Mark was doing. I rattled off "he's started on some new book but he's not sure yet what it will be." He asked what it was about and without thinking I started ... "A Dead..." then, I just stopped.

He was waiting expectantly on me to finish that sentence. "A Dead, ...what?" he said.

I slowly finished with... "It's not what you think, it's a western, and it has monsters or something..." I finally told him the working title. I can still see his reaction. He thought it was shockingly funny and all Mark, though. I got home and told Mark about the conversation with Sheriff Cooper hearing the title, that he thought it was funny and it was never called anything else.

Mark was so excited about these characters. Richard O'Malley (Mark always wanted to be a Newspaper Reporter. It was such a Noble Profession in "The Front Page", Jack Lemmon, Walter Matthau), Cheveyo (for his Good intentions of righting wrongs, for whatever reasons he had. Think of all of your favorite Unintentional Hero's) and, of course, the Dead Sheriff. As for the cast of characters, I thought they couldn't get wilder than the first book. Well, just wait until you read the sequel! "The Dead Sheriff

Volume 2 Cannibals and Bloodsuckers"!

As far as future characters (I hope there are many more) I've only seen a few lists. I've saved a few notes here and there when I find them. Knowing Mark, though, it boggles my mind to think what else he would have done, with these characters alone. I do know, that during this creative period, he started making plans to create another anthology. He had already named it "Bullets and Brimstone." I can barely imagine how that would have turned out. If I could show you the responses to invitations he received, all the yeses, you may a moment of sadness, too, that it was never created. Heather May photographer. Quite a few big names in our story-tellers' world said yes. At least I still have those letters, and my imagination of what could have been.

This is probably my one chance to at least start thanking people. I'm still reeling, from the loss, and once again, the list would be a mile long. Old friends. New friends. I think about how hard Dr. Charles Rhodes fought for Mark. His entire staff has been here for me for so long. Ada, Amy, Angie... the medical team during the last minutes who fought to keep him with us. The Greenup 911 Responders. The people who have been here for me, Johnda and Greg Dowdy, Kitty Watson Dogoud, Randy Russell, Tom and Doris Haynes, Mayor Bob and Judy Crager, Dr. Dave Gallo, Nancy Kalanta, Connie Jones, Les and Diane Hayes, Audrey, Angie and Andy Cann, Debbie and Jeff Justice, Mike and Jodi Wilson, Kathy Dougherty, Margaret King, Geoff Moore, Jim Forrest, Ernie G. Anderson, Jeff and Vickie Elswick, the staff of WLGC Radio KoolHits1057, Bobby Leach, the entire Flatwoods Police and Fire Departments, Dr. Tim Brom. I could never forget Brian Spears, who coordinated manuscripts to make this book possible. I'm about to get myself in trouble, now. Because once again, I have a mile long list and I'm so afraid of leaving someone out.

My biggest "thank you" of all has to go to My "Fairy Godfather" Ron Fortier. Ron gave Mark the first "Dead Sheriff" book he hoped it could be, dreamed it could look like. He never got to see it. But, I already know what his face would have looked like at first glance. He would have been thrilled. Ron then turned around, took the manuscript Mark had written for the sequel and—Ron, I can't tell where Mark's voice ends and yours begins. You have no idea how humbled and beyond thrilled Mark would be knowing an author, Wwriter, gifted storyteller of your caliber took what he started and made it magnificent. You, Rob, Art and Zachary— There aren't enough words in the Universe to tell you how grateful I am.

Oh, one more thing. As it turns out. I found out a little about myself the last couple of years. Marky truly was wrong. I do love westerns. I love these characters. Gore and all. I love so many things because of Mark Justice.

Mrs. Norma Kay Ison Justice
Dec 19, 2018
Flatwoods, Ky.

ABOUT OUR CREATORS

WRITERS -

MARK JUSTICE (23 Sept 1959 – 10 Feb 2016) was a writer, podcaster and radio personality. His published include Deadneck Hootenanny, Looking at the World with Broken Glass in My Eye, Dead Earth: The Green Dawn and Dead Earth: The Vengeance Road (both with David T. Wilbanks). He edited Appalachian Winter Hauntings. His short fiction appeared in four volumes of Legends of the Mountain State, two volumes of Horror Library, In Laymon's Terms, Dark Discoveries, The Horror Garage, Dark Jesters, The Green Hornet Chronicles, The Phantom Chronicles Volume 2, The Captain Midnight Chronicles, The Avenger Chronicles, Damned Nation, and he contributed to The Book of Lists: Horror. Mr. Justice produced and hosted the popular genre podcast Pod of Horror. He also hosted a morning radio show in Kentucky, where he resided with his loving wife, Norma Kay and their contentious cats.

RON FORTIER – Comics and pulps writer/editor is best known for his work on the Green Hornet comic series and Terminator – Burning Earth with Alex Ross. He won the Pulp Factory Award for Best Pulp Short Story of 2011 for "Vengeance Is Mine," which appeared in Moonstone's The Avenger – Justice Inc. and in 2012 for "The Ghoul," from the anthology Monster Aces. He is the Managing Editor of Airship 27 Productions, a leading New Pulp Fiction publisher and writes the continuing adventures of both his own character, Brother Bones – the Undead Avenger and the classic pulp hero, Captain Hazzard – Champion of Justice. In 2017, he was awarded the first, Pulp Grand Master by the Pulp Factory.

Fortier also writes the highly popular Pulp Fiction Reviews blog. You can find him at (www.Airship27.com)

INTERIOR ILLUSTRATOR -

ART COOPER - is a Canadian artist/writer/editor who was a founding partner of Spectrum Publications, which published three bi-monthly fanzines in the early '70's. Art was a member of the inaugural Cartooning program at Sheridan College in Oakville, Ontario, where the guest instructors included such luminaries as Joe Kubert, Neal Adams and Will Eisner. Art contributed to a number of fan publications and penciled two stories for Orb Magazine before getting married and completing his engineering degree. Art has worked as a project manager in the Mining and Metals industry for the past few decades, and has done some freelance advertising work on the side. Art is the proud father of two grown sons, and lives in Mississauga, Ontario with his current wife and daughter.

COVER ARTIST -

ZACHARY BRUNNER – graduated from the School of Arts with a degree in filmmaking. Upon graduation, he realized that he would rather pursue a career in illustration, needing a more creative job than the high-stress environment of film production. He began working with comic writer Jim Krueger on two graphic novels, "The High Cost of Happily Ever After," and "Runner." Both are available at Amazon.

While studying at SVA, Zachary worked as a concept artist on an animated film called "Brother," directed by Sari Rodrig. The short film went on to win countless awards all over the world, having been shown at festivals such as Cannes and the Student Emmys. Zach currently is working on Sari's second short animated film, "Essence."

He has also worked as a storyboard artist for Torque Creative, the in-house advertising agency for Mercedes-Benz. He is also currently working on several storyboards for short independence films.

Other print projects included "Christopher Rising," "Penny Dreadful" and "The Poisonberry Fortune" and "Foot Soldiers,Volume 1." He plans on furthering a career in concept art and in the comic book industry.

What's come before...

Richard O'Malley is a hard working Boston reporter in the years following the Civil War. He is fascinated by tales of the wild west and the colorful frontiersmen who are taming it. None captivate him more than the stories of the Dead Sheriff; a dedicated lawman who had risen from the grave to continue his mission. Taking his life savings, O'Malley embarks on a personal quest to find this mythical figure and chronicle his exploits. What he finds will make them both legends.

Airship 27 Productions is thrilled to bring pulp fans Mark Justice's most original creation in this new, expanded edition; the first of a brand new series starring THE DEAD SHERIFF.

More Western Weirdness...

TERROR ON THE PLAINS

Former Union scouts and saddle tramps Durken and McAfee are more than satisfied with their lives as cattle-punchers for Homer Eldridge and his Triple Six ranch. But fate has other, more sinister and weird plans for the two cowpokes...

Writer Fred Adams, Jr. spins weird western tales that will have readers on their edge of their seats and jumping at shadows. Mixing a heady brew that is half H.P. Lovecraft and half Louis L'Amour, SIX-GUN TERRORS volumes one through three are creepy adventures not soon forgotten.

Airship27Hangar.com

NEW PULP

PULP FICTION FOR A NEW GENERATION!

FOR AVAILABILITY: AIRSHIP27HANGAR.COM